ASSUME NOTHING

*The new novel from the critically acclaimed
and award-winning author*

When Joe Reddick and his family are threatened
in their LA home by a masked, knife-wielding
intruder, it means serious trouble for a gang of
desperate criminals. The threat sends Joe Reddick over the edge. He's lived the nightmare of
losing a family to a crazed killer once, and he's
not going to let it happen again. After sending
his wife and son to safety, he goes to war, determined to kill those responsible. Soon Reddick's
living nightmare will finally be over. One way or
the other...

*A Selection of titles by Gar Anthony Haywood
available from Severn House*

CEMETERY ROAD
ASSUME NOTHING

ASSUME NOTHING

Gar Anthony Haywood

Severn House Large Print
London & New York

This first large print edition published 2012
in Great Britain and the USA by
SEVERN HOUSE PUBLISHERS LTD of
9-15 High Street, Sutton, Surrey, SM1 1DF.
First world regular print edition published 2011 by
Severn House Publishers Ltd., London and New York.

British Library Cataloguing in Publication Data

Haywood, Gar Anthony.
  Assume nothing.
  1. Suspense fiction. 2. Large type books.
  I. Title
  813.6-dc23

ISBN-13: 9780727898838

Severn House Publishers support The Forest Stewardship Council
[FSC], the leading international forest certification organisation. All
our titles that are printed on Greenpeace-approved FSC-certified paper
carry the FSC logo.

Printed and bound in Great Britain by the
MPG Books Group, Bodmin, Cornwall.

In Memory of Richard Deroy

Great fathers come in all shapes and sizes, and they go to war for their families in myriad ways. If the proof of a man's parenting is in the quality of the people his children become, this guy had to be one of the best.

Acknowledgements

The author is indebted to the following people, who can be credited with making this book a more credible read than might have otherwise been possible:

Sylvia Longmire
Author of *Cartel: The Coming Invasion of Mexico's Drug Wars*

Lukas Ortiz, Triana Silton & Rigo Orozco
Cómo se dice muchas gracias en español?

Anna Deroy

D.P. Lyle

Paul Bishop

Bob Bravo

Mark Haskell Smith

Marcus and Chy

PAST TENSE

WEST PALM BEACH, FLORIDA

His last night in Florida, Joe Reddick remembered the blood in the goldfish bowl.

And just like that, he knew he was doomed to fuck up again. Drive the heel of a pool cue into a rude drunk's eye, or throw an insolent yuppie down a long flight of stairs. He could see it coming the moment the nightmare released him and his eyes opened wide on to the dark, empty reaches of his bedroom, sweat rolling down the ridges of his spine like water rushing from an open tap.

He had been living with the recurrent nightmare for almost two years now but its occasional surprises could still bring him to his knees. From time to time, a long-forgotten detail or two from the longest day of his life would bubble up to the dream's surface and his reaction to the shock was always the same: recoil and strike. Walk around in a white hot daze until his freshly stoked rage egged him into sharing his pain with someone, anyone, who might marginally deserve it.

Tonight, the nightmare's new prop had been a trivial one, all things considered: just a flat-bottomed globe of glass filled with crimson water, sitting atop a hallway table next to a face towel striped with blood. An eerie tableau, perhaps, but hardly haunting – unless of course, like

11

Reddick, one were privy to the front end of Donovan Sykes's twisted little joke.

Sykes had thought he was being funny, using Little Joe's fishbowl for a wash basin after his demonic work in Reddick's home was done. The two Palm Beach PD detectives who had questioned Sykes later told Reddick he had fallen all over himself describing how Fenster and Gomez, Little Joe's pet goldfish, had tasted going down. Laughed so hard he cried, they said.

Reddick imagined Sykes's laughter now, twenty-six months and eleven days later, and leapt from his bed like a man fleeing from a burning house.

He tossed his clothes on without showering and took a taxi straight to the airport, leaving his Gotham Court apartment for good. It was only a few minutes after six a.m. His flight to Los Angeles was over three hours away, but the airport seemed the safest place for him now. Maybe if he hid in the empty bar with his eyes closed, drank himself into a state of benign semi-consciousness until his plane began boarding, he could get out of Florida without doing any more damage.

But no.

The mindnumbing somnolence of West Palm Beach Airport before eight in the morning offered him no diversion from the images of the nightmare that kept filling his head. By nine a.m., a successful escape to California still over an hour away, Reddick could feel the blood in his veins burning like oil in a skillet and he couldn't keep his fists unclenched.

He was relocating to Los Angeles in the hope life could be different somewhere else, that after months of psychotherapy he was a sane and stable man who only needed a change of scenery to be made whole. But that was a dream that would evaporate like smoke if he let the wheels come off again now. He could run to LA or Chicago, Dallas or St Louis – to the far corners of the fucking earth if he wanted – and it wouldn't make a damn bit of difference, because he'd still be the same old Joe Reddick, a sick, wounded wreck of a man for whom there was no hope for a life of normalcy.

The American terminal was packed now and everywhcrc hc looked he saw something that angered him, ordinary nuisances that right at this moment rubbed his nerves raw. Every spoken word, every click of a laptop keyboard raged in his head like an amplified scream.

He heard the guy in the Dolphins jersey before he saw him. He was a big hulk with massive arms and a pitted red face, standing before an observation window next to a woman Reddick imagined was his wife. The guy called himself being discreet, holding his voice down to a low rumble, but the malice in his body language, and the fear in his woman's eyes, left little doubt about the nature of their exchange.

He had a grip on the lady's left biceps that Reddick noticed right away.

Reddick had seen such holds before: vise-like expressions of male authority meant as much to break the spirit as to bruise the flesh. It was the weapon small men liked to use to re-establish their will over wives and girlfriends when an open right hand was, for one reason or another, a socially untenable option.

Reddick looked away, but only for a moment.

The guy kept asking the woman if she was listening. 'Are you listening? Are you *listening*?' Talking to her like a child he'd lost all patience with.

Take it somewhere else, asshole, Reddick thought. *Do us both a favor*.

But the guy never moved, of course. He just went right on playing the dick, the foul-mouthed, high school jock gone to seed who thought the world was his own private oyster and everything in it had his name on it.

Reddick got up, intending to move to another part of the terminal, but then he got his first good look at the guy's face and whatever chance he'd had of holding things together went out the window.

Because, hell, if the sonofabitch didn't have Junior Greene's teeth.

The man named Junior Greene whom Reddick knew during his old days on the Riviera Beach Police Department was tall, black, and ugly as homemade sin. And it only made matters worse that he had the teeth of a bull moose.

When Greene smiled, he looked like a fighter trying to eject his mouthpiece. His grin was an unnerving flash of pale yellow he used to great effect, a calling card all his enemies knew him by, and Reddick had despised it even before

14

Greene had shown it to him that day almost two years ago up on the jailhouse steps, stretching his lips back as far as they would go to punctuate a victory over an old adversary.

Greene had cut a large letter 'H' for 'Hollywood' into the side of a sixteen-year-old girl's face eleven days before, trying to break her of the habit of going to the movies instead of walking her stroll, but thanks to Reddick, the charges against him had been dropped. Reddick and his partner Charlie Post had busted Greene only three months after the triple funeral that would haunt Reddick to his grave, and Reddick had been getting more volatile and out of control by the day. Knowing what he and the rest of the world did about Reddick's troubles, Greene should have granted the cop a wide berth, but the arrogant fool had chosen instead to respond with a hearty 'fuck you' when Reddick asked him to produce the weapon he had used on the girl. Reddick returned the insult by breaking the pimp's left arm in two places.

Not surprisingly, an Assistant DA subsequently decided the case against Greene was too tainted to take to trial, and set him free.

Post had tried desperately to talk him out of it, but Reddick had insisted on being there the day Greene was released from custody. Squinting into a blinding noonday sun, the pimp had stepped out of the county jail, immediately spotted Reddick and Post sitting in their unmarked Chevy – and smiled his best smile.

It had been all Post could do to keep Reddick from killing him right there.

Less than five weeks later, Reddick was an ex-cop. He'd already been on course to be booted from the job before Greene's final act of defiance, but having the pimp laugh in his face that day, knowing full well what Reddick had only recently endured, had sent his downward spiral into overdrive.

For a long time afterwards, Reddick dreamed about payback. But payback never came. Greene became part of a past Reddick needed desperately to put behind him, to bury and forget like a bad dream, so that was what he did. He gave Greene a pass.

In fact, he couldn't remember the last time the thought of Junior Greene, standing outside the Palm Beach County Jail with that goddamn equestrian grin on his face, had even entered his mind.

But it sure as hell was there now.

'Can I help you, buddy?' the guy in the Dolphins jersey asked.

He'd finally taken note of Reddick staring and left his woman alone long enough to return a stare of his own. Reddick could see now that his teeth were – incredibly – actually larger than Junior's had been. Whiter and more inhumanly symmetrical. He wondered how in hell the guy could ever get his lips to close around them.

'Hey. I'm talking to you,' the big man said, closing in on him.

'Sorry,' Reddick said, finally finding his voice. He still had a chance to escape without incident, if only—

16

'This is a private conversation, asshole. You got a problem with that?'

Reddick only glared at him at first. Then: 'You should treat the lady with a little more respect.' Not knowing he was going to say anything at all until the words were out of his mouth.

'Say what?'

Enraged, the big guy took three steps, put his face right up in Reddick's.

Some things, Reddick thought, fate just wouldn't let a man walk around.

A few minutes shy of six o'clock that same day, a Riviera Beach cop named Dick Glavin walked over to Charlie Post's cubicle and said, 'Hey, Big Stuff. You'll never guess who just broke a guy's face into a hundred different pieces out at West Palm Beach Airport.'

Post didn't even bother looking up, just kept right on typing the arrest report he was struggling to get through. He knew it was Glavin talking, and he knew the white man was grinning. The Robbery and Homicide detective had a smirk you could fucking *feel* when he talked to you.

'So there ain't no point in my trying, right?'

'Your old pal Joe Red. That's who.'

'What? Aw, *damn*!' Post said, having just misspelled the word 'intersection' for the third time in three tries. He groped around for his bottle of correction fluid, finally gave Glavin a taste of his attention. Taking his best shot at faking disinterest. 'Joe Red, huh? That right?'

'But not to worry. No damage done,' Glavin

17

said, his grin smearing itself across his mottled face again. 'Asshole he did the nose job on took the first swing. We couldn't've held him if we'd wanted to.'

Post started re-correcting the flaw in his document, said, 'So what happened?'

'What happened is, he wigged out again. Saw this gorilla jerkin' his old lady around and decided to offer him a little relationship counseling.' Glavin finally started to laugh. 'I guess the guy didn't appreciate it.'

'Jesus.'

'Yeah. Wrong Good Samaritan to fuck with, right?'

'Where's Red now?'

Glavin made a pair of wings out of both hands, flapped them overhead. 'Gone west. We let him go just in time to catch a two o'clock to Los Angeles. He says he's movin' out there permanently. What, he never told you?'

'Me? Why would he tell me?'

'No reason. I just thought—'

'Hey, Dick. Me and Red are ancient history, all right? Now, put a sock in it and go think somewhere else, I got work to do here.'

Glavin looked at him, measuring the level of his sincerity. Then he threw his head back and laughed one more time before turning and walking away.

Post watched the white man cross the crowded squad room, his mind wandering. He waited until Glavin had completely disappeared, then opened the top drawer of his desk and shuffled through the small landfill inside, looking for something. After a moment, he found the greeting card, the one he'd received just over a week ago and then quickly put away. It was one of those sexually suggestive numbers designed to titillate horny old men and easily excited college boys. There was a photograph on the front of two immense, perfectly tanned white breasts spilling out of a skimpy red brassiere, and the text inside read:

'I'm going to miss you, TWO.'

Someone named 'Red' had scribbled a short note about leaving for California, then signed his name at the bottom.

Post propped the card up on his desk for display and shook his head, like a weary mother hen pondering the fate of her most troublesome chick. It was nice to see his old partner still knew how to kick a little ass every now and then, but it was also unsettling to see that he hadn't yet learned how to *stop*. Some cops, ex or otherwise, never did.

Post used to hold out hope that the man he once thought of as a brother would someday come around, stop suffering these momentary lapses of self-control that always seemed to cost one deserving asshole or another a quart of blood. But no more. He had given up that pipe dream well over a year ago. Red was *entitled* to crash and burn occasionally, perhaps more so than any cop ever born, and Post had eventually grown tired of pretending not to feel that way himself. Because he had seen the bodies too, that cold November night. First Kaye's in Reddick's living room, then the two smaller ones upstairs. It was a sight he would never forget.

Post stared for a moment longer at the greeting card his old friend had sent him in lieu of a proper goodbye, then tossed it into the wire wastebasket beside his desk, shrugging. If Joe Reddick was indeed still a headcase after all this time, it was truly a crying shame. But it wasn't Charlie Post's problem anymore.

It was California's now.

PRESENT TENSE

LOS ANGELES, CALIFORNIA
Seven Years Later

ONE

You've done this sort of thing before,' the cop said. The nametag pinned to his left breast said his name was Connelly.

Reddick just looked at him.

'I remember you. You split a guy's head open with a garbage can out at Castaic Lake, about six, seven months ago. When I was still with the County Sheriff's.'

Reddick couldn't believe it. Of all the LAPD uniforms to catch this call ... 'That's got nothing to do with this,' he said, now vaguely recognizing the guy.

'He roughed your girlfriend up or something. Or was it your wife?'

'Look. I need to know. You gonna take me in, or not? My kid's gotta get home, he's dead on his feet.'

The cop glared at him, didn't even bother to glance over at the little five-year-old Reddick was talking about, curled up asleep on a couch nearby. He was trying to be civil, the uniform, treat Reddick like a person instead of an animal, and all Reddick could do by way of thanks was crack wise, act like he wasn't staring down the wrong end of some serious shit.

23

'Please answer my question, Mr Reddick,' the cop said. Not fucking around anymore.

'She was my wife,' Reddick said.

'The boy's mother?'

Reddick nodded.

'And what'd the guy do to her again? Refresh my memory.'

Grudgingly, still pretending he couldn't see what the earlier incident had to do with this one, Reddick obliged, told him how he had indeed used a metal garbage can to try and crush the skull of a bearded biker with a tattooed beer belly out at Castaic Lake the previous July. Before Dana had finally lost patience with him and asked him to move out.

'Yeah. I remember now,' the uniform said.

Reddick remained silent.

'They got into it out in the parking lot. The biker almost ran her over on his way out and she said something to him, got his ass all bent out of shape.'

Reddick still didn't say anything.

'As I recall, though, he never actually touched her. Just threatened to punch her lights out, or something along those lines.'

'That was enough.'

'You almost killed the man, Mr Reddick.'

Reddick shrugged. 'He said he was gonna knock her teeth out. If he was just talking to hear himself speak, he picked the wrong day to do it.'

The cop nodded, studied him in silence for a moment. 'Like this kid tonight. Guess he picked the wrong night to knock your kid down, too.'

Reddick shrugged again, still offering no

24

apologies. 'I guess so.'

They had just been horsing around. Three body-pierced skinheads in their late teens, white skin translucent as tissue paper, forearms and biceps stained blue with tattoos, pushing and shoving each other like drunken sailors as they stood in one of two long order lines at a Glendale McDonald's, just after ten on a Saturday night. Their language was blistering, an endless onslaught of 'fuck yous' and 'motherfuckers' that could have peeled paint from the walls, but their routine was being tolerated until one of them threw an elbow out, knocked a drink off a woman's tray as she tried to ease past. Orange soda exploded across the floor like liquid shrapnel and the restaurant's manager finally appeared, made a brave if ill-fated attempt to usher the trio out.

He was a mousy looking East Indian with a long neck and a bald, luminescent pate, and the skinheads showed him all the respect his mild appearance demanded. Which was to say, they laughed in his face, told him to get his 'black nigger ass' back behind the counter before they had to put their collective foot in it. Then, just to clarify their point, the largest of the three put his hands full in the manager's chest, shoved him backward into the group of people still standing in line behind him.

Reddick's son Jake hit the floor beneath the Indian's weight like a blindsided quarterback, the back of his head making an audible *whack* as it smacked off the hard linoleum.

And then the big skinhead laughed.

25

He never saw Reddick coming, a rocket launched from a nearby table, so he couldn't anticipate the overhand right Reddick threw at him, caving in the left side of his face like a papier mâché construct. The kid's friends watched him go down in a heap, blood spewing between his fingers as his hands went instinctively to his nose, and never thought twice about retaliation. They could see in Reddick's eyes that he was hoping they'd try it, give him any excuse to go after them, too.

Afterward, in the deafening silence that took over the restaurant, every customer in attendance had gazed at Reddick in open horror, as if he were something wild that had wandered in off the street to attack and feed off the innocent.

It was a reaction to which Reddick was no stranger.

'You don't think you might have overreacted a little?' the uniform asked now. 'I mean, this kid you hit's no Boy Scout, I grant you, but he didn't *intend*—'

'I don't give a damn what he intended,' Reddick said. 'He hurt a five-year-old boy during the commission of an assault. Damn near broke his neck. Far as I'm concerned, he got off easy.'

The cop fell silent again, in an awkward spot. He was professionally obligated to admonish Reddick, to make some concerted effort to condemn his attack on an unarmed man damn near half his age, but his heart clearly wasn't in it. Reddick knew the nature of his confliction, because he'd seen it in others before: Just as he

26

had out at Castaic Lake six months ago, the uniform probably admired him. If he had a wife and kids of his own, how could he not envy the zeal with which Reddick seemed determined to defend his family from all the scumbags of the earth?

'Tell you what, Mr Reddick,' the cop said eventually, closing his little notebook up to announce that he was all through asking questions. 'We're gonna let you go. Again. The kid wants to sue you in civil court later, that's his privilege, but I'm not gonna bust you for protecting your boy from someone who, as you just pointed out, was in the act of committing an assault of his own.'

Reddick waited for the 'but.'

'But I'd like to offer you a little bit of advice, if I may.' He fixed his eyes on Reddick's, made sure he had his full attention before going on. 'You know that expression "chill out"? I think you'd better learn how to do that. Because if this sort of thing happens to you as often as I think it does...' He shrugged. 'Sooner or later, the wrong people are gonna get hurt. It's only a matter of time.'

Thirty minutes later, Dana took her own turn making Reddick feel like an ass.

Dropping their son off at home at the ungodly hour of one a.m. had been an easy tip-off that something had gone wrong. Reddick could be irresponsible, but never where Jake was concerned. That much, at least, she knew about him.

'What happened, Joe?' she asked, after he had

27

laid the sleeping boy down in his bed and she had escorted Reddick back to the door, like a prison guard showing an inmate the way back to his cell.

'Nothing,' Reddick said. 'The movie ran late and we ate after instead of before. I should've called, but I didn't. I'm sorry.'

'You're lying,' Dana said.

Reddick stared at her, his cheeks burning. Eight years his junior at thirty-three, his estranged second wife was a big-boned, auburn-haired beauty whose luminous green eyes had always disarmed him, but never more so than at times like this, when he was trying to feed her a line. So he cut to the chase, gave her a short version of the evening's events, doing what he could to make them sound innocuous. She wasn't fooled one bit.

'Jesus, Joe,' she said.

'Yeah, I know. Same old Red. Thank God he's soon to be your ex, huh?'

'Don't do that. Don't start talking about *us* when we were talking about *you*.'

'Let it go, Dana. No damage was done, all right?'

'You can't go on this way, Joe. You need to start seeing Dr Elkins again. If you don't—'

'Hey, I've gotta go. Do me a favor, tell Jake I'll call him tomorrow or Monday, come by to see him again next week. OK?'

He turned to leave and Dana let him, both of them lacking the energy to resume their favorite pastime of late, arguing endlessly over things that would never change. She had disappeared

28

inside the house before he could even back his car out of the driveway.

The five-mile drive to Reddick's apartment in Echo Park was a long one. He deliberately took the surface streets to extend it, to give himself time to gear down before any attempt at sleep could prove futile. He even put the radio on, scanned the dial until he found an FM station playing the most sedate pseudo-jazz imaginable.

But his mind raced helter-skelter all the same.

He'd come a long way in nine years. That much was irrefutable. The recurring nightmare that had chased him out of Florida rarely visited him anymore, and when it did, he could deal with it, shake off its effects before he did something stupid to make the pain go away. He had some semblance of self-control now.

But in many ways, he was still damaged goods. Just another crazy waiting for his next dark impulse to come unglued. That he had been moved to violence tonight by more noble motives than usual did little to change this fact.

Still, Reddick was all but unrepentant. A return to normalcy would have been nice, but normalcy had its drawbacks. Complacency, in particular. Belief in the idea that nothing bad ever happened to those who didn't somehow ask for it, either by omission or commission. Or that the safety and security of the people you loved was something you could purchase with cold, hard cash, rather than forge in blood, time and time again. These were all mere delusions, lies people told themselves to give them comfort at night, and

29

every day they cost some poor bastard dearly.

But not Reddick. Reddick was one of the enlightened. And being enlightened, he felt little fear, because now he knew what was necessary to hold on to what was his, to keep those who peopled his private little universe out of harm's way: Vigilance. Constant vigilance. That, and a ready and unapologetic willingness to do unto others long before they could do unto those he loved. Reddick's rule to live by was a simple one: No one hurt his family for free, *ever* – and nothing would ever make him abandon it. Not Dana's threats of divorce, not being separated from his son – nothing.

He had been burned once. It would never happen to him again.

With home less than five minutes away, Reddick sped south through a yellow light on Fletcher Drive just before the Glendale Freeway exit ramp, saw nothing but clear sailing ahead and then a white van on his right came out of no-where to leap into his path.

Reddick stood on his brakes and turned his wheel hard left to avoid the collision, sending his Mustang across the double yellow line dissecting the street. Conversely, the driver of the white Chrysler hit the gas, burned rubber in his own quest to keep the two vehicles apart. But both men were attempting the impossible. Inevitably, the Ford and Chrysler slammed to-gether, right headlight to left rear quarter panel, then skidded to a halt, both gouged and dented but otherwise intact.

Reddick's Mustang sat there making ticking noises on the wrong side of the street, the stench of burning rubber thick in his nose.

'Crazy sonofabitch!'

He looked over at the van, wired with adrenaline, watched in amazement as, its engine still running, it began to roll forward and then accelerated.

The guy wasn't going to stop.

Incredulous, Reddick restarted the Mustang, slammed it into gear, and mashed on the gas to go after the idiot.

It only took him forty seconds to catch up with him.

Driving home less than a half-hour later, hands still slick with sweat, Andy Baumhower knew he was in big trouble.

It would have been inaccurate to say he was surprised, however, because he'd been waiting for disaster to strike all night. Disaster was the fate of all amateur felons eventually, and that was what Baumhower was tonight, an amateur. Just a white collar criminal playing a big league game. If he hadn't fucked up by causing an ill-timed car accident, he would've found some other way to do it.

Still, he considered himself lucky. He'd managed to escape from this guy Reddick, the Mustang's driver, without having to deal with the police. They had exchanged addresses and phone numbers, and insurance and driver's license info, and that was it. The damage to both vehicles had been minimal and no one, thank

31

God, had been hurt. Reddick had wanted to call the cops anyway, enraged by Baumhower's foolish attempt at hit-and-run, but Baumhower had talked him out of it, playing the remorseful, apologetic sop who couldn't afford another hike in his insurance rates to the hilt.

Not that Reddick had been an easy sell. He'd no more bought Baumhower's reasons for not wanting the police involved than he had the younger man's explanation for why he'd been where he was when the accident occurred: coming off an LA River access road that should have been closed to the public. Baumhower had said he'd mistaken the dark access road for an on-ramp to the adjacent Glendale Freeway and quickly reversed his field, not bothering to watch for opposing traffic upon re-entry to Fletcher Drive. Reddick hadn't asked him to elaborate, just accepted his story in silence, but Baumhower could tell he wasn't fooled. He'd only acted like he was for reasons of his own.

Which was why Baumhower was worried now, sweaty palms sliding all over the wounded van's wheel as he raced home to Chatsworth. The feeling Reddick had left him with was that he wasn't a man easily duped. That he had seen through Baumhower like an open window and would come back to haunt him later. Maybe even as early as tomorrow.

When Baumhower would have to explain to his three accomplices why they should have never asked him to dispose of Gillis Rainey's body in the first place.

TWO

That night, as Reddick might have guessed it would, the nightmare revisited him. Beginning, as always, in his old green Pontiac, rolling through a dark Florida landscape toward home...

... and from his first sight of the house, he knows something is wrong.

It's a few minutes past ten on a Wednesday evening in November, the end of a long day. Just short of twenty miles and a seemingly interminable drive north of downtown West Palm Beach, the sleepy suburb of Lake Park is cold beneath a black, disinterested sky, and the short little cul-de-sac which the Reddick home terminates is empty and silent, devoid of life. Kaye's station wagon, a Mercury Sable in gun-metal gray, is in the driveway out front, where he has come to expect it, but the house is pitch black, and this is the aberration that alarms him immediately.

Because he knows Kaye has no patience for the dark.

The demented sadist she had for a father once locked her in a closet as a small child, to punish her for crying too long and too hard over something she has never been able to recall, and she has spent half her life surrounding herself with light ever since. By the time the sun has fully set each day, she has already made her rounds, moving from room to room to illuminate the house, repelling the forces of darkness with all the singlemindedness of a priest performing an exorcism. It is an eccentricity she seems powerless to contain, and, in fact, never has in all the nine years she and Reddick have been married.

Until now.

Jumping out of his old Firebird, its feeble and unwilling engine having died of its own volition before he could actually kill the ignition, Reddick rushes to his front door, fumbling with his heavy ring of keys, and is relieved to find the door locked and deadbolted, showing no sign of forced entry. Rational explanations for the darkened house only now begin to occur to him. In the time it takes to open the door and step inside, he convinces himself that his fears are unfounded, that Joe Reddick the cop has yet again brought his job home and overreacted to harmless, after-hours stimuli. If the problem battery in the wagon outside has finally gone dead on her, Reddick can, with a little imagination, see Kaye picking the kids up from school in a neighbor's car and taking them shopping afterward, losing all track of time. Or finally blowing a fuse with her nightly 6,000-watt light show and, having no idea how or where to change it, staying at a friend's house until Reddick can come home from work to do it himself.

Only a few seconds inside the house, however, he knows such optimistic speculation is but wishful thinking. Reddick has smelled blood

34

before, too many times to mistake it for anything else, and its telltale stench is here, filling the darkness before him with an undeniable warning of things to come. He tests the wall switch nearby, determined to prove his instincts wrong, but instead only confirms their reliability when the foyer is flooded with light.

As a dizzying swell of nausea quickly begins to overtake him, he calls out at last, his voice barely recognizable as his own:

'Kaye!'

He finds her in the living room. Laying face down, half-naked, on the floor, blood staining the shag carpet beneath her like black dye. The hilt of a large kitchen knife protrudes from the back of her neck.

Reddick retches into his open hands, blinking back tears that burn like ammonia, then races without thinking up the stairs to look for his children. Halfway up the blood-dappled staircase—

He woke up. Mouth open but silent, a fistful of bed sheet in each hand.

He was rigid with fear and his breathing was ragged, but he wasn't screaming. He had learned to stop screaming long ago. The mattress beneath him was soaked with sweat. He looked at the clock on his bedside table, saw that it was only four a.m. He hadn't been asleep more than two hours.

Once upon a time, there had been no rhyme or reason to the timing of the nightmare's appearances. It came and went as it pleased, requiring

35

no inducement to show itself. But no more. Nine years and two shrinks had at least seen to that. Now when the dream came to him, it was as a reflex action, a delayed response to some sudden anxiety. A deep sense of guilt or rage; even sexual excitement could sometimes precipitate the nightmare's invasions of his sleep.

This time it was fear.

Or at least, the odd sensation that trouble, in one shape or another, lay just ahead. Good cops learned to sense trouble coming from miles away and Reddick was no exception. Even after years away from the job, his instincts about such things remained unassailable.

This guy Baumhower, the dickhead in the white Chrysler van tonight, had been bad news. His story about why he'd come flying off that LA River access road the way he had was bullshit, and there'd been more to his reluctance to file a police report than any fear of having his insurance rates go up. A stone-cold killer the guy wasn't – he was too much of a wuss for that – but Reddick was fairly certain that, whatever he'd been doing just prior to plowing his van into Reddick's Mustang, it had probably been something a real cop might want to investigate.

Why he should have cared what the truth was, no longer being a real cop himself, Reddick didn't know. His only interest in Baumhower now should have been a check from him for the damages to his car, plus any medical expenses he might incur later. And yet, Reddick couldn't shake the feeling that Baumhower was an omen of some kind. The tip of some disastrous iceberg

36

that would soon be in his path.

And he worried that this would not be the last restless night he endured on the little asshole's account.

THREE

'For Chrissake, Perry, let me kill the dumb fuck,' Ben Clarke said. 'Please.'

Clarke was sitting in one of the two leather chairs opposite Perry Cross's office desk, glaring at Andy Baumhower with what could only be described as utter contempt. Clarke was a big man with a flat, linebacker's face, and when he scowled, his black eyes all but disappeared beneath the overhang of his slab-like brow. It was a countenance that had to be seen to be properly appreciated.

The whippet-thin Baumhower, meanwhile, one of Clarke's three equally white, twenty-something partners in the fledgling consortium of diverse businesses they called 'Class Act Productions,' was perched on a stool at Cross's wet bar, right alongside Will Sinnott, who was already hard at work on tomorrow morning's hangover.

'Fuck you, Ben,' Baumhower said.

Drunk or sober, he wasn't fond of Clarke, and had never gone out of his way to disguise the fact. On several occasions, in fact, in order to receive the respect he felt his Herculean stature deserved, Clarke had found it necessary to demonstrate to Baumhower just how easily he

38

could break the smaller man's neck. Another such demonstration seemed to be in the making until Cross, to whom Clarke deferred shamelessly, raised a hand to freeze him in his tracks.

'Take it easy, Ben. Andy ran into a little bad luck, that's all.'

Cross was standing before the wall of dark, one-way glass that stretched from floor to ceiling behind his massive rosewood desk, watching an elderly woman with a head full of alarming white hair blow a five-foot putt by a mile. From his office suite up on the nineteenth floor of the Century Court Towers building in Century City, his view of the Los Angeles Country Club's back nine was without limit, and he often liked to show his back to his three friends in order to follow play down on the greens.

'Bad luck my ass,' Clarke said. 'He fucked up. We're all dead now, and he knows it.'

'It wasn't my fault, asshole,' Baumhower said.

'Yeah? You should've run away, you dipshit! The guy can place you at the scene now. He's got your name, your address—'

'It doesn't matter, Ben,' Cross said flatly, shaking his head. 'Better that it weren't true, yes, but as long as this fellow never comes to connect Andy to Gillis's body...'

'What, and you don't think he *will*? The master criminal here dumped Rainey in an open storm drain, for Chrissake. After we told 'im to lose the body where nobody'll ever find it.' He turned to Baumhower again. 'In case you never heard, Einstein, the homeless hide out in those storm drains all the time. If one of 'em doesn't

39

come across Rainey before the week is out, it'll be a goddamn miracle.'

'All right! I made a mistake! I think we all get it, Ben, Jesus!' Baumhower had had enough of Clarke's constant harping. 'But let's not forget whose idea it was for *me* to get rid of the body in the first place, shall we? If you're such a goddamn expert on the proper disposal of dead bodies, why the hell didn't you and Perry take care of Rainey's yourselves?'

'Because you're the one who killed the poor bastard,' Sinnott said. It was the first time he'd opened his mouth all morning.

Baumhower turned to face him, surprised. He and Sinnott weren't allies, exactly, but they often found themselves on the same side of an issue whenever Cross and Clarke, the master and his lackey, joined forces in a company debate. Baumhower couldn't help but feel a little betrayed, having the fat and inebriated wuss that was Will Sinnott turn on him now.

Even if every word he'd just said was true.

They were just four little rich boys with money. Murder was supposed to be out of their league.

Clarke's old man was a *Fortune 500* communications magnate; Baumhower's father was an internationally renowned orthopedic surgeon and his mother an equally famous divorce attorney; Sinnott's parents were just plain filthy rich, born to money made three generations ago in the newspaper and textile industries. All the wealth and power Cross possessed, however, he had amassed himself, in spite of his parents. His

40

father was the alcoholic owner/operator of a fast food franchise in North Hollywood, and his mother was a part-time stenographer. Neither had ever given Cross a dime.

Clarke and Sinnott had attended Stanford together and had hooked up with the other two after graduation through various intermediaries. Cross had been a regular at McCullough's, Clarke's Westwood area nightclub, and the two hit it off immediately, Clarke all but mesmerized by the other man's moviestar good looks and unflappable cool. The four became inseparable – two sociopaths and a couple of weak sisters who admired them – and they all shared the same ambitions toward fame, fortune, and autonomy from the moral boundaries that lesser men had to abide by. They formed Class Act Productions so as to pool their resources and unify their efforts to become billionaires by the time they were each thirty-five. That they might find it necessary to break a law or two along the way concerned none of them in the least, though only Clarke would not have blanched at the idea of murder.

But murder was what they had committed, however inadvertently.

Baumhower and Sinnott had been against Cross's insane plan to kidnap Gillis Rainey from the start. They wanted no part of it. But Rainey owed them money he seemed determined not to repay and Cross was insistent that such desperate measures were necessary to get it back. He not only wanted a unanimous vote on the old fool's abduction, he demanded they all take an active role in the enterprise, something only Clarke was eager to do. Sinnott, being the gutless wonder that he was, eventually caved in to them both, and that left Baumhower no choice but to do likewise, certain that the fifty-one-year-old Rainey's kidnapping would somehow blow up in their faces.

It did exactly that – and Andy Baumhower was to blame.

He was to blame because, less than sixteen hours after their former 'financial advisor' had been snatched from his West Hollywood home and left in Baumhower's charge, Rainey was dead, putting the $100,000 refund they had been hoping to extort from him forever out of reach. Cross had forgotten that Rainey was a diabetic. Baumhower had thought all the thrashing about he'd been doing inside the storage room Clarke had locked him up in at the back of McCullough's had simply been the man's feeble attempts to either escape, or attract a would-be rescuer's attention. Who could have guessed the sonofabitch was having a diabetic seizure?

Certainly not Andy Baumhower. He sat outside that storage room door all of last Saturday afternoon without making a single move to go inside, certain there was nothing more to Rainey's frenetic groaning and foot stomping than desperation and rage. Imagine his surprise when Rainey turned up dead.

It was a mistake any of the others could have made just as easily, but since Baumhower had been the one to make it, Cross had assigned him

42

the task of disposing of the dead man's body. He said it was the only fair thing to do.

Cross couldn't believe his accursed luck.

Clarke was laying the blame for their predicament entirely at Andy Baumhower's feet, but everyone knew it was really Cross who was responsible. He was the one who'd brought Rainey into the Class Act fold to begin with.

His friends had always been able to see the low-rent real estate tycoon and self-proclaimed 'investments broker' as the silver-tongued shyster that he was, but not Cross. Forever on the lookout for another mentor, Cross had met Rainey at an otherwise boring dinner party and immediately insisted the Class Act *wunderkinds* do business with him. Rainey promised he could turn $100,000 of Class Act's money into a hundred and twenty-five in only six months, and Cross wouldn't rest until his partners had bought in, dismissing all their objections as the murmurs of small men who were terrified of becoming big ones.

It was a decision he deeply regretted now, of course.

Almost eight months later, Rainey had yet to return their original investment, let alone produce a profit from it, and it had seemed he was determined to go on punking them that way indefinitely, counting on their reluctance to spend money he knew they didn't have by taking him to court. Now the asshole was dead, and every dime of their hundred grand was gone.

It was a huge setback, to be sure, but only

Cross knew the full extent of it. Clarke was blowing a gasket over this guy Joseph Reddick, when Reddick was actually the least of their problems. Their real problem was Ruben Lizama. Cross had managed to keep Ruben's name out of things up until now, not wanting to hear all the wailing and gnashing of teeth he would have to endure if his friends found out what he'd done, but he couldn't keep them in the dark any longer. They needed to recoup their hundred grand, fast, and put together another $150,000 to go with it, and the sooner they figured out how to do both, the better.

They were all just dead men walking if they didn't.

FOUR

Of Ruben Miguel Lizama's three older brothers, Jorge Junior, the eldest, was his favorite.

Which really only meant that his tolerance for Jorge was greater than it was for either Juan or Roberto. Juan and Roberto liked to get in Ruben's business, while Jorge never did. As the heir apparent to Jorge Lizama Senior, one of the most powerful Mexican drug lords operating out of North America, Jorge was too self-secure to have any interest in the private affairs of his brothers, no matter how his knowledge of them could be used to his own advantage.

Ruben liked that.

What Jorge liked about Ruben, conversely, was his baby brother's complete indifference to power. While the prospect of someday inheriting the family business from the legendary *El Principito* ('The Little Prince') had both Juan and Roberto openly salivating, Ruben seemed almost put off by the idea. The amenities of wealth gave him great comfort but, unlike his older siblings, he had no use whatsoever for the influence wealth had on other people. Ruben had ways of his own to secure the cooperation of others, and none of them had anything to do with money.

45

This last was something Jorge Junior *didn't* like about Ruben, but for which he had a great deal of respect, nonetheless.

'So. *Que pasa, manito?*' Jorge said.

It was late Monday afternoon in Manhattan, only hours after Perry Cross and friends had gathered together to discuss Andy Baumhower's car accident with Joe Reddick on the opposite coast. The two Lizama brothers were sitting in Jorge's lavish suite at the Hotel Pierre on Fifth Avenue, enjoying a panoramic view of Central Park at dusk, the $40,000 in chump change their father had sent Ruben here to deliver having already exchanged hands. Rene, Jorge's chief bodyguard, sat nearby, watching soccer on a muted television, face folded up in deep concentration.

Ruben shrugged, said, *'No mas aqui.* I'm tired. All this running around...'

'You're an errand boy. That's what errand boys do, run around.'

'I know.'

'There are more important things you could be doing. If you wanted—'

'I don't want to do anything "important." I'm just tired, that's all.'

Jorge saw the look Ruben was giving him, knew it was an order to back off. Ruben was perfectly satisfied being his father's personal messenger, and maybe always would be. If he had any burning ambition at all, it was to someday become his father's most trusted enforcer, a job no member of a major crime family ever held, due to all the risks it entailed. Aspiring to

46

be a lowly soldier, a thug who did all the messy blood work the drug trade demanded, was crazy, and Jorge Junior didn't understand it. But that was Ruben. He had a morbid fascination with blood, and he had established himself as someone who could spill it in creative, memorable ways that often worked to the family's advantage.

Jorge was thirty-two, Ruben only twenty-six, and yet the two men could have practically passed for identical twins. Only the ten extra pounds Jorge was carrying around made them distinguishable from one another. Both had the same dark complexion and smooth, angular jaw as their father, and both were thick in the chest and narrow in the waist, the exact opposite of Juan and Roberto and the portly Jorge Senior. The pair even wore their raven black hair the same way, combed straight back and tied in a simple ponytail.

'OK. *Lo siento*,' Jorge said. 'Let's talk about something else, hmm?'

'Like what?'

'Like your four friends in California. The rich little *gabachos*.'

Ruben was slow to say anything. 'What about them?'

'It's none of my business, of course. And what's none of my business, I usually treat that way. You know that, yes?'

'I know it. What is it, Jorge?'

His brother glanced over at Rene, said, 'Roberto knows about them, little brother. He knows about *everything*.'

47

'What everything?'

'Please. No games. I didn't have to tell you this, I could have just kept quiet. But I don't like to see you fucked with, so I'm telling you: He knows about the money you gave them. I don't know how, but he does.'

Ruben studied his brother carefully, letting him see the suspicion behind his eyes. 'Maybe he found out the same way you did. By spying on me like a woman.'

Jorge shook his head. 'I don't spy. But people tell me things. I pay them well to tell me things.'

'OK. So Roberto knows. So what?'

'So if Papi doesn't know already, he soon will. And if anything goes *wrong*—'

'Nothing's going to go wrong. I know these guys, I checked them out. They'll deliver as promised, don't worry.'

'Me? *I'm* not worrying. I'm not the one doing business with fucking *hueros*. You know how Papi feels about—'

'Working with white boys, yes, yes. I know all about it. But Papi's not me. I have my own way of doing business, I'm my own man.'

'Yes, but—'

'Roberto can tell Papi whatever he likes. Juan, too. It makes no difference to me.'

'No?'

'No. My brothers forget that Papi will die soon, and you will be *el patron*, not them. And when that happens, all the ass kissing and back-stabbing they've done to get ahead will be for nothing. And I won't have to pretend I don't despise them anymore.' He stood up, brushed the

48

lint from his suit as a prelude to leaving. 'Tell them that the next time you see them, huh?'

'Ruben...'

Ruben turned at the door, said, 'Relax, big brother. I know what I'm doing. I always do.' He grinned, then walked out before either Jorge or Rene could stop him.

During the long elevator ride down to the hotel lobby, alone in the car throughout, Ruben thought about the news he had just received, and what, if anything, he should do about it. His father would be furious to learn he had entrusted $250,000 of the cartel's money to four baby-faced *Americanos*, it was true, but nothing of consequence would come of *El Principito's* anger as long as Ben Clarke delivered on his promises. That was the key. Clean money was clean money, no matter where it came from, and if Clarke and his three partners could launder the quarter million as promised, when promised, Jorge Senior and his two overly ambitious sons, Juan and Roberto, would have little to complain about.

The Class Act boys were due to produce the money in exactly eleven days. Ruben had planned to fly into Los Angeles a day or two early just for the occasion, but now he had a better idea. He would fly in a full week early instead. Relax and enjoy himself over the weekend, then say hello to Clarke and the others first thing Monday morning. Long before they were expecting to see him.

Just to make sure they weren't planning to make him look stupid in front of his family.

49

FIVE

Orvis Andrews was looking for a big payday. The biggest of his life, in fact. The figure his lawyers were throwing around was eleven million, but many observers believed he could get more than that, if he and his legal team played their cards right. Two of the LAPD's finest had beaten Andrews senseless nine months earlier out in Woodland Hills, trying to take him in on a spousal abuse charge without having to kill him first, and the black man was now suing the department and the city which funded it for all his injuries were worth.

And what injuries he had. A broken pelvic bone, one shattered kneecap, a broken left eye-socket, and three broken teeth, two upper, one lower. Witnesses said when the cops brought him into County/USC Hospital prior to booking, he looked like somebody the tanks had run over in Tiananmen Square.

On the surface, it appeared to be the Rodney King fiasco all over again, except that this time, no one had been around with a handy camcorder or cell phone to record Andrews's beating for posterity, leaving certain aspects of it open to debate. Like how it happened and why, for instance. Not surprisingly, Andrews's story was that the cops had seen a brother who needed some knots on his head and immediately proceeded to administer them, whether such action was called for or not. The cops, meanwhile, were crying self-defense, claiming the six-foot-six-inch, 230-pound Andrews had resisted arrest with a vengeance, fueled by rage and controlled substances of unknown origin. The truth was probably somewhere in-between, but since eyewitnesses to the incident were scarce, and what there were had only conflicting opinions about what, exactly, they had seen that night, it seemed the court was going to have to decide for itself what precipitated Orvis Andrews's beating, and what, if anything, he was entitled to in the way of compensation.

Fortunately for Andrews, this decision would be made based entirely on the merits of the evidence at hand, rather than the sympathies of the court. For if ever a plaintiff appeared undeserving of the court's sympathy – or anyone else's sympathy, for that matter – Orvis Andrews did. Because Andrews was not a particularly nice man. He was a career criminal with a bad temper whose eclectic rap sheet was exactly six pages long, and counting. Which, while it didn't grant the LAPD license to beat him within an inch of his life for sport, did help to explain why the officers involved might have thought it necessary to treat him differently than their average, law-abiding citizen.

With Andrews's case scheduled to go to trial in less than three weeks, Reddick's surveillance of the big man had just gone into high gear. As a chief investigator for the City Attorney's office, it was Reddick's job to investigate the validity of civil claims made against the LAPD, and in that role, he'd been following Andrews around now for almost a month. It was the most boring work Reddick had ever done.

Among the many injuries Andrews was claiming to have sustained in his late night waltz with the police was a spinal contusion that had left him partially paralyzed on the right side of his body, and he'd been hobbling about, first on crutches, then with the aid of a cane, ever since leaving the hospital. In twenty-six days of surveillance, Reddick had yet to see the big man move an inch without the benefit of one or the other, the crutches or the cane, making him about as exciting to watch for eight hours a day as an ant farm.

Still, Reddick was convinced that Andrews's partial paralysis was just a sham, a mere gilding of his actual injuries designed to make $11,000,000 in damages seem woefully insufficient, and Reddick had not lost hope that he would be there, digital video camera in hand, when Andrews finally let his guard down and proved it.

Today was the day.

Every man had a weakness, a passion over which he had limited control, and Andrews was no exception. He had a vice that had been calling him for over nine months now, something he could not properly indulge in while pretending to be handicapped, and this was the day it broke him down, led him to risk everything just for a momentary taste of its bittersweet rewards. For some, the mistress who could not be denied was blow; for others, rock or smack. Gambling or alcohol, porno or phone sex.

For Orvis Andrews, it was bowling.

Three o'clock on a Wednesday afternoon, four days after Andy Baumhower's mini-van had exchanged sheet metal with Reddick's Mustang, Andrews limped into Arrowhead Lanes way the hell out in Lancaster and rolled six games. Reddick sat at the opposite end of the near-empty building and, lower back aching for the fourth day in a row, discreetly aimed a compact video camera at the black man as he bowled four 200-plus games and one in the high 190s, after starting off slow with a 145. And all with a house ball and his right arm, the one the LAPD was supposed to have rendered useless.

Reddick hoped Andrews hadn't already spent that eleven million.

Meanwhile, seventy miles to the south of Bakersfield, an amateur bird watcher named Angela Cromartie was walking along a stretch of the LA River in Silverlake when she spotted something with her binoculars that was most definitely not a Blacknecked Stilt. It was a man's leg, protruding from the shadows engulfing a storm drain opening in the north wall of the basin. She thought it had to be something else, a pile of old clothing with a shoe jutting out of it at an odd angle or something – but no. She kept the binoculars trained on it until she was sure: It was a man's leg, fully clothed, and it wasn't

53

moving.

It didn't have to belong to a corpse. There were dozens of other explanations for it. But as she pulled her cell phone from a windbreaker pocket and started inching her way up to the storm drain, moving as if through slabs of mud, she couldn't make herself believe a single one of them.

SIX

The next morning, Thursday, the story was on page twenty-two of *The Los Angeles Times*. It was only four paragraphs long.

It said that the body of an unidentified Caucasian male, age approximately fifty, had been discovered in the LA River near the Atwater area of Los Angeles late Wednesday afternoon. An Eagle Rock resident named Angela Cromartie had stumbled upon the fully clothed corpse while walking the river and alerted authorities. Cause of death was unknown pending toxicology tests, but a police spokesperson told reporters the body, which investigators estimated had been in the river about a week, showed no obvious signs of foul play.

Reddick never saw the story, but Will Sinnott did. He'd been waiting for such a news report to make the papers, or appear somewhere online, ever since Andy Baumhower had told his Class Act partners about the car accident he'd had immediately after dumping Gillis Rainey's body in the river. Like Ben Clarke, Sinnott had recognized the accident, and Andy's mishandling of it, as a catastrophe rife with danger. If Rainey's body were ever discovered and identified, and this guy Andy had crashed into – Joseph Reddick – heard about it, and put two and two together ... the cops would be knocking on Andy's door within hours. And after that?

End game.

Oh, Cross talked like he didn't believe it, like Ben was just overreacting to the most remote of all possible outcomes, but Sinnott knew better. There were only so many blunders a group of amateur criminals could make before their incompetence finally caught up with them, and Sinnott and his friends had already committed more than their fair share.

Rainey's body turning up now, less than a week after Baumhower had disposed of it, had been all but inevitable, and Sinnott had little doubt it was the harbinger of even worse things to come.

As bad as the news was, however, he knew it wasn't going to warrant anyone's full attention, because the boys behind Class Act Productions had a much more immediate problem on their hands.

In eight days, they were due to pay Ben's psychotic friend Ruben Lizama a quarter million dollars, and they were still trying to figure out how the hell they could scrape up that kind of cash in so short a period of time.

Unlike his three spineless business partners, Ben Clarke actually relished the idea of becoming a serious criminal.

At this stage in his young life, with no felony arrests to his credit, the twenty-four-year-old Stanford grad with the lumberjack build and gravel pit voice was merely a bully who aspired to the next level; he could talk the talk, but he had yet to walk the walk. Clarke found this deeply annoying, and he was bound and determined to change it.

Though he had no practical experience in serious crime himself, he had many casual acquaintances who did. It was a natural byproduct of the business he was in. Clarke's end of the Class Act consortium consisted of three highly profitable Los Angeles area nightclubs – McCullough's out in Westwood, where Gillis Rainey had died, Nightshades in Santa Monica, and Primo Joe's, just around the corner from Cross's office in Century City – and all were popular hangouts for the most beautiful young gangsters Los Angeles had to offer. Pimps, dealers, call girls, and gangbangers – Clarke entertained them all, and was thrilled to do so.

But no one intrigued him more than Ruben.

A regular guest of all of Clarke's establishments, Ruben was rich, beautiful, and effervescent, everything Clarke demanded to see in his clientele, and the man drew desirable women to him like a magnet. Clarke liked to think that the LA nightlife began and ended with his three clubs, and that never seemed a more justifiable conceit than when Ruben and his tiny entourage were somewhere in attendance, igniting the room with light and laughter.

Of course, Clarke had recognized Ruben as a drug trafficker immediately, but this only added to his allure. Ruben was living the life Clarke dreamed of having himself someday, one unaffected by the moral and ethical constraints smaller men were forced to adhere to, and Clarke considered every minute spent in Ruben's company an education he couldn't get anywhere else.

It was with this kind of fawning admiration that Clarke eventually offered Ruben entree into the Class Act inner circle. He was hoping that, merely by linking his own fortunes with Ruben's, some of the Mexican national's magic might somehow rub off on him. Clarke and his three partners had been looking for seed money at the time, struggling to get the fourth and last segment of their combined businesses – Will Sinnott's exotic car detailing service – off the ground, and they'd been too hungry and over-zealous to much care where it came from. Had they known who Ruben really was, Clarke's friends would have wanted nothing to do with him, but Clarke led them all to believe he was just a common coke peddler trying to go legit, and they bought it. They were too green to do otherwise. Baumhower fretted and Sinnott whined, but in the end, with Cross's blessings, Clarke took $250,000 of Ruben's money and promised him Class Act Productions would clean, press, and return it in one year.

Now that money was gone. Fucking Cross had gambled it away. Gone out to Vegas with his goddamn girlfriend and burned up a quarter million dollars belonging to an enforcer for one of the three biggest and most dangerous drug cartels in Mexico.

'You had better be fucking kidding me,' Clarke

had said when Cross made the confession Monday.

But Cross hadn't been kidding, of course – who the hell would joke about such a thing? – and Clarke had his hands locked around the smaller man's throat, before either Baumhower or Sinnott could stop him, the moment this became obvious.

Killing Gillis Rainey had been a bad mistake. Leaving his body in the LA River, then getting involved in a traffic accident with somebody immediately afterward, had been a monumental blunder. But fucking with Ruben Lizama's money was suicidal. It was the kind of thing a man did when life held no meaning for him anymore, and he didn't care how much pain he would have to endure just to see it come to an end.

'I *told* you, Perry. Jesus Christ, *I told you*!' Clarke bellowed when Sinnott and Baumhower, working as a team, had managed to put some distance between him and Cross. 'This guy's crazy! The man hammers ice picks into people's ears, for Chrissake!'

'Come on, Ben. You don't really believe that?'

'You're goddamn right I do!'

Clarke had never seen it himself, but the people he'd heard it from were not in the habit of making up such colorful stories.

'Oh, Christ,' Sinnott said, whimpering, and Clarke turned to look at him just in time to see him vomit on to his own shoes.

Cross pretended not to have noticed. 'I had a run of bad luck. I thought we'd get our money

59

back from Gillis.'

'And then?' Clarke said. 'Gillis only owed us a hundred thousand, Perry. Where the hell did you think Ruben's other hundred and fifty was going to come from if you're only just now bothering to tell us this shit?'

Cross didn't answer.

'I don't believe it,' Baumhower said, almost laughing. 'He was going to roll the dice again!'

'I told you, I had a run of bad luck. It wasn't going to last, it never does. I would have made Ruben's money back, and more.'

'Two hundred and fifty thousand? You crazy sonofabitch!' Sinnott said, wiping his face and hands with a bar towel. 'You're sick, Perry. You need help!'

'Excuse me?'

'You heard the man,' Clarke said. The others had never heard him speak to Cross this way before. 'You're sick. You've got an illness, and you told us you were gonna do something about it. You were gonna see a doctor, you said.'

Jesus, Perry thought, he sounds just like Iris.

'I intended to,' he said. 'I just thought ... Well, I thought I had things under control.'

The four men fell silent as one, the magnitude of their dilemma slowly sinking in.

'So what are we going to do?' Sinnott asked.

The question was meant for everyone, but Perry took it upon himself to answer it. 'Well, for one thing, convert as many assets to cash as we can, as quickly as we can. After that...'

They all looked at him, waiting for the other shoe to drop.

'...as much as I hate to suggest it, I think the tried and true would probably be best.'

Baumhower began shaking his head from side to side as if he were trying to break something loose within. 'Not a chance. No way. You're talking about what, two hundred thousand dollars? I couldn't get another dime out of my folks if I put a gun to their fucking heads.'

'And that goes double for me,' Sinnott said. 'My father's cut me off. He's all done loaning me money.'

'Perhaps if your parents were made to understand the gravity of the situation, they'd reconsider,' Cross said.

'And exactly how are we supposed to do that?' Clarke asked him. 'Make them understand the gravity of the situation? "Hey Mom, Dad, we owe a drug dealer two hundred fifty thousand in a week, and if we don't come up with the scratch, he's gonna cut our balls off." Is that what we're supposed to say?'

'Of course not. What I would do is make up a story in which, if you don't get the loan, your family's good name will become front page news for all the worst possible – and most socially embarrassing – reasons. Your folks may not give a shit about your balls, but they sure as hell care about their reputations. Feel free to correct me if I'm wrong.'

No one even bothered to try.

In the four days since that time, Cross had proven to be a prophet. Using bullshit cover stories along the lines of what he had proposed, Clarke and Baumhower had already managed to squeeze roughly a hundred thirty grand, in total, from their respective parents, and each was hopeful they could get another ten or twenty between them if it became absolutely necessary. Only Sinnott's parents had refused to cave, his father holding fast to his promise that the bank of Harmon Sinnott was closed to his son forever.

All four partners were cash poor and buried in debt, Cross most especially; by selling what little they could at fire sale prices, they anticipated being able to pull together a little over $50,000, at the most, over the next several days. That, even added to what Clarke and Baumhower had received from their respective parents, wouldn't be near enough. Sinnott's old man had to come around for at least another seventy, and fast, or Will and his friends were going to find out just how much truth there was in the horror stories people liked to tell about Ruben Lizama.

When Clarke read Will Sinnott's email, referring his Class Act partners to the online version of the *Times'* story on the discovery of Gillis Rainey's body the day before, he could barely believe it. It would have been funny had it not been so terrifying. The burial pit they'd dug for themselves just kept getting deeper and deeper.

Rainey's body being found so soon was a complication they didn't need. To survive, over the next seven days everyone had to be thinking about one thing, and one thing only: scraping the rest of Ruben's money together. But Clarke knew his weak sister associates couldn't be counted on to do that and worry about facing a murder rap, too. As long as there was a chance the police could connect them to Gillis Rainey, no matter how remote, Baumhower and Sinnott, and perhaps even Cross, were going to be distracted by the possibility.

This guy Joseph Reddick was the problem. He was the one who could put Rainey and Baumhower together. The odds were a hundred-to-one against that he ever would, but it could happen. It would be just their luck. The only way to reduce the discovery of Rainey's body to a non-issue was to make Reddick a non-issue.

Baumhower and Sinnott would bitch and moan, and Cross would probably object strenuously, but this time around, Clarke was going to tell his best boy where he could stick his objections and play lead dog for once. He'd raised his share of Ruben's money and the others were going to need clear heads to do the same.

This dumb shit Joseph Reddick had to disappear and Ben Clarke, felon in training, knew just how to make it happen.

SEVEN

Reddick's boss at the City Attorney's office was a self-important little prick named Carl Hart. Hart was a short, dark-haired man in his late twenties who had eyes like a squirrel and the build of a weekend marathoner determined to run himself straight into the grave; there was more fat and muscle on one of Reddick's fingers than there was on the arms that stuck out of Hart's ubiquitous short-sleeve shirts. His emaciated appearance and perpetually foul attitude made for an asshole Reddick could hardly stand to be in the same room with without wanting to throw a chair out the window.

'Tell me you've got something for me this time,' Hart said.

They were up in his office on the eighth floor of City Hall East, surrounded by photos of Hart crossing various finish lines in near-death triumph, and he was bouncing the tip of a pen on his desk with an impatience no meeting only thirty seconds old should have warranted.

Reddick said, 'He's a bowler.'

'Excuse me?'

'You know. A ball with holes in it. Ten pins at the end of a long stretch of hardwood. Bowling. He likes to bowl.'

Hart tapped the pen two, three more times, then stopped. Catching on. 'With his right arm?'

'With his right arm.'

'And you have video?'

'I have video.'

Hart nodded and grinned. It was the grin of a shark with capped teeth and a bad need for braces. 'I knew it. I knew this one was bullshit.'

Hart thought every excessive force case brought against the LAPD was bullshit, especially when the charges were coming from somebody of color, but Reddick didn't bother to point this out. Hart thought he was doing the Lord's work, and anyone who questioned his impartiality was just a bleeding heart looking for employment elsewhere.

'How soon can I see it? The video?'

'I'll work on it over the weekend and have something for you by Monday,' Reddick said. In truth, he could have come to today's meeting with a copy of the video in hand, but he liked making Hart wait. It was one of the few ways he had of punishing the asshole for replacing the man who had originally hired Reddick five years ago. Compared to Hart, whom Reddick had been enduring now for a little less than a year, Ed Flores had been a goddamn candidate for sainthood.

'OK. Stay on him in the meantime,' Hart said. 'Until I see that video, I want as much physical evidence of his bogus incapacity as we can gather.'

He stood up and opened his office door. He'd heard all he needed to hear and lacked the com-

65

mon courtesy to offer a simple goodbye.

Reddick smiled, choosing amusement over some other emotion that might have moved him to change the position of Hart's nose on his face, and walked out.

'Finola, what are you doing?' Finola Winn asked herself out loud. She'd been doing a lot of that lately, holding conversations with herself like a crazy homeless person, and it worried her a little. She let the wrong person hear her do it, a Northeast watch commander or news reporter, say, and the brass would have her on administrative leave before she even knew what hit her.

But there was no one around to hear her today. She was alone, wasting her lunch hour wandering the cement bed of the Los Angeles River, working a John Doe case that in all probability wasn't even a homicide. Her partner, Norm Lerner, had refused to join her in this exercise, choosing instead to do what sane people did between the hours of twelve and one p.m. and eat. Norm thought Finola was nuts, doing legwork on a case they'd only caught the day before, and one he was sure was going to turn out to be some bizarre form of LA suicide rather than murder, at that, and Finola couldn't really argue with him. This *was* nuts, which was why she was behaving like a lunatic off her meds and talking to herself now.

Something about the body they'd found in a storm drain down here yesterday wouldn't leave her be. A fully clothed white man spread out on his back in a pool of black water, ripe as a rotten cantaloupe and crawling with maggots after what the coroner's tech guessed had been maybe three-to-five days of curing. The clothes had been nice: high-end slacks and a silk sport shirt, the shoes soft leather loafers that had Norman drooling. A TAG Heuer watch was on the dead man's left wrist and a gold ring was on each of his middle fingers. He carried no wallet, no ID, no cash.

It was way too soon to rule out homicide, but nothing at the scene had suggested it. The body bore no obvious wounds and neither blood nor a weapon – nor shell casings, for that matter – had been found anywhere around it. It looked as if the guy had just wandered into the mouth of the storm drain and collapsed in a heap. The idea seemed far-fetched, but Finola knew she had seen much crazier things happen, more times than she cared to admit.

Still, the incongruity bugged her. The deceased and the river just didn't jibe. Whoever he was, he wasn't the kind of person one regularly saw down here – vagrants and gangbangers, indigent poor folks scavenging for recyclables. This guy had money, and probably, somewhere, a home. Why come down here to die?

The barrel-chested black woman with the LAPD detective's badge clipped to her belt, neatly corn-rowed head shining in the sun, scanned the river's cluttered floor for answers. Not knowing what she was looking for, or why she was bothering to look for it.

'What are you doing, Finola?' she asked herself again.

No sooner had their waitress set their coffee cups down than Dana said, 'I'm going to see a lawyer next week, Joe.'

'Yeah? What about?'

'Don't. Please don't. This is hard enough for me as it is.'

He thought about saying something smart, despite her warning, but it had taken him all week to get her to agree to this lunch meeting and he was afraid she'd storm out before he'd even had a chance to speak.

'You don't want to do that, Dana,' he said, and the words came out sounding just as pathetic as he felt.

'No. I don't. But I don't know what else to do.'

'You could give me another shot. That's something you could do.'

She shook her head. 'I've tried. It's just too hard.'

'And being alone would be easier? Raising my son on your own, without his father?'

'His father's a crazy man. A hot-tempered headcase who's going to get him seriously hurt someday – or worse – if I don't do something to stop him.'

She was losing her own temper, the way she always did when Reddick refused to admit he was demented. He thought he saw the guy in the booth behind her turn his head, her sudden anger drawing his attention, but Reddick wasn't sure. The coffee shop was just too damn crowded to suit him.

'I'm sorry,' Dana said. 'I didn't mean that.'

'Yeah, you did. But you've got it all back-wards. I'm the reason Jake *hasn't* been seriously hurt yet. And as long as I'm around, he never will be.'

'You can't say that. Nobody can. That's your problem, Joe. You're trying to guarantee some-thing you can't possibly control.' She waited for two women headed for the cash register to pass their booth, then went on, making a concerted effort to be kind. 'People get hurt. Bad things happen to them. It's life, and you can't make Jake and me exceptions to it, no matter how hard you try. It just isn't possible.'

'That's what you say. I say, it's better to attempt the impossible than do nothing. Life's a rigged game, Dana. The man who doesn't try to improve the odds for himself and everyone he cares about gets fucked. *That's* your "guaran-tee."'

The man sitting behind Dana visibly flinched, and now Reddick was sure he was listening in. Reddick was going to give the asshole ninety seconds to mind his own business before getting up to suggest he have his lunch somewhere else.

'Look,' Dana said. 'I didn't come here to argue with you. I just wanted you to know what I plan to do. I'm going to file, Joe.'

'No.'

'Separation is just delaying the inevitable. You won't change and Jake and I can't be around you the way you are. Let's try to end this thing amicably, for Jake's sake, while we still can, before it turns into something completely ugly.'

'No. I'm not walking away and neither are

69

you,' Reddick said. 'OK, so I come off the rails every now and then, maybe even more than I should. But it's only because I love you, and I don't want to see anything happen to you. I've got that right, Dana. To protect what's mine. I've earned that right as much as anyone in this world, and you know it.'

'Joe...'

'You want to tell me you're calling it quits because you don't love me, that's a different conversation. But that's not what I hear you saying because it isn't true. Is it?'

'Yes. It is.'

'You're lying.'

Dana pushed herself out of the booth, attempting to flee, knowing she was only proving him right. Reddick jumped up to catch her by the left wrist and turned her back around to face him.

'Wait! Don't go.'

'I have to get back to work. And we've said all there is to say. It's over, Joe. Whether we love you or not, Jake and I don't want to be your excuse for waging war against the world anymore.'

She pried his hand off her wrist to free herself and walked out. Reddick let her go. The coffee shop was dead silent, every eye in the place aimed in his direction, but he barely noticed.

He sat back down in the booth and drank his coffee.

Clarke had been following Reddick around for hours – ever since early this morning when he'd driven out to the Echo Park address Reddick had given Andy Baumhower at the scene of their accident and this guy fitting Reddick's description had come out – and now he was faced with a dilemma. Stick with Reddick, or follow this big, nice looking brunette he'd just tried to have lunch with at the Eat Well coffee shop on Sunset? Clarke thought Reddick 'tried' to have lunch with her because it looked like lunch hadn't worked out, the lady storming out of the joint in a huff before anything more than coffee could be served.

From his parked car across the street, Clarke watched the brunette scurry down the block as Reddick, clearly visible behind the coffee shop's big picture windows, just sat there sipping his joe, looking like he'd just lost the family dog to cancer. Or, Clarke thought, having an epiphany, like his old lady had just told him they were through. He'd noticed the wedding band on Reddick's left hand when he'd had the binoculars on him earlier, so unless she was some kind of piece he had on the side, it stood to reason the brunette was Reddick's wife.

His decision suddenly made, Clarke started up his BMW and watched as the lady got into a blue, late model Ford parked a block down the street. He eased away from the curb, did a U-turn well out of Reddick's sight, and started east down Sunset after the Ford, keeping his distance, in no great hurry.

If Clarke was right about the woman he was tailing, Reddick was a family man, maybe even one with kids, and that could only make him that much easier to deal with. A man with a wife and kids had no choice but to listen when you spoke to him; he had more than himself to think about when making critical decisions. A man without, on the other hand, could blow you off if he felt like being a hero because he had nothing to lose but his own life. Your leverage against him was severely limited.

Driving on in the air-conditioned car, keeping the blue Ford in plain sight, Clarke reached into the bag of chocolate chip cookies on the passenger seat beside him, next to the nine-inch assault knife and fresh roll of duct tape, and hoped Joe Reddick knew how to lay down when somebody gave him the order.

EIGHT

Because of the strange holes he liked to put in people with assorted sharp instruments, both his friends and enemies in the Mexican drug trade had come to call Ruben Lizama 'La Aguja,' or 'The Needle.' Pencils, steak knives, screwdrivers, garden shears – it seemed nothing with a hard edge or point was too esoteric to be used by *La Aguja* to either torture a man, stop his heart from beating, or both.

It was no doubt this proclivity of Ruben's that was foremost in the minds of the five men he had come to see today in the city of Tampico, at the southern-most tip of his home state of Tamaulipas, Mexico. The five men were arranged in a neat row, face down on the dusty floor of the machine shop in which they worked, as Ruben and the three family soldiers he'd brought with him loomed over them, automatic weapons at the ready. The men knew why Ruben had come – all had spoken to the Federal Police about a murder they had witnessed one of the Lizama soldiers commit, and one of them had actually said something other than *'Yo no vi nada'* – and so they also knew they were all dead. What they didn't know was what kind of death Ruben had in mind for them, and it was

73

this mystery above all else that had two of the five pissing into the floor through their overalls.

Ruben let them squirm for a long time; he was in no particular hurry. They had the machine shop all to themselves. Upon his arrival, he had ordered it to be evacuated of all but the five men on the floor, and without anyone issuing a single word of argument, the building had emptied out like a burning movie theater. Now it was almost deathly silent, with only the sound of a few running machines providing background for the prayers some of those on the floor were uttering.

Finally, Ruben pointed to one of the five, a short, older man with jet-black hair and skin nearly as dark, and said, in Spanish, 'Him.'

The soldier closest to Ruben reached down with his free hand to lift the little man off the floor. The other offered no resistance; instead, he came to his feet and stood with his back straight, head up, making no attempt to avert his eyes from Ruben's. He was afraid, but not a coward, and he understood that anything he said or did now to try to save himself would only serve to disgrace his family name. Ruben saw all this and grinned, satisfied he had chosen the right man.

He glanced over at the three Lizama soldiers, almost offhandedly, and nodded his head.

Instantly, the shop roared with gunfire, blinding sparks and muzzle flashes lighting up the walls. The four men prone on the floor died in a hail of bullets, a barrage that only seemed to stop when their assassins had grown weary of the exercise.

With great interest, Ruben watched the little

man standing before him and saw him flinch once, then close his eyes up tight. That was all. When the shooting stopped, he opened his eyes again without being asked and waited, trembling but silent, as unwilling to dishonor himself by pleading for his life as ever.

'*Cómo te llamas?*' Ruben asked.

The little man told him his name: Guillermo Leal.

'Were you the one who gave the police a description of my friend?' Ruben asked in Spanish, already knowing the answer.

'No,' Guillermo Leal said, shaking his head.

Ruben leaned in close to study his hard, impassive face for a moment, just to make sure his instincts were correct, and decided he believed him. The *alcahuete* he had come here to find was one of the four dead men on the floor.

'*Bueno*,' Ruben said, patting the little man on the back. He looked around the shop, searching for something, and eventually his eyes locked on to to a hulking green machine several feet away. It was a drill press of some kind, fitted with a bit the size and length of a hatchet handle. Ruben took Leal by the elbow and gently guided him toward the press, the three gunmen trailing behind. 'Come,' he said.

When they reached the machine, Ruben asked the little man which of his two hands he used the most. Leal gestured with his right, hesitantly, because he knew, like the other three men watching, what was coming.

At Ruben's signal, one of the soldiers – Poeto, his personal bodyguard – started the press running and waited, hand on the wheel that would lower the whirring drill bit down toward the machine's table.

'I have left you alive so you can honor me with a favor,' Ruben told Leal. 'When we are gone, I want you to show your left hand to anyone you think may be talking to the police about my family's business. To warn them what could happen. Do you understand?'

Leal nodded. Tears welled in his eyes, but he made no move to wipe them away.

Later, after the deed was done, Ruben sat in the back seat of the car as Poeto drove him and the other Lizama soldiers away, and marveled at little Guillermo Leal's courage. He had accepted the punishment they had seen fit to visit upon him without complaint, honoring them with silent capitulation and nothing more. Ruben wondered how many other men could have done as well, and the thought brought his mind around to Ben Clarke and Clarke's three friends in America. In Leal's place, waiting for the terrible pain to come, how would such pampered *nenes de mam*á have behaved? Like men or like children?

Ruben thought he could guess. He didn't take Clarke for a coward, per se, but he knew the *Americano* was far more flash than substance, and what little he had seen of Cross, Baumhower, and Sinnott had not impressed him. Still, the evidence of their joint success seemed to speak for itself; whatever their short-comings in the way of real balls, Clarke and his Class Act partners clearly knew how to make money, and that in itself made them useful to Ruben. Because he loved Los Angeles – the parties, the women, the movie stars – and with the help of Clarke and his friends, he hoped to someday become a real player there. Not simply Jorge Lizama's youngest son, who made the A-list now by virtue of his father's drugs and grisly reputation, but a bright young man who had learned the filmmaking game and mastered it. Ruben didn't want to buy or terrorize his way to stardom in Hollywood – he actually wanted to earn it – and doing business with Ben Clarke and company was his idea of a first step toward that end.

If it turned out to be a false step – if trusting Clarke to launder $250,000 of Lizama family money proved to be a foolish mistake – Clarke would pay for it with his life. Later today, *La Aguja* would fly out to Los Angeles and spend the whole weekend partying.

After that, he would go see Ben Clarke and find out what kind of man the big white boy was compared to brave, little, one-handed Guillermo Leal.

Aside from the Orvis Andrews surveillance, Reddick had several other assignments for the City Attorney's office on his plate. One of them involved a woman named Gina Delgadillo, a thirty-six-year-old mother of three who was suing the city of Los Angeles to the tune of thirteen million dollars. Delgadillo was claiming she'd been seriously injured at Angel's Gate Park in San Pedro six weeks earlier when a pair of clowning maintenance workers had backed a small utility truck into her. As in the Orvis Andrews case, Reddick was supposed to determine if her injuries were as extensive as Delgadillo's attorneys would, given the chance, lead a jury to believe.

He was out at the park where the accident had taken place late Friday afternoon, interviewing one of the maintenance men who'd allegedly caused it, when he received a text from Dana on his cell phone. A text from his wife wasn't particularly unusual, but after their lunch earlier in the day, he hadn't expected to hear from her again any time soon, and this was the first time he could remember Dana resorting to a text without first attempting to reach him in person. Her message was short and maddeningly ominous:

nd 2 see u @ home rt awy. xplain when u get here. pls hurry!

His immediate thought was that something must have happened to Jake. It didn't make sense, her texting him about something as grave as that, but Reddick couldn't imagine what else such a dire message could mean. He tried to get his wife on the phone and only got her voicemail. He tried twice, left a crazed demand for a call back after the second attempt, and then thought to reply to Dana's text with one of his own:

whats gng on? what happened?

His text went unanswered. He waited two minutes, then ran to his car and started for his old home.

He was furious by the time he arrived, having almost convinced himself his panic would prove to be unwarranted. Dana was blowing a non-life-threatening situation way the hell out of proportion and had sent him a message far more cryptic and mysterious than necessary. And she still wasn't answering the phone. She had to know what he would think, the conclusions he would jump to. If this turned out to be no big deal...

Please, God, let that be it.

Throughout the drive out to Glendale, he had been tempted to call the police, demand they send a car out to precede him, but now he was glad that he hadn't. The normalcy he saw outside his old home seemed to prove what an embarrassing overreaction that would have been. There were no ambulances, no squad cars, no crowds of neighbors milling about on the sidewalk out front; instead, there was only silence and tranquility, and Dana's Volvo parked with perfect precision in the driveway. Not halfway in and skewed to one side or the other, the way someone rushing home in hysterics might have parked it, but straight in toward the garage.

Reddick allowed the merest wave of relief to wash over him, then rushed to the front door.

Dana answered on his first ring of the bell. Still dressed for work, she looked ashen, like someone who'd just witnessed her own death. There was no sign of Jake anywhere.

'Jesus. What the hell's going on?' Reddick asked, stepping inside.

Someone standing behind the door hit him at

79

the base of his skull with something anvil-hard and dropped him face first on the floor. His hold on consciousness lasted only long enough for him to hear Dana shriek his name, and then his ground-level view of the world was swallowed up in black.

The first thing Reddick saw when he came to was Dana, stretched out on the couch above him, bound and gagged with duct tape. She was blinking at him furiously, eyes brimming with tears.

He immediately recognized that he, too, was bound in a similar fashion, tape binding his ankles together and his wrists behind his back, a long strip wound completely around his head to cover his mouth. He was still on the floor, on his back, but he'd been moved away from the door to the center of the living room, which was dark now, suggesting he'd been out for some time.

'I'm gonna make this quick,' he heard someone behind him say.

Reddick turned to one side, head throbbing, to see a big man standing several feet away, a dark ski mask covering his head, a knife approaching the size of a small machete clutched tightly in one gloved hand.

'I got your kid tied up in the bedroom,' the guy said. 'If you wanna keep him alive...'

Reddick didn't hear the words that followed. His vision blurred and his head filled with a deafening static, all the air rushing out of his lungs at once.

I got your kid tied up in the bedroom.

80

Reddick began to scream, the tape around his mouth barely containing the full intensity of his terror and rage. His eyes rolled up toward the top of his head and his body convulsed, every muscle pulled as taut as a violin string.

The man in the mask just stood there and watched, stunned, as Dana's sobbing grew to a fever pitch.

'What the fuck?' the big man said.

He walked over to Reddick and kicked him hard in the midsection, once, twice. 'Hey. Hey! Shut the fuck up and listen to what I'm telling you, asshole!'

But Reddick was beyond his reach. Something inside him gave way and the room flared white, before darkness engulfed him again like the wings of death itself.

'I don't know what your problem is, buddy, but you better get over it fast.'

The man in the mask was looming over him, breathing straight into his face. Everything else was as it had been before: Reddick on the floor, Dana on the couch. He had no idea how long he'd been out.

'Now, I'm gonna try to explain things to you one more time, and if you freak out on me again, your little boy's dead. Understand? Nod your head if you understand.'

The sound of the man's voice was like something out of a dream, muffled and undulating. The room before Reddick's eyes kept blinking in and out as if illuminated by a light bulb threatening to die. Questions without answers clattered around inside his head, company for a single thought that refused to fall silent: *Not again. This can't be happening to me again.*

But Reddick understood. He didn't know who this man was or why he was here, but he knew one thing with absolute, unshakable certainty: He had to hold on long enough to hear what the man in the mask had to say. The comfort and release of total madness beckoned; he had nothing but a whisper-thin thread of sanity left. But he either held on to that thread now, with all the power he possessed, or Jake, and probably Dana as well, were dead. It was as simple as that.

Reddick nodded his head.

'Good,' the man in the mask said, standing erect. 'Here's the deal. I need you to forget something. A car accident you had a few nights ago with a friend of mine. His name's Baumhower. Remember?'

Reddick did, but he couldn't believe it. This was all about that whimpering fool in the minivan Sunday night?

'I'm waiting for you to nod your head,' the man in the mask said, nudging Reddick in the chest with the toe of his right shoe.

Reddick nodded again.

'For reasons you don't need to know, Mr Baumhower can't have word of your accident go beyond you and him. So you're gonna pretend it never happened, Reddick. You're not gonna report it to your insurance company, the cops, no one. Ever. Do I have to tell you why?'

Reddick shook his head. The threat that this maniac would come back to harm his wife and son was implicit.

'Well, just to be sure, I'm gonna tell you both anyway.' The masked man walked over to where Dana lay, put his face an inch from her own and turned the blade of his knife to and fro, right in front of her nose. 'You paying attention, sweetheart?'

Dana nodded, frantic.

'Your boy over there breathes a word about the accident to anybody, you're all dead. I'll start with the kid and leave you for last. After you and I have some fun first, of course.'

Reddick could feel himself slipping away, becoming something more animal than human. Desperate as he was to remain silent, a low, rumbling moan began to roll through him like thunder.

'Would you like that? You an' me havin' a little fun first?' the man with the knife asked Dana.

And then Reddick was screaming again, helpless to do anything else. Images nine years old, of three corpses strewn about a bloodstained house in West Palm Beach, Florida, streamed through his mind in an endless loop, all he had left of a family he'd once loved the way he loved Dana and Jake today. The giant in the ski mask looked over to see him making a silly, futile effort to get to his feet, flopping around on the floor like a decapitated chicken. Without a word, he sauntered over and kicked Reddick under the chin, seemingly trying to take his head off.

Reddick fell on to his back and finally let go, blinking up at the ceiling spinning above him until the lights went out for good.

NINE

They found Jake asleep in his bedroom. He'd been knocked out with chloroform, but was otherwise unharmed. Despite what their intruder had said to the contrary, he hadn't even bothered to tie Jake up or gag him, one small favor for which they could be thankful. Had Jake awoken and found himself alone, trussed up and gagged like his parents, things could have been much worse. As it was they had to lie to him, tell him the big man in the mask who'd scared Mommy and covered his mouth with the funny smelling cloth was just a friend of Daddy's playing a stupid game. He clearly found the story incredible, but he didn't question it.

Naturally, Dana wanted to call the police. Had she done so when she had the chance, having been first to slip out of her bonds before Reddick had even regained consciousness, he would have had no say in the matter. But she'd waited until she was sure Jake was safe and Reddick was OK to go to the phone, and by then it was too late.

'No police,' Reddick said.

'Joe...'

'You heard me! We're not calling the police!'

They sat in the dining room together, both of them shaking like heroin addicts in withdrawal,

Jake back in their bedroom where they'd perched him in front of the TV. Dana was sure Reddick was either insane or suffering the effects of a concussion, possibly even both. Bruised and ashen-faced, he looked more like a dead man than a live one, and he wasn't making sense. How could they not call the police?

But Reddick was adamant. From the moment he'd heard the words that were pounding in his head, even now – *I got your kid tied up in the bedroom* – he'd been thinking it through, considering every possibility if he and Dana did what almost anyone else would do in their position and seek help from the authorities, and no matter how he looked at it, one thing was an irrefutable constant: risk. The chance that something could go wrong and, for all their efforts to protect his wife and son, the cops or the Feds would let the man in the mask make good on his threat to kill them. The odds said it couldn't happen, that such a thing was as unlikely to occur as the same number coming up twice in a single lottery, but Reddick didn't give a damn.

Infinitesimal or not, he wasn't going to play the odds in this, the most important game of his life.

'But what else can we do?' Dana asked. 'Wait for that bastard or this Baumhower friend of his to come back?' She'd already asked him who Baumhower was and he'd told her what little he knew, confessing he had no clue why the little shit would want so desperately to keep the car accident they'd had five nights ago a secret.

'They won't be back,' Reddick said.

'But how can you know that?'

Reddick just looked at her, making no effort to disguise the demon, freshly unleashed, roiling about within.

'Oh, my God. You can't seriously be thinking of taking care of these people *yourself*????'

'You don't need to worry about it. You and Jake are getting out of here. Tonight.'

'What?'

'There's no guarantee the police can protect you. I've seen what happens when they can't. As long as you and Jake are somewhere safe, I can make sure those assholes never threaten either one of you again.'

'How?'

'Like I said: You don't need to worry about it.'

Dana shook her head, fighting back tears. 'This is insane. You're hurt, Joe. You need a doctor. And we need to call the *police*. Now, before anything else happens.'

'No!' Reddick slammed the heel of a fist into the dining room table, salt and pepper shakers leaping into a midair dance. Terrified, Dana fell silent and inched her chair away from the table, making ready to flee. She had never seen her husband this far gone before and the thought of him laying a hand on her or their son – something he had not done once in the six years they'd been together – was suddenly not so difficult to imagine.

Reddick saw the fear on Dana's face and froze, immediately aware of what he'd done. This wasn't what he wanted. He wasn't the monster here.

86

He withdrew to his side of the table again and waited for the rage to subside. Dana was right to be afraid of him and he knew it; pushed or prodded the wrong way, he was capable of anything now, and once he let his thirst for blood out of the box, he would never get it back in. He either learned to keep himself in check, or all was surely lost.

'Please,' he said, his voice a dry, barbed whisper. 'You have to trust me on this, Dana. I've got to handle this situation alone. There's no other way to be sure.'

'Sure of what?'

He took a long time to answer. Tears and images of the wife and two children he'd once thought were his forever began to cloud his vision like a veil. 'That I won't have to bury you or my son. Been there, done that.' He shook his head and swallowed hard. 'I'm never going there again.'

Dana remained far from convinced. Not going to the police for help ran counter to everything her instincts were telling her to do. But there was truth in her husband's words to her, truth she couldn't deny even to herself. Seeking police protection was no guarantee of her safety or that of their son, and nothing short of a guarantee would suffice. She hadn't suffered what Reddick had suffered, could only imagine the depths of his pain and heartbreak, but she had seen enough over the years to know that he would never survive it if anything were to happen to her or Jake. Asking him to entrust their lives to others while people who had threatened them with death were still breathing was asking the impossible.

Even so, Dana might have held her ground and insisted they call the police over Reddick's objections were it not for the simple fact that Jake was her son, too. She loved Reddick, but Jake was her life, the center of her universe. If Reddick needed to know with absolute certainty that Baumhower and his friend would never again touch a hair on the boy's head, no less so did Dana. And, it shamed her to realize now, she didn't much care what such certainty would ultimately cost.

'All right,' she said, reaching out to take Reddick's hand.

He held on to her tight, drawing all the strength from her that he could. He knew he would need it. He'd been an emotional cripple for a long time, a borderline psychopath walking a razor wire between normalcy and madness, and now he'd been pushed over the edge. His head throbbed and his body ached, and he felt like the only thing holding him together was his skin, that if he turned too quickly in one direction or another, he'd crumble into a pile of ashes that would then scatter to the far winds. But he couldn't let that happen. Not yet. He had work to do first, dirty work, and to do it he would have to retain some level of functionality. One day or two, that was all he needed.

After that, he'd gladly surrender in full to the darkness that had been calling him for the past nine years.

TEN

It didn't take Clarke long to begin having second thoughts. He should have just killed Reddick and been done with it.

Cross, of course, were he aware of what Clarke had done, would say just the opposite: Clarke should have never approached Reddick in the first place. So what if he heard about Gillis Rainey's body turning up in the river? Was that any reason to assume he'd put the dead man and Andy Baumhower together, ever? Why make a pre-emptive move to guard against something they had no reason to believe would ever happen, and one so fraught with risk, at that? Instead of improving the odds that Reddick would never go to the police with word of the car accident he'd had with Andy last Sunday morning, Clarke had all but ensured it.

Unless the scare he'd put into Reddick proved to be big enough.

That was the one thing Clarke was becoming less and less sure of as time wore on. By early Saturday morning, one long restless night after he'd fled Reddick's home, Clarke was as convinced as ever that trying to silence Reddick before he could become a problem had been the right thing to do. Sitting back and doing nothing, playing the percentages that Reddick would never connect Gillis Rainey to Andy Baumhower, would have been a punk move, the equivalent of hoping and praying for the best. Clarke never hoped or prayed for anything; what he wanted to happen, he took action to *make* happen. But maybe in Reddick's case, he hadn't taken action enough. That was his growing suspicion.

Reddick's behavior at the house – all the screaming and thrashing about – had been troubling. It had been above and beyond what Clarke would have expected to see from a man who was simply afraid for his wife and child. There had been an electric quality to it that brought to Clarke's mind the clinically insane, and if that was the case – if Reddick was in one way or another deranged – how he would react to Clarke's invasion of his home once his hands were untied and the gag removed from his mouth was anybody's guess. A sane man could be counted on to do what was reasonable, but a crazed one was unpredictable.

Adding further to Clarke's sense of unease was the fact that, from the beginning, Reddick hadn't looked like the kind of man who would scare easy. Appearances could often be deceiving, but the man Clarke had followed around for most of the day Friday, before he'd been reduced to a trussed-up crybaby curled up in the fetal position on his wife's living room floor, had resembled nothing as much as a cop or a Marine, somebody who was far more comfortable going through things than around them. He wasn't a cop, because Clarke never once saw him flash a badge, and if he was US military, he was no longer active. But he had spent over an hour on Friday inside the City Hall East building downtown, where Clarke knew a number of law enforcement agencies had offices, so his being associated with the law in one capacity or another could not be entirely ruled out.

Were do-overs possible, Clarke would have gone back in time to the moment Reddick walked into his wife's home and the trap Clarke had set for him there and whacked them both. He hadn't thought such an extreme measure was necessary then, but he could see now how killing them would have left much less to chance. What he'd done instead was done, however, and Clarke couldn't change it. All he could do was prepare for the worst in case Reddick chose not to play ball and went to the authorities. First, he had to tell Baumhower what he'd done so the fool didn't get caught by surprise if the cops came calling. Andy would surely spill his guts otherwise.

After that, Clarke would spend a few hours throughout the weekend checking in on Reddick and his family, looking for any sign that Reddick had tragically mistaken his threat to kill them all for a bluff.

Clarke's suspicions about Reddick were well-founded, but he would prove to be too late getting around to having them. While Clarke was deciding to keep an eye on him and his wife over the next two days, Reddick was already

91

taking steps to make such surveillance impossible.

He had started by driving Dana and Jake all the way down to Irvine late Friday night, hopping off and on the freeway throughout just to make sure they weren't being followed, and finding a motel room there for the three of them. Once they were checked in, he remained awake while his wife and son slept, then dozed for a couple hours himself as soon as Dana awoke Saturday morning. She didn't want to touch the SIG Sauer P220 handgun he'd stopped at his apartment the night before to pick up, along with several other things, but he'd forced the weapon into her hand and shown her how to operate it anyway, determined to leave nothing to chance.

The minute Jake awoke, they all showered and dressed and found a quiet place near the motel to have breakfast.

'What now?' Dana asked immediately after they'd placed their orders. Sitting between them, Jake was in his own little world, listening to his mother's iPod while working the games on a children's menu, so speaking freely wasn't a problem.

'Nothing. You two sit tight here until I come back for you.'

'Here? Why here? My brother—'

'No.' Dana's brother Ken lived out in Moorpark and the home he shared with his wife and three kids there was big enough to accommodate another half-dozen people. 'I want you where these guys will never be able to find you, and depending on their resources, hiding out with a family member might not be good enough.'

Dana's silence, and the look she gave him, said she thought he was taking his paranoia to new heights.

'They found you once, Dana. They had my address, not yours. Until I know who these assholes are, I'm going to err on the side of caution.'

She nodded, satisfied with his reasoning. 'How long?'

'I don't know. A couple days at least, maybe more.'

'Do you know what...' She reconsidered, glancing at Jake, and tried again. 'Do you have a plan?'

'Not yet. But something will come to me.'

It was a lie. He'd had a plan for hours now. It just wasn't anything his wife would have wanted to hear.

They'd both had over fourteen hours to sleep on things now, so Dana's next question hardly surprised him. He'd asked it of himself more than once today. 'Are you sure we're doing the right thing? There isn't anything else we can do?'

'Other than go to the police?' He shook his head.

'I'm afraid, Joe.'

'Yeah. That makes two of us.'

'No, I mean for you. I don't want you to get hurt or...' She glanced at Jake again. 'Or to see you do something that can't be undone.'

Reddick spooned some sugar into his coffee, gazed absently into the vortex he created stirring it around in his cup. 'Let me tell you how things go down if we do the only other thing we can do and turn Baumhower and his pal over to the cops. They take Baumhower in for questioning right away but they don't know who his friend is and Baumhower isn't saying, so he remains at large. Maybe for a week, maybe for a month, maybe for as long as it takes them to squeeze a name out of Baumhower, and they can't do that until they know what the hell this is all about.

'They'll expect me to tell them and I won't be able to, because I don't have a clue myself, which will only make them wonder if Baumhower isn't right when he says I've got to be some kind of wack job off his meds who's making all this shit up. You'll corroborate my story, of course, but then they'll talk to Jake, and what will he say?'

He looked up at Dana and waited for her to answer.

'He'll say the big man in the mask was just a friend of yours playing a game.'

'Exactly. Because that's what we've told him, right? And now the cops aren't just thinking I'm crazy, they're thinking me and my "friend" in the mask are trying to set Baumhower up somehow. Trying to run some kind of bizarre extortion scam, or something. So they let Baumhower go and turn their attention to me, and now both Baumhower and his pal are free to look for you and Jake, find you, and kill you like they promised they would.'

'But that would be crazy! The police would know Baumhower did it immediately.'

94

'Sure they would. But they still wouldn't have a motive for his threatening me in the first place, and without that, I'd look like a better suspect to them than he would. Estranged husband with a history of mental illness – I'd be tailor-made for the rap. And Baumhower – depending on what it is he's trying to hide by keeping me silent about our accident – might actually prefer to take his chances killing us all than have the cops find out about it.'

Dana's head wagged from side to side, the color all gone from her face. 'OK, enough. I don't want to hear any more.'

Reddick understood how she felt. He was long past caring, because caring was a luxury he couldn't afford anymore, but he could have easily been sickened by it all himself. Knowing what he had to do – what the fates were giving him no choice but to do if he ever wanted to live a moment without fear again – made him feel like a caged animal. But a cage was exactly what he was in, and turning the man who'd put him in it over to the authorities was not the way out, for all the reasons he'd just given Dana, and more.

They tried to make small talk for the duration of their breakfast, but it was a wasted effort. Their mutual dread for what lay ahead hung over the table like a foul odor, robbing them both of the will to so much as crack a halfhearted smile. When Jake picked up on their mood and inquired about it, as they'd known he would eventually, Dana volunteered a lie before Reddick could, explaining they were sad because she and Jake couldn't go home for a while. Something bad had happened with the plumbing and until Daddy could go back and fix it, she and Jake would have to stay at the motel. It was a ridiculous fable that Jake questioned like a military interrogator, but in the face of receiving no other details, the boy had no choice but to accept it as an at least partial form of the truth.

Reddick drove his wife and son back to the motel, hugged Jake goodbye as if for the last time in his life, then gave Dana $300 in cash and left her with a few last minute instructions: 'Keep your eyes open, stay close to your phone, and avoid using credit cards whenever possible.' This last was taking things to yet another extreme, but Reddick didn't give a damn; they'd had to use a credit card just to get the room and that was where Reddick wanted it to end. If Dana thought he was being ridiculous, she was smart enough not to say so.

At the door, he put the SIG Sauer in his wife's hand and said, 'Don't give me any shit about this. If somebody comes through this door you don't want to see, you're going to have to stop them on your own. I won't be able to get here in time to help.' He nodded in the direction of Jake, sitting on the bed behind her reading a comic book. 'Understand?'

Dana nodded and took the gun, looking bone tired, then surprised Reddick with a kiss and promised to do exactly as he'd instructed.

ELEVEN

As Finola Winn's luck would have it, Gillis Rainey was a momma's boy.

Winn and her partner Norm Lerner might have spent weeks trying to identify the dead man's blackened, gas-swollen body otherwise. The Coroner had managed to pull a fair set of prints off the corpse but they hadn't matched those of any criminal presently in the system; Rainey had no arrest record and so he had no prints on file. And though the preliminary autopsy had given them a cause of death – diabetic ketoacidosis – no medical alert bracelet that could have borne the dead man's name was found on his body.

It was looking like Rainey would remain a John Doe indefinitely until, in her last official act before shutting down her computer late Friday night, Winn checked Missing Persons one more time and came across the report Rainey's mother had filed on him less than twenty-four hours earlier. Lorraine Rainey's description of her son fit Winn's John Doe to a T, right down to his Type 1 diabetes and fondness for $900 Ermenegildo Zegna shoes.

According to the report, Gillis Rainey was a fifty-one-year-old real estate broker and con-firmed bachelor from West Hollywood who hadn't been seen or heard from in almost a week, or since late the previous Friday night. He wasn't the kind of son who called his mother every day, nor she the kind of mother who needed that kind of attention, but neither had ever before gone more than three days without at least trading phone messages. Six days was a new record for them, and to Lorraine Rainey it suggested something was wrong. Gillis Rainey – her only child – was diabetic and he didn't always take care of himself right. If he'd gone off somewhere with one of his wild friends and forgotten his insulin kit, or gotten too busy dancing at one party or another to take his insulin as prescribed, he could be in serious need of medical attention. It wouldn't have been the first time his foolish, overgrown frat boy life-style had nearly killed him.

Late Saturday morning, Detectives Winn and Lerner drove down to Cheviot Hills to see Lorraine Rainey at home, a set of carefully selected crime scene photos in hand. They were hoping she could positively identify their John Doe as her son. Visits like these were always tough on a cop, but Lerner was damn near whistling on the drive out. He was certain this trip would close the door on a case he'd had figured as a suicide or accidental death all along, and nothing made him more unbearably happy than proving to be more perceptive about something than Winn.

Lorraine Rainey lived in a little three-bedroom house on Beverly Drive that dated back to the early 1950s. It looked like every other single-story house on the block, clean and well kept, one big picture window facing the street off an open porch adorned with white lattice work. The lawn out front was so green and perfectly trimmed, it could have been cut from right field at Dodger Stadium.

She answered the door just as Winn was trying the bell for the second time. Winn guessed she was a woman just entering her seventies, and not without a fight. Short and lean, with a mop of sandy brown hair laced with gray, Lorraine Rainey didn't wear the standard-issue senior uniform of pale gray Nike sweatsuit and running shoes like other people her age; on her, the outfit resembled that of an infantryman heading off to war. It was all Winn could do not to salute under the weight of her coal-black, hawk-like gaze.

'Yes?'

They were the police; surely she had to suspect as much. Who else could this salt-and-pepper pair be? And yet no hint of the dread Winn had expected to see was there.

'Good morning, ma'am.' Winn flashed her badge and introduced herself and her partner. 'We're here to see a Ms Lorraine Rainey.'

Finally, she got a reaction.

'Goddamnit!' Lorraine Rainey said. Not fearing the worst, but cursing like a drunk over a spilt beer.

'I'm afraid we're here about your son Gillis,' Winn said, thinking that maybe the old girl had misunderstood the purpose of their visit.

'He's dead, isn't he?'

Winn and Lerner exchanged a look. Lerner said, 'A body's been recovered we believe may be that of your son, yes ma'am. But we haven't yet made a positive ID.'

'We were hoping you could take a look at a few photos,' Winn said, 'tell us if you think the body is in fact your son's.'

Lorraine Rainey let out a heavy sigh and nodded, her anger replaced by something resembling mere exhaustion. 'Come on in.'

They settled in the living room, a pristine re-creation of the American good life, circa 1950, the detectives seated on one side, their hostess on the other. A ticking clock on the fireplace mantel was the only sound in the entire house. Winn removed the photographs from her purse, a half-dozen in all. 'I know this may be difficult for you. But please do the best you can to look these over carefully.' She passed the photos to Lerner, who handed them over to Lorraine Rainey.

Gillis Rainey's mother saw the first photograph and immediately closed her eyes against the sight. She let her chin drop down to her chest, paused a moment, then raised her head up again, eyes glistening. Through a film of tears she refused to wipe away, she studied the rest of the photos one by one, taking her time, a low rumble now and then escaping from somewhere down deep in her throat.

She nodded her head when she was done, handed the photographs back to Lerner. 'Yes, that's my son,' she said. And then: 'Goddamnit!'

'You're sure?' Lerner asked, only because either he or Winn had to.

Lorraine Rainey glared at him. 'Yes, I'm sure!

Those are his clothes and his rings. I was with him when he bought that watch. You don't think I know my own son?'

'We're very sorry, ma'am,' Winn said, grateful that Lerner was the target of the woman's wrath and not she.

'What happened to him? Why does he look like that?'

Winn told her where and when the body had been discovered, and how, checking to see how she reacted to each piece of the news. It all seemed to be a complete surprise to her.

'In the river? You mean the concrete one?'

'Yes, ma'am. Up near Atwater Village,' Winn said.

'I don't understand. What the hell would he have been doing down there?'

'We don't know. To tell you the truth, we were kind of hoping you could tell *us*. As of now, it doesn't appear he was a victim of any foul play. The Coroner says cause of death was diabetic ketoacidosis, which, in simple layman's terms, means he hadn't taken his insulin for quite some time.'

'Can you tell us if your son was good about that? Taking his meds, I mean?' Lerner asked.

'No. Not hardly,' Lorraine Rainey said, suddenly angry again. 'Gillis could be very irresponsible at times. He liked to party like a man half his age and anything that got in the way of that would often go ignored. Including the warnings of his mother.'

'Warnings?' Winn asked.

'I had to constantly tell him to slow down. Be

careful. Those kids you run around with don't need to eat or sleep, but you do. You'll kill your-self trying to keep up with them, I said. But do you think he'd ever listen? Not on your life.' She shook her head with disgust.

'What kids were these?'

'What? Oh. Young boys, mostly. People he worked with, clients and colleagues. I never met any of them, but I heard all about them. How much money they had, what kind of cars they drove. And of course, how much they all loved to dance. Gillis couldn't go a day without danc-ing.' She smiled, forgetting her outrage for a brief moment, then caught herself and melted down again, finally starting to cry outright. 'The damn fool! Now look what he's done! Left me all alone, the selfish sonofabitch!'

The cops let her go for a while, as afraid to intrude as they were reluctant. She pulled a monogrammed handkerchief from her sweat-pants' pocket, dabbed her eyes and blew her nose a couple times, and only then did Lerner say, 'Can we get you anything? A glass of water from the kitchen, maybe?'

Gillis Rainey's mother shook her head in-dignantly. 'No. I'm all right. But thank you.'

Winn jumped right back in, anxious to get this interview over with before the subject could keel over dead herself, the victim of either a broken heart or an aneurism, it was impossible to tell which. 'This is a difficult time for you, we know. We only have a few more questions.'

Lorraine Rainey nodded and blew her nose into the white handkerchief one more time.

'You say your son liked to go out dancing. Would you happen to know where?'

'Where?'

'The specific clubs he frequented. I'm wondering if any of them would have been near the river where he was found.'

She shook her head again. 'I wouldn't know where he went. That's something you'd have to ask his little friends about.'

'If you could give us a name or two, and phone numbers if you have them, we'd be happy to do that.'

'I can't help you with phone numbers. And all I ever heard were first names. London. Tony. Perry. Does that help?'

It didn't in the slightest, but Winn put the names down in her notebook anyway.

'You say you don't know what your son would have been doing down in the river where he was found.'

'No. I can't imagine.'

'I hope you'll forgive me if you find this next question objectionable, but it has to be asked: Is there any chance he was down there trying to buy illegal drugs? Did he use marijuana or any other narcotic that you're aware of?????'

'Absolutely not. Never.' Lorraine Rainey appeared angry enough to leap from her chair and take Winn by the throat. 'And yes, I *do* find the question objectionable!'

Winn glanced over at her partner, who raised an eyebrow in lieu of a shrug. Gillis Rainey being a drug user would have gone a long way to explain his presence in the river, where buys

103

of everything from grass to meth were routinely made from sundown to sun-up. But the Coroner had found no trace of drugs in the dead man's body and his mother was clearly of the opinion he had no use for such diversions.

'Again, I apologize,' Winn said. 'But we're trying to make sense of what happened to Gillis, and why his body turned up where it did.'

Maybe he liked to walk the river to clear his head,' Lerner said to Lorraine Rainey. 'Is that possible?'

She glared at him, trying to decide if she liked him any better than she did Winn. 'I don't know. I suppose so.'

'We understand that diabetics can become seriously disoriented when they've gone too long without an insulin injection,' Winn said. 'In fact, it's not uncommon for them to wander off and go missing for extended periods of time. Perhaps that's what happened in this case.'

Winn waited patiently for Gillis Rainey's mother to recognize the statement as a question.

'Are you asking me if anything like that ever happened to Gillis before?'

'Yes, ma'am.'

'Then the answer is yes. It happened to him at least once that I'm aware of, and I'm sure it happened to him on several other occasions that I was never told about.'

'Can you tell us about the one instance that you know of????'

'He woke up alone in a stranger's bed way out in Desert Hot Springs and called me in a panic. He said he had no memory of whose house he

104

was in or how he'd gotten there, and he didn't have his insulin kit. I had to call nine-one-one to have an ambulance sent out to save him. He couldn't call himself because he was slurring his words so badly he would have never been understood. If I hadn't known better, I would have sworn he'd been drinking.'

'But he hadn't been.'

'No. I told you. My son enjoys—' She stopped, took a deep breath, and pushed on. 'I mean, he *enjoyed* taking chances with his health, as I've mentioned, but he wasn't crazy. He didn't use drugs and he hadn't touched a drink in over nine years, or since the day he was first diagnosed.'

'So if I may,' Lerner said, desperate to move things along so he and Winn could get the hell out of there and file this case away under 'Not a Fucking Homicide' where it belonged, 'it sounds like what you're telling us is, in your opinion, what happened to your son was just an accident. He went out partying last Friday night, forgot to take his insulin as he sometimes did, and for one reason or another, went down into the LA River where he died.'

'Yes. I don't know what else I *could* think.' The question was a baffling one to her. 'What do *you* think happened to him?'

Both cops remained silent.

'Oh, no, no. You don't mean to suggest he was *murdered*?'

'As I mentioned a moment ago, we've found no evidence to that effect as of yet,' Winn said, reasserting her role as the lead detective in the

room. 'But it's our job to consider all the possibilities, no matter how remote. Can you think of
anyone who might have wanted to harm your
son, Ms Rainey? Anyone at all?'

'No.'

'Friends, relatives, romantic interests...?'

'No. No one.'

'What line of work was Gillis in?'

'He was in real estate. He bought properties
and helped others do the same.'

'He worked for himself????'

'Yes.'

'Was he doing well?'

'Well? He was a goddamn millionaire. *You*
should be doing so well.'

Winn bore the blow without flinching, taking the old woman's tragic loss of a son into
account, and said, 'Then money would have
been no problem for him recently.'

'A problem? Certainly not.'

'What about the people you say he helped? His
clients? Were they doing equally as well?'

'I don't understand the question. What does
any of this have to do with what happened to my
son?'

'We're trying to determine if he could have
been having any serious disagreements with
someone he worked for or with,' Lerner said,
having decided he may as well play the part of a
real, on-duty homicide investigator since Winn
was determined to do so, with or without him.
'It's just routine, ma'am.'

'If his clients were all happy with the work he
was doing for them, it's a moot point,' Winn

106

said. 'But if they weren't—'

'No one can satisfy everybody,' Lorraine Rainey said irritably. 'I told you, my son was in real estate. Sometimes you make money in real estate and sometimes you don't, and some people just don't understand that. They think every investment is guaranteed a return and when they don't get it, or have to wait too long for it, they cry bloody murder.'

'Are you thinking of anyone in particular?'

'I already gave you his name. Perry something or other. Gillis said he was making him crazy, complaining because Gillis couldn't turn a property they'd bought together around fast enough.'

'Do you know if threats were exchanged?'

'Threats? Certainly not. Gillis thought the whole thing was funny.'

'Funny? In what way?'

'He used to laugh whenever he talked about it. The young man was a friend of his, they went out dancing together. Haven't you been listening to what I've been telling you?'

'Yes, ma'am, I have,' Winn said, finally at the end of her patience with this obnoxious old witch. She stood up and signaled for Lerner to do the same. 'We want to thank you for your time. And of course, you have our deepest condolences.'

She handed Lorraine Rainey a business card. 'Please feel free to call if you have any questions, or if you can think of anything else in the next few days that might help us with our investigation.'

'Investigation? What the hell is there to in-

107

vestigate?' Gillis Rainey's mother threw Winn's card to the floor at her feet. 'My goddamn selfish son finally killed himself, just the way I always told him he would if he didn't take better care of himself. He got what he deserved. What the hell is there to investigate?'

Out in the car, Winn looked over at Lerner and said, 'You want to go solo next time, Norm, all you have to do is say the word.'

'Come on...'

'We don't need to be sweating this one. I get it. But going through the motions before kicking it to the curb wouldn't kill you, would it?'

'Hey, I've got no problem busting my ass when a murder has actually been committed. If you see something here that says "homicide" to you, I'll be happy to hear about it.'

'Nobody's saying it's a homicide. I'm just saying it's not clear to me what the hell it is. What's this guy who lives out in West Hollywood doing down in the fucking LA River near Atwater Village? Even if he was off his meds and half out of his mind, how in the hell would he end up down there? Without his wallet or any ID?'

'You heard the old girl. He was a party animal, No,' Lerner said, using the nickname her fellow cadets had given Winn way back in her first days at the police academy. 'He ran the club scene with boys half his age, and he didn't much give a damn for doctor's orders.'

'So?'

'So despite what his mother seems to believe, he probably wasn't declining every time his pals passed the bong or the blow. Chances are good he was an occasional user, at least, and every user has to go out and make a buy sometime, right?'

'Except he didn't make a buy that night. The Coroner didn't find anything in his body and we didn't find anything on or around it.'

'So he died before he could make a connection.'

'And his wallet?'

'That one's easy. He got rolled after the fact, by somebody who found him before the bird lady who called us in did.'

Gillis Rainey had been down in the storm drain for days. Winn had to admit that was plenty of time for his body to have been noticed by one of the river regulars who would've had no problem relieving a stiff of all his cash and credit cards. And yet...

She shook her head and started the car. 'I don't like it,' she said. 'Everything you say could be right, but it doesn't feel that way to me.'

Lerner fell silent for a moment, then gave in. 'OK. Our man was murdered. Kindly tell me what the method was that left no marks on the body, or traces of toxins in his system. And it'd be nice to hear a motive, if you can spare one.'

Winn could only wish she had an answer or two for him. Accidental death may not have added up completely, but what kind of cockeyed murder was she suggesting this was instead? She put the car in gear and started driving. 'Give me some time to think about it,' she said. 'I'm sure I'll come up with something.'

TWELVE

Iris Mitchell had threatened to leave Perry Cross before. She didn't need his bullshit; she was drop-dead gorgeous, Harvard educated, and only twenty-six years old. If she wanted to, she could replace Perry with someone else just as rich and pretty in less time than it took the Earth to make one complete revolution around the sun. But replacing Perry with more of the same – just one more iteration of the ideal, storybook partner she'd been struggling to find since the braces had come off her teeth at the age of fourteen – would be pointless. She finally understood that. It was time to compromise: rich *or* pretty, she couldn't have both, because men who were both always thought those things were all a girl had any right to ask for.

Perry wasn't the worst fiancé she'd ever had; in fact, he was better than most. He was even-tempered and generous to a fault. He was punctual and courteous and never forgot a birthday, and he made love with a soft, refined touch. But he was a pathological liar unlike any Iris had ever encountered before. While most liars of her experience were victims of compulsion, Perry was nothing of the kind. He lied selectively and with premeditation, and always about things of

110

the utmost importance. Things that could spell the difference, for instance, between his being a prosperous, self-reliant life partner, and one she dared not turn her back on for a minute.

This time, Iris had not only caught him in a lie, but in the act of defrauding her to the tune of seventy-five hundred dollars. That was the amount of the personal check he had stolen from her purse, forged her name to, and then cashed, all in the space of the last forty-eight hours.

'*I* didn't sign that check,' he said. 'You did.'

'*I* did?'

'You don't remember because you were half asleep. I made it out but you signed it while you were still in bed.'

'No,' Iris said, shaking her head repeatedly. She'd been fucked up that morning, true enough, suffering the aftereffects of her friend China's kick-ass book launch party on the Strip the night before, but there was no way she'd been so far gone that she could sign a check made out to Perry for seventy-five hundred dollars without remembering it now. Hell, no.

'Well, that's what happened,' Perry said, 'whether you believe it or not.'

She glowered at him, sitting there in the den of his Venice condo with a ball game on and a beer in his hand, looking like her accusations of theft were hardly worth being distracted from the score. She could scream at him for another two hours and it wouldn't change a thing; he had given her his explanation for the check and, other than repeating it, he had nothing else to offer her. He had needed a small loan to cover a transfer of funds between accounts that had been slow to occur and she had agreed to give it to him while half asleep Wednesday morning. He'd taken a check from her purse, she'd scribbled her name on it, and then drifted off to sleep again. The end. It was a straightforward, uncomplicated lie that he was, as always, totally committed to, and how she chose to react to it was her business.

'You've been gambling again, haven't you?'

She'd gone to Vegas with him a month ago and seen him lose more money than even he could laugh off convincingly, and he'd promised her then he was through, that he'd cut his right arm off at the shoulder if he wagered another cent before seeking help.

'*Life* is a gamble,' Perry said. He'd turned his full attention back to the football game.

'This is it, Perry. I'm done,' Iris said.

And this time, she wasn't just talking. She stormed out of the room and went off to the bedroom to pack her things, cursing herself for having ever kept more than a toothbrush here in the first place. She didn't expect Perry would follow and he didn't, giving her one less reason to think she was making a mistake.

As she gathered her clothes together on the bed, the same bed she and Perry had made love in only hours earlier, she tried to understand what it was about Perry Cross she had found so irresistible. She had dated men with more money and better looks, who came from better families and had gone to better schools. Smarter men, men who made her laugh more and treated her

112

with greater respect. What the hell did Perry bring to the table that these men hadn't?

Confidence. That was what. Not the kind that any man who'd achieved some level of success in his chosen profession could always claim, but the kind that threatened to change worlds. An unshakable, unrelenting sense of self-worth Perry filled a room with just by entering it. It was a message a woman could read in his merest glance, one that said he intended to have his way, right or wrong, and you could either move aside, come along for the ride, or lose everything you possessed trying to stop him.

Iris had chosen to go along for the ride.

Exactly eighteen months later, almost to the day of their first meeting at a Grammy awards after-party at Staples Center, the thrill of it had finally worn off. The downside to Perry's ex-hilarating power had proven to be addiction and treachery, character flaws she might have been able to handle individually, but not in combination. Perry was a compulsive gambler and a liar, and now he had taken up stealing from her, and that was where Iris had to draw the line. You could fuck around with other women if you wanted to, and tell all the stupid, unbelievable lies to cover your tracks you could come up with; Iris could live with that kind of deceit because she'd been there, done that, too many times to count, and had learned how to recipro-cate. But ripping her off – treating her like some clueless fool who'd left her bank card in an ATM machine just for your convenience – was un-forgivable. It was one thing to be a man's bitch,

113

and quite another to be his punk, too.

Iris Mitchell was nobody's punk.

She was halfway through packing a bag when the doorbell rang. One of Perry's friends, no doubt, she thought. Fuck him. But then it occurred to her that Perry would only sit there on his lazy ass and scream at her from the other room to go get it, and rather than submit to one more minute of his bullying, she went to the door.

It was Will Sinnott. Will was a souse with a ten-year-old's sense of humor who'd been trying for years to drink his way out of the closet, but he was far and away the least repulsive of Perry's three business partners. Iris was almost relieved to see him standing there, despite the hangdog look on his face.

'Hey, Iris. Is Perry here?'

'In the playroom,' Iris said, tossing the words over her shoulder as she rushed back to the bedroom to finish packing.

Iris rarely seemed happy to see him, so Sinnott was surprised only by the severity of her rude welcome. Left to do so on his own, he showed himself in and found Cross exactly as promised, swallowed up in the cushions of a black leather divan in the den, staring blankly into the nonsense of beer commercials on TV.

'What's with her?' Sinnott asked.

Cross didn't bother looking up. 'Who?'

'Iris. Who else would I be talking about?'

Cross shrugged, fired the remote control at the flat-screen to change the channel. 'I had to borrow some money. She doesn't remember giving it to me. Whatever.'

Sinnott stepped back to peer down the hall, saw Iris through the open door moving frantically around the bedroom, piles of clothes in hand.

'Looks like she's moving out,' he said.

'Ask me if I give a shit,' Cross said. He still hadn't taken his eyes off the TV.

Sinnott understood the situation immediately. Cross had 'borrowed' his fiancée's money the same way he'd 'borrowed' Ruben's. He was desperate, as were all the Class Act partners. It wouldn't have been beneath Cross to treat someone he allegedly loved so callously under the most normal of circumstances, and now he was in the bind of his life. To him, simply taking what he needed from Iris, rather than wasting time asking for it, must have seemed like a complete no-brainer.

'What can I do for you, Will?' Cross asked.

'I've been trying to call you all morning and you never called me back. Is your phone on?'

'No. It's Saturday. I'll turn it on after lunch. What is it?'

The man was insane. They were thousands of dollars in debt to an enforcer for the Lizama drug cartel, and he didn't think it important to have his cell phone on outside of normal business hours.

Sinnott said, 'My father agreed to help.'

Cross finally turned around to face him.

'It's not the seventy grand we were hoping for, but it's something.'

'How much?'

'Fifty. With conditions.'

'Shit. You couldn't get the seventy? With conditions, you should've insisted on seventy.'

'Perry, you asshole, you should be grateful he gave me a fucking dime!'

Cross had no idea how hard it had been, to what extent he'd had to prostrate himself to win his father over. Harmon Sinnott was a cold-hearted bastard who despised Cross with a passion, believing him to be both a destructive influence on his son and an associate beneath Will's station. He hadn't worked for a cent of the vast fortune he'd inherited from his own father but, if only for the sake of appearances, he'd always been gainfully employed running one business enterprise or another, and without the aid of others. Partnerships, in his mind, were for losers. Hence, his view of Class Act Productions, and the three young men Will was allied with under its banner, was that of a sieve, a glorified boys' club that would never have anything to teach his son about capitalism other than how to make a failure of it and look like a drunken fool doing so.

'So what are the conditions?' Cross asked, finally turning off the television to fully acknowledge Sinnott's presence in his home. 'Aside from getting off the bottle?'

Sinnott didn't say anything, having hoped Cross wouldn't broach the subject until much later.

'Ah. It's come down to me again, hasn't it?' Cross stretched and yawned, then grinned broadly. 'Well, don't sweat it, Will. Daddy's en-

116

titled to his opinion. And I'm sure the boys and I can figure out a way to get along without you, given thirty seconds or so to think about it.'

'Fuck you.'

'You're right. That was uncalled for. Can I get you a drink? Wait, don't tell me. Of course I can.'

Cross went to the wet bar and fixed Sinnott his usual libation, a Bulldog gin martini, dirty. It was barely noon. Sinnott watched him work the shaker, trying to generate the will to walk away, but in the end he simply walked over and took the glass from Cross's hand, cursing his lack of backbone every inch of the way.

Maybe his father was right. Maybe he *was* just a puppet on Cross's string.

'So how short are we?' he asked, sipping his drink with the casual, detached manner of a man on a blind date. 'With the fifty I just brought in, I mean. Can you make up the difference, or...?'

'Not at present, no. We're still a good twenty Gs short.'

'Christ.'

'Yeah. Bummer.'

Sinnott looked to see if he'd meant the comment as a joke, but as Cross poured bourbon over ice into a glass for himself, there was nothing on his face to suggest as much.

'So what now?'

'I don't know. Stall for time, maybe? Have Ben talk to Ruben to see if he'll grant us an extension.'

'An extension?' Sinnott finished off his drink and immediately went to work fixing himself

117

another, an act that by now had become an automatic reflex to him. 'Perry, this is an assassin for a Mexican drug family we're talking about, not a loan officer for B of A.'

'Business is business. Doesn't matter where the money comes from. And just because he's supposed to be crazy, that doesn't mean he can't be reasonable. We give him two thirty now and promise to deliver the remaining twenty in thirty days, plus interest, why shouldn't he find that acceptable?'

'Because that's not what we agreed to do. We gave the man our word he'd get his full quarter million back by Friday. If we don't do that—'

'What's he going to think? That we're stiffing him? This guy who jams ice picks through people's heads, if Ben is to be believed? I doubt we look that stupid to him, Will. Ruben will understand. He'll have to.'

'And when he asks why we don't have the full two hundred fifty thou? What do we tell him?'

Cross rolled the ice cubes around in his glass, said, 'We tell him what he's probably heard from a hundred other business associates lately: The world economy's been in the toilet for two years, with the US stock market leading the way. As a result, we've suffered a few unexpected losses that have left us a little short, but not so short we can't pay him an additional thirty grand in thirty days if he'd be willing to wait. How the hell could he argue with that?'

Sinnott shook his head and shrugged, growing tired of testing Cross's powers of persuasion. He left his stool at the bar for an armchair, where he nursed his drink as if determined to make it last for hours. Amid their silence, the two men could hear Iris still knocking about in the bedroom, drawers slamming shut and pieces of luggage being bounced across the floor.

'We should have never taken his money in the first place,' Sinnott said. 'And we should have never given Gillis ours.'

'Fuck Gillis,' Cross said, deflecting Sinnott's implied accusation. 'He got what he deserved.'

'Maybe so. But he may get the last laugh yet. Jesus, Perry, why did they have to find his body so goddamn soon?'

'Now or later, what's the difference? They still have to ID it. And even then, what's that to us? The asshole died of natural causes.'

'Yeah, but—'

'Chill out. You sound like Andy. We've got enough to worry about without worrying about fucking Gillis.'

'Andy?'

'You think *you're* a nervous wreck? I've been trying to talk him down off the ledge ever since you sent that email around about Gillis's body being found. He's convinced that guy he had the car accident with is going to do like Ben said and report it to the cops. What was his name? Roddick?'

'Reddick. Joseph Reddick,' Sinnott said.

'I told him, so what if Reddick goes to the cops? They'll take the report and forget about it. If they had some reason to believe Gillis was murdered, they might give a shit about some guy driving like an idiot near the spot where his body

119

turned up. But Gillis *wasn't murdered.*'

'Not technically, no,' Sinnott said. 'But he died during the commission of a crime. A crime that we committed.'

'And do the cops know that, Will?'

'No. I mean, I don't think they do.'

'They don't. There's no way they could. Gillis's body was clean, we didn't leave a fucking mark on it. Even if the police knew the body was his – which they apparently don't, at least not yet – they'd have no reason to suspect foul play.'

It was true. Aside from binding his hands and gagging him with duct tape, Sinnott and his friends had never subjected Rainey to any physical abuse that he could remember.

'There's nothing for them to think but that Gillis was just some poor schmuck off his meds who wandered down into the river and died,' Cross said. 'God knows, Andy could've picked a less conspicuous place to dump him, but he also could've chosen worse. We're in the clear, Will. Believe me.'

Sinnott wanted to believe him. Oh, how he wanted to believe him. But Cross had established long ago that he was the last person in the world to trust in matters of risk assessment.

'What does Ben say about it?' Sinnott asked, but before Cross could answer, they heard something crash to the floor out in the hall.

Cross jumped to his feet, muttering, 'Goddamnit,' thinking Iris had finally taken her temper tantrum too far. But when he got to the door and peered out, there was nobody there.

The only sign that someone had been was a shattered crystal flower vase, uprooted from its perch on a side table, spilling water and Dendrobium orchids across the hardwood floor.

'Iris?'

Without his noticing, he realized now, she had grown abruptly silent. He went to the bedroom, found it empty. No clothes in the closet, no travel bags on the bed. He checked the rest of the condo. As near as he could tell, Iris was gone, along with anything that might have proven she'd once spent substantial time there.

Cross returned to the den, Sinnott watching him for clues, and flopped back into his original seat on the divan. He grabbed the TV remote, turned the game on again, and said, 'Whatever.'

Iris hadn't been standing outside the door of the den for long, but she'd been there just long enough to overhear more of Perry's conversation with Will than either would have ever wanted to share. She'd gone to the den intending to leave Perry with a proper goodbye, only to flee his condo instead like a rabbit from a pack of hounds.

They'd murdered Gillis Rainey.

At least, that's what it had sounded like to her. Or was she just reading something into their exchange that hadn't really been there?

Will: *He died during the commission of a crime. A crime that we committed.*

Perry: *Gillis's body was clean. We didn't leave a mark on it.*

And Perry had gone on to say something about

121

Andy Baumhower 'dumping' a body. What else could any of it mean but that the three of them – and in all likelihood, Ben Clarke, as well – had murdered this man Gillis Rainey? The same Gillis Rainey, no doubt, Perry had been cursing to hell for months now as a liar and a thief????

Iris was driving away from Perry's condo, her foot heavy on the gas to put as much distance between herself and Cross as possible, when a sudden lurch of nausea forced her to pull the car over to the side of a freeway on-ramp. She got her door open just in time to avoid vomiting all over the leather seats of her Audi TT. A truck flying up the ramp barely missed shearing her door off and taking her head along with it, but she didn't care. Right now, she had to wonder if she didn't deserve to die, being such a fool as to fall in love with a piece of work like Perry Cross.

She had known he was narcissistic; he had proven that almost daily. And of course he could be cruel. Anyone as driven to succeed as Perry would have to be cruel, on some level. But capable of murder? She would never have imagined it. There should have been signs of such a terrible potential that, try as she might now, she couldn't recall ever seeing.

Still, there was no denying what she'd heard. This man Rainey was dead, and Perry and his friends had murdered him. As revenge, Iris could only imagine, for refusing to pay them the $100,000 Perry claimed he owed them. One hundred thousand dollars was a lot of money by any reckoning, but it shouldn't have been enough to drive men like these to such extremes. That it had could only mean that one or more of them was in some kind of serious financial trouble. Trouble that had to start with Perry. That was the only reasonable explanation for both Rainey's murder and Perry's forging her signature on a seventy-five hundred dollar check.

Tooling down the 405 freeway aimlessly, windows down to keep cool air blowing in her face, Iris went from shock to terror in less than a heartbeat. What if Perry and Will knew how much she'd overheard? She had tried to slip out of the condo without making a sound, but in her rush to back down the hallway, she'd knocked a vase full of flowers off a table on to the floor, where it exploded with what felt to her ears like a thundering crash. Surely, one of the two men in the playroom had heard the vase shatter and, finding her gone, put two and two together. What would they do now? If they were capable of killing Rainey, why would they not be just as capable of killing her to keep her quiet about it?

She thought about going to the police, but she didn't entertain the idea for long. Thinking through the story she would have to tell, she realized how little there was to it. They would ask a million questions she had no answers to, along with one she did: Had Perry or Will actually used the word 'murder'? No. Neither man had. Upon hearing this admission, the police would then wonder if she hadn't simply misunderstood what she'd heard, or leapt to a wild conclusion unsupported by any facts. They would treat her like a crazy woman.

No. She couldn't go to the police. But she couldn't go home, either. Not until she knew, one way or the other, if what she suspected about Perry and his friends was true.

She drove through the night and contemplated her next move. Hours away from the realization that her wallet, and every piece of ID she owned, was still back in Perry's condo where she'd left it.

THIRTEEN

Like Iris Mitchell, Andy Baumhower was afraid to go home.

He was also equally reluctant to talk to the police, though not for fear they would think he was crazy. He was afraid they would think he was guilty of murder, which, of course, he was. That and kidnapping, and now – thanks to Ben Clarke – attempted blackmail.

Clarke had found him this afternoon at the Woodland Hills offices of Baumhower's limo service company, Prime Rides, Inc., and told him about his visit to Joseph Reddick's home the day before. He'd made the confession like it wasn't a confession at all, just a status report he was doing Baumhower a favor by passing on.

Baumhower was stunned beyond all belief. The big oaf actually thought what he'd done was something to be proud of.

'You stupid bastard,' Baumhower had told him, barely able to exhale enough to speak. 'Here we are accusing Perry of being out of his fucking mind, when it's really you who's certifiably insane.'

'You better watch your mouth, little man,' Clarke said.

'What the fuck were you thinking? Reddick

will go to the cops now for sure!'

'Yeah? Then why aren't *they* here talking to you instead of me? He's had plenty of time to go to the cops if that's what he's gonna do, and he hasn't. I've been out to his place and his wife's a couple times already today and there ain't a whiff of the police anywhere. Reddick's a problem solved, Andy, because *I* fucking solved it.'

Baumhower wanted to call Cross immediately, but Clarke threatened to shove the phone up his ass if he dared try. 'Don't worry about Perry. I'm having dinner with him tonight, I'll tell him then myself.'

'And what the hell am I supposed to do in the meantime, Ben?'

'Nothing. Behave normally. Keep your eyes open for the cops, and if they contact you, remain calm. Reddick can't prove a fucking thing, Andy, and if he goes to the police, he won't live long enough to even try.'

Baumhower blinked at him. 'What do you mean?'

'What do you think I mean? I told the man what I'd do if he opened his mouth and I wasn't fucking around.'

'Ben, for God's sake—'

'God ain't got nothing to do with this. We're all up to our necks in shit, man, and I for one ain't going down without a fight.'

He wasn't just talking; Baumhower could see that. He had always worried that Clarke's barbaric tendencies would go too far someday, and it seemed that day had finally arrived. The man was prepared to kill three people, including a child, to spare himself a prison term, and he seemed to have no qualms about admitting it. If Baumhower had ever doubted before that the three friends to whose fortunes he had bound his own would someday lead to his total and complete destruction, he was no longer so misguided.

Now, in the wake of Clarke's visit, Baumhower sat in his office like a figure chiseled in ice, so paralyzed by fear the mere thought of leaving his chair made his stomach turn. He picked up the phone twice to call Perry, despite all of Clarke's warnings, only to put it down again, unable to imagine what Cross could possibly say or do to change anything. Baumhower could only hope that Clarke's foolish gambit had, by some miracle, actually worked. His memory of Joseph Reddick was that of a man who would be difficult to rattle, somebody whose natural response to being threatened would not be fear but fury, but Clarke said he had a wife and child to consider, and that could make all the difference. Maybe, if Baumhower and his friends were lucky, Reddick cherished his family too much to risk doing anything that might result in their deaths at Clarke's hand.

Maybe.

As the hours passed, and no calls or visits came from the police, Baumhower's anxiety level slowly fell away. Reddick never left his thoughts for long but Baumhower became less and less convinced that the world would come crashing down upon his head any minute. He eventually left his office and, following Clarke's advice, went about his business as normally as possible, an occasional glance over his shoulder the only outward sign of his diminishing paranoia. At the end of the day, dusk filling the sky black, he arrived at his ranch-style home in Chatsworth wary but unafraid, concerned for his safety only enough to check the street outside for police cars before pulling his Benz first into the drive and then the garage.

The garage door was almost fully closed behind him, the garage itself growing oddly dim, when he realized the overhead light was out. The door banged shut and he was plunged into total darkness. He hit the remote to open the door again but nothing happened; he could hear the sound of the opener's motor running above his head but that was all. In a panic now, Baumhower threw open his car door, not intending to get out, but merely to bring the Benz's interior lights to life...

... and had what felt like the hard, metallic nose of a gun pressed into the back of his skull, just above his left ear.

'Make a sound and you're dead. Any sound at all,' Reddick said.

Baumhower knew it was Joe Reddick even before he spied his silhouette out of the corner of his eye, standing in the dark garage right beside him. His voice had the same ragged edge to it Baumhower had noticed six days ago out in Atwater Village, only tonight, it sounded a thousand times more sinister.

'Please...'

'That's a sound. Shut your face or I kill you

128

right here. Nod if you understand me.'

Baumhower nodded, fighting the urge to faint.

'Slowly: Kill the engine, then get out of the car and into the house. Now,' Reddick said.

Baumhower did as he was told, keeping his hands out to his sides to demonstrate how determined he was to cooperate. Reddick used the gun at the back of his head as a prod to steer him over to the door leading into the house, the one that was normally closed and locked but was standing open now. The idea that Reddick had already been inside his home, undeterred by the security system that should have detected his presence, added a whole new dimension to Baumhower's fear and sense of violation. Who- or whatever Reddick was, he clearly had talents the average family man did not possess.

Reddick pushed Baumhower through his own home, beyond the kitchen off the garage, down the hall and into the spare bedroom Baumhower used as an office. The whole house was dark but Reddick was unfazed; he had obviously already staked the place out and knew the lay of the land. Terrified now, Baumhower was unable to hold his tongue any longer. 'Please listen to me. If you're here because of what happened to your wife and son—'

Reddick smashed the heel of his gun off the side of his head, knocking him to his knees. Baumhower brought a hand up, feeling for blood, and the tears he'd managed to hold off up to now filled his eyes.

'You wanna talk? That's good,' Reddick said. He reached across Baumhower's desk to turn on a small reading lamp, cutting the darkness only enough to cast them both in shadow. 'Start talking.'

Baumhower blinked up at him, still on his knees, and got his first good look at Reddick's gun and the right hand that was holding it. He was wearing surgical gloves, more evidence yet that he hadn't come here just to talk.

'What do you want me to say?'

'Start with a name for the asshole who broke into my home yesterday and go from there.'

'I don't—'

'I've got no particular interest in torturing you, Mr Baumhower, but if you lie to me – just *once* – I promise you you'll regret it.'

'Ben Clarke,' Baumhower said.

'And who the hell is Ben Clarke to you?'

It took Baumhower a few seconds to decide how best to describe Clarke. 'My business partner.'

'OK. Now you can tell me why you sent him out to threaten the lives of my wife and son with a goddamn K-Bar knife.'

'I didn't send him out to do anything! I swear to God, I didn't even know what he'd done until this morning!'

Reddick took a step forward, nudged the snout of his handgun into the side of Baumhower's nose, hard.

'It's the truth!' Baumhower cried, his eyes screwed tightly shut.

Reddick slowly backed off, eased himself into the chair sitting in front of Baumhower's desk. 'What's this all about? Why's it so goddamn

130

important to you and Clarke that I not tell the police about our accident?'

Baumhower was slow to answer, nearly as terrified to speak as he was to hold his tongue.

'We were afraid,' he said finally.

'Afraid of what?'

Again, Baumhower hesitated. 'We didn't want them to know I was there.'

'Who? There where?'

'The police. Near the river. We thought...' He saw a vein in Reddick's neck pulse, went on before the man could get up out of the chair and strike him again. 'We thought if they found out about the accident, they'd know I was the one who ... who...' He couldn't get the rest out.

'I'm running out of patience, Andy,' Reddick said, and if his words hadn't conveyed this message, the edge to his voice, and the crushing weight of his gaze, would have.

'They'd know I was the one who dumped Rainey's body,' Baumhower said, all in one breath, before he could lose the nerve.

Reddick fell silent, considering Baumhower's answer. It made perfect sense, of course; a white panel van, leaping from a river access road on to the street in the dead of night, precipitating a collision Baumhower had at first attempted to ignore, then begged Reddick not to report.

'Who was Rainey?' Reddick asked.

'Please. I can't tell you any more. It was an accident. Nobody intended to kill anybody!'

Reddick rose to his feet. 'One more time. Who was Rainey?'

'Gillis Rainey. A friend of Perry's who owed

131

us money. He called himself a financial advisor but all he was was a con-man. A fucking liar and a thief!'

'Hold it. Perry? Who the hell is Perry?'

Baumhower didn't answer, cursing his own stupidity. He was needlessly giving Reddick more information than he was demanding to know.

Reddick sat back down in the chair, rolled it on its casters over to Baumhower until he was close enough to hold the gun an inch from his head.

'OK. We're gonna start over, from the beginning,' he said. 'And this time, you aren't gonna leave out the slightest detail.'

Baumhower told Reddick everything, no longer giving a damn whether he was saying too much or not. Reddick asked few questions, and those only for clarification's sake, content to let his hostage do all the talking. His expression had grown ever darker as the enormity of the bumbling criminal conspiracy he'd stumbled into became clear to him. By the time Baumhower was done, insisting he'd said all there was to say, Reddick resembled nothing as much as a hanging judge about to pronounce sentence. He'd known coming in that Baumhower and the big man who'd terrorized his family the day before were bad guys, deserving of his contempt if not an ounce of his mercy, but he hadn't counted on discovering they were only two parts of a larger and more menacing whole. The knowledge raised the danger they represented to an entirely different level.

132

Baumhower saw the change in him and was justifiably alarmed by it. He'd been holding out the faint hope that telling Reddick what he wanted to know, without making any effort to save himself, would appease the man enough to spare his life. But now he wasn't so sure. Now, Reddick was looking at him like the only thing he had left to decide was where in Baumhower's body he should put the first bullet.

'What are you going to do?' Baumhower asked, voice quavering.

Contrary to what his hostage thought, Reddick had yet to make up his mind. His intent all along, insofar as his premeditation went, was to question Baumhower only long enough to learn Clarke's identity and what secret he and Baumhower were so desperate to hide, then kill them both. Not to exact revenge or dispense justice, but to remove them as a threat to the people he loved in the most certain and permanent way possible. But now the game had changed; he had four people to worry about, not just two, and he might need to keep Baumhower alive, at least for a while, to get to the other three.

Reddick stood up and ordered Baumhower to do the same.

'Please. What are you going to do?' Baumhower asked again, getting slowly to his feet.

'I heard you the first time. Shut up and let's go,' Reddick said. He waved his gun at the door.

It wasn't the answer Baumhower wanted to hear. He had convinced himself that Reddick was going to kill him, no matter what he did, and the only reason he could think Reddick might

133

have to take him out of the house was to do it somewhere remote, where no one would hear the shots and his body would neither soon nor easily be found.

'No,' Baumhower said. It had taken all the courage he could muster.

Reddick grimaced, his patience wearing thin. 'One way or another, you're going out that door,' he said. 'By your own power or mine, it makes no difference to me.'

'I think you're forgetting something, aren't you? What Ben told you? If anything happens to me, your wife and little boy are *dead*.'

He hadn't meant it as a personal threat. It was just a last ditch effort to save himself. But Baumhower could not have miscalculated any worse. Reminding Reddick of Clarke, and the promises of death the big man had made to Reddick the day before, did nothing but snap his tenuous hold on reason like a twig. In a single instant, any rationale Reddick may have had for keeping Baumhower alive was erased from his mind.

If anything happens to me, your wife and little boy are dead.

Recognizing his mistake immediately, all Baumhower had time to do was watch Reddick point the gun at his face and pull the trigger.

FOURTEEN

At Cross's insistence, he and Ben Clarke had dinner Saturday night at *Koi* in West Hollywood. Clarke hated sushi and wanted to dine at Nightshades, his club in Santa Monica, within the familiar and noisy confines of his private office overlooking the dance floor, but Cross wouldn't hear of it. He was in a somber frame of mind and had no interest in trying to talk to Clarke amid the hedonistic trappings of one of his clubs.

They sat at a booth in the darkest of four dining rooms, candlelight casting bands of shadow across the walls, Cross eating avocado rolls and Yellowtail sashimi with gusto, Clarke picking at a bowl of white rice and roasted duck like a kid searching for a live bug. Neither paid any attention to the A-list celebrities occupying various other booths in the room, Cross because he didn't give a damn and Clarke simply too miserable to notice.

'Try him again,' Cross said.

'Fuck that. We've tried him three times already, he ain't gonna answer the phone.'

'He will eventually. He has to. Try him again.'

Clarke glowered at him but Cross wasn't looking, too intent on eating to raise his eyes from his plate. Clarke thumbed the redial button on

135

his phone one more time, listened as the call rang through yet again to Andy Baumhower's voicemail.

'Voicemail,' he said, tossing the phone aside to bounce with a clang off his water glass. 'What'd I tell you?'

Cross shook his head, facing Clarke directly now. 'I don't like it, Ben.'

'You don't like what?'

'I can see how he might want to avoid talking to me, but you? Why shouldn't he want to talk to you?'

'Who said he doesn't want to talk to either one of us? So Andy's not answering his voicemail. Man could be catching a movie or something. He could be someplace where he can't have his ringer on, or just can't hear it.'

He was reaching and he knew it. Baumhower had been AWOL now for going on two hours and Clarke didn't need Cross to tell him how unlike their friend this was. Cell phone, email, online social network – it didn't matter. Baumhower was fucking OCD when it came to answering every message left for him in thirty minutes or less, rain or shine.

He didn't want to panic, but Clarke was beginning to think the worst. As was Cross, obviously. Clarke had told him over appetizers what he'd done the day before to Reddick and his family, making it all sound like the only move a wise man could have made. The news enraged Cross, no surprise, but not to the vitriolic level Clarke had been expecting. Instead, Cross took it with surprising calm, betraying more in the way of bemused astonishment than unadulterated out-rage. He considered what Clarke had done to be unbelievably stupid, and he said so, but he confessed to a mild suspicion that it could lead to the desired result, nevertheless. It all depended on Reddick, Cross said, and whether or not he would take Clarke's threats to heart and scare.

Having never laid eyes on Reddick himself, he asked Clarke for his opinion.

'The last time I saw him,' Clarke said, teeth bared in a crooked smile, 'he was all curled up in a ball on the floor, crying like a little bitch. He's gonna scare, all right.'

He was neglecting to mention, of course, all the other things he had seen in Reddick aside from simple fear: pain, anger, confusion – and frothing, violent, wild-eyed madness, the kind most commonly found in padded rooms. Whether this last made Reddick more or less likely to follow his instructions, Clarke didn't know, but he thought he could guess how Cross would feel about it. Cross would see it as a bad omen.

Which was precisely how he was taking Baumhower's state of incommunicado now. The timing of it bothered him. Maybe, as Clarke would have him believe, there were explanations for Baumhower choosing this moment to go uncharacteristically silent that had nothing to do with Joe Reddick, but until he heard them from Baumhower himself, Cross was going to operate as if all hell was about to break loose.

'Get Will back on the phone,' he said. 'Tell him to go by Andy's crib and check on him.

Right away.'

'And if he wants to know why?'

They'd talked to Sinnott once already tonight to ask if he'd heard from Baumhower recently, but they hadn't told him anything about why they were asking.

'Just tell him Andy looked like shit when you saw him this morning and we want to make sure he's OK.'

'And he's supposed to believe that?'

'Hell, Ben, I don't care if he believes it or not. Just get Will over to Andy's, all right?'

The only thing Clarke had a mind to do was tip the table over on to Cross's lap and walk the fuck out. He was sick of Cross's Jap food and tired of his orders, and the creeping fear that Baumhower had grown quiet because he was *gone* – halfway to Belgium or Israel or God-knew-where by now in some pointless, idiotic flight from the authorities – was burning a hole in Clarke's gut from the inside out. But because Cross was right, because it only made sense to send Will out to Andy's place to see what the fuck was going on, he kept his seat in the booth and made the call.

As he predicted, Sinnott wouldn't go without asking a host of questions first. Clarke told him he and Cross were concerned about Baumhower because he'd been talking about turning himself in to the police, convinced that the discovery of Gillis Rainey's body was bound to lead them to his door any minute. It was a lie not too far from the truth, and it did the trick; duly alarmed, Sinnott couldn't get off the phone fast enough to go check on Baumhower as requested.

Sinnott had a house up in the hills of Encino, less than a twenty- minute drive from Baumhower's place in Chatsworth. Cross and Clarke ordered fresh drinks while they waited for Sinnott to report back, making small talk neither really wanted to hear just to fill the time. When, thirty minutes later, it was Cross's phone that rang instead of Clarke's, they both had the same thought at once.

Sinnott wasn't calling to say that all was well.

They found him sitting in the dark interior of his car out front, his face as white as an albino Koi. An open flask of brandy was in his lap, standing upright between his thighs. They could tell just from the smell of the car that the flask had long been empty.

'I can't go back in there,' Sinnott said.

All they'd been able to get out of him over the phone was that Andy was dead, and that they needed to get their asses over there right away. Cross told him not to call anyone else – especially not the police – and to stay put until they arrived.

The front door was ajar when they reached the porch, presumably as it had been upon Sinnott's arrival. Clarke led the way inside, gesturing for Cross to avoid touching anything. The house was dark except for a room off in the back, the one both of Baumhower's friends recognized as his home office. They crept to the open door and were greeted by the sight of Baumhower's body, sprawled out on the floor above a pool of his own blood. One eye was open and the other was simply gone, replaced by a black, red-rimmed hole.

'Fuck!' Clarke said.

They entered the room and looked around, trying to piece together the circumstances of Baumhower's death. As near as either man could tell, his killer had left little in the way of evidence behind. Everything in the room seemed to be in its proper place, exactly as they remembered it. Except:

'Where's his MacBook?' Cross asked.

The black laptop Baumhower never went anywhere without was absent from its usual perch atop his desk. Cross and Clarke canvassed the room, checking every inch of the floor and the surfaces of furniture, and saw no sign of the computer anywhere.

'Maybe he put it down somewhere on his way in,' Clarke said.

They went back to the front of the house and looked, starting in the hallway, then moving on to the kitchen, where Baumhower would have first entered from the garage. They scanned end tables and countertops, all the places Baumhower might have laid the laptop before retreating to his office.

The MacBook wasn't there.

'Ben, look.'

Clarke turned, squinted in the dark to see Cross standing in the living room next to a big-screen TV that appeared to be hanging by a thread from one wall. A phalanx of power and A/V cables that should have been plugged into

140

its back sprouted in a loose jumble from a hole in the wall above it, some showing signs of having been ripped from their connectors by force. As Clarke drew closer, he could see that the display itself had been similarly torn away from its bracket, a de-installation job done in haste and left woefully incomplete.

'What do you think?' Cross asked.

'I think we should take a good look around, see if anything else is missing besides Andy's MacBook,' Clarke said.

They split up and worked quickly, going from room to room, elbowing light switches on and off to avoid leaving fingerprints behind. Nothing glaring stood out in its absence, but they found every drawer in an armoire and dresser in Baumhower's bedroom yanked open, and a leather jewelry box that lay empty and turned on its head atop his bedside table. When Cross went back to Baumhower's office, Clarke was gingerly going through the dead man's pockets.

'His wallet's gone and so's his cell phone,' Clarke said. 'There's no cash on him, either.'

'So...'

'You thinkin' what I'm thinkin'?'

'Looks like the poor bastard walked in on somebody jacking the place.'

'Exactly. TV, MacBook, cash and credit cards ... What else could've happened?' Clarke's sense of relief almost brought a smile to his face.

'You don't think this could've been Reddick?'

'What?'

'Maybe he killed Andy and set everything up to look like a burglary. That's possible, isn't it?'

'Possible? Anything's possible. But Reddick didn't do this. Who the fuck do you think he is, James Bond?'

'You've met him, I haven't. You tell me.'

'I already did. Reddick's under control. He ain't got the balls to go to the cops, and he sure as hell ain't got enough to do all this. Gimme a break.'

Cross fell silent as if convinced, but Clarke knew he still had his doubts. Remembering the convulsing, howling wild man Reddick had been the last time he'd seen him, Clarke only halfway believed what he was saying himself.

'And if you're wrong?' Cross asked finally. 'If he left his prints all over this house and they lead the cops directly to him? He could ruin us all, Ben.'

'He could. But he won't.'

'There's only one way to really be sure about that, though, isn't there?'

He waited for Clarke to return his look and properly interpret it. It didn't take long.

'No problem,' Clarke said.

They both turned at what sounded like a small whimper, discovered Sinnott listing to one side in the open doorway, holding back tears with no success whatsoever.

'So,' he said. 'Who are we planning to kill now?'

Reddick couldn't remember killing Baumhower. His memory was just a cold, black hole in the moments before he found himself down on one knee, checking Baumhower's body for a pulse

142

he knew wasn't there.

He'd grabbed everything he could carry that he thought might be helpful in running down the dead man's three partners – his wallet, laptop computer, and cell phone – and then did a rush job of doctoring the scene to resemble a home burglary interrupted, acting on sudden inspiration. There was only one course of action for him to take now – find Baumhower's trio of friends, starting with Ben Clarke, and kill them all post haste – and every second he could keep them guessing about his intentions would be critical to his success. If they realized too soon he was coming for them, they'd likely scatter to the four winds, and the lives of his wife and child would remain in the very state of peril he was seeking to render impossible.

Retreating to his Echo Park apartment, Reddick gathered Baumhower's things together on a dining room table and subjected them to a thorough inspection, working through a haze of guilt that kept threatening to overwhelm him. He was a murderer now, pure and simple, someone who had taken another man's life without the excuse of professional duty or self-defense, and it was going to take Reddick some time to get used to the idea. Time he didn't really have, because he had yet more killing to do, and remorse would only get in the way. He had to keep reminding himself that none of this had been of his own choosing, that fate had thrown him and Baumhower together through no fault of his own. He wasn't an evil man, just an astoundingly unfortunate one, and whatever damage he was destined to do in the days to come he could not be held accountable for.

Baumhower's iPhone was a wealth of information, an unsecured storehouse of names and phone numbers, addresses and notes, but Reddick knew the data on the dead man's laptop would be far more useful to him. Almost as if to prove the point, the black MacBook booted up to a login screen and no further, demanding a username and password Baumhower's phone had not. Reddick would have been done had he been forced to rely on his skills as a hacker to proceed; short of trying the most obvious and inane username/password combinations imaginable, he would have had no clue how to go about determining the right one.

But Baumhower, it seemed, had been nothing if not consistent, and so had treated computer security with the same ineffectual lack of sophistication he had shown in securing his home. Reddick had managed to successfully break into Baumhower's residence in part because the dead man had left all the pertinent passcode info regarding his home security system on a note in a kitchen drawer for Reddick to find, allowing him to kill the alarm and assure the security firm that had installed it all was well when a dispatcher officer called the house to investigate. Now Reddick was relieved to discover that Baumhower had stored a similar note-to-self regarding his MacBook login in the memo section of his unsecured phone. It was a lucky break, certainly, but Reddick knew it was also an error all too typical of people like

Baumhower, jittery milquetoasts afraid to trust critical information to the vagaries of memory.

Reddick entered the correct username and password – a predictably inane 'Primerider1'/ 'UCLA2007' – and watched as the laptop booted up completely. He did a quick inventory of the files on its hard drive, opening only enough to become satisfied the MacBook was indeed the fount of information on Baumhower and his Class Act friends he'd been hoping for, then shut the machine back down. He would examine the files in detail later, taking copious notes, but right now he wanted to check in on Dana and Jake before they bedded down for the night. His wife's voice would serve as a reminder of what he was fighting for and give him the strength to go on, even if by talking to her so soon after Baumhower's death, he ran the risk of somehow revealing to her what he'd done.

'Oh, Joe, thank God,' she said, sounding half-asleep, when he'd identified himself. 'I've been worried sick.'

'No need. I'm fine.'

As he'd anticipated, she wanted to know everything: how he was, where he was calling from, how he'd spent his day. He answered the first two questions but not the third.

'We've already been over this. I'm doing what I have to do,' he said. 'Let's just leave it at that.'

She fell silent, knowing she was doomed to imagine things now that were likely to be far worse than the truth.

'Where's Jake?' Reddick asked.

'In bed. He's beat.'

'Already?'

'He's been in and out of the pool all day. We may have told him we're here because the house is flooded, but he's treating this like a vacation.' Before Reddick could offer a response, she said, 'Joe, please. You can't not tell me *anything*.'

He thought it over, putting himself in her place. Relenting, he said, 'I can tell you that what we're up against is bigger than what I thought this morning. Turns out it isn't just Baumhower and his friend with the knife we have to worry about. There are at least two others.'

'Two others?'

He gave her a greatly abbreviated version of the story Baumhower had told him, leaving just enough on its bones to explain why Baumhower and his friends had been so desperate to keep him silent about the car accident he'd had with Baumhower six nights before.

'Oh, my God. I think I read something about that somewhere,' Dana said.

'About what?'

'The murder. Yesterday or the day before, I can't remember which, I read something about a body being found down in the LA River.'

'Did the story say whose body it was?'

'No. The police were still trying to identify it.'

'But the story said it was murder?'

'I think so. Or maybe ... No, wait.' She thought it through. 'Maybe it didn't say anything about it being murder, at that. I think all it said was that the cause of death had yet to be determined. Still, it has to be the same guy, doesn't it?'

146

'Most likely.'

'Then our problem's solved, isn't it? If the police are already looking for Baumhower and his friends—'

'No,' Reddick said.

'Joe, just listen to me for a minute—'

'It won't work, Dana. We can't just turn these assholes in.'

'Why not?'

'Because for one thing, it wasn't technically a murder. According to Baumhower, the victim's death was accidental. California law may not recognize the difference, but a judge handing down sentence just might. And that's assuming they're all convicted, which is anything but a safe bet.'

'What do you mean?'

'I mean that these are people with enough money and pedigree to beat almost any rap. Their lawyers are the kind that either make murder charges vanish completely, or get prison time reduced to the bare minimum.'

Just in the fifteen minutes he'd had Baumhower's laptop up, he'd learned enough about the Class Act quartet to know that all this was true. Baumhower and his friends weren't just four brown-skinned thugs off the street the system could be counted on to lock up and throw away the key; these were young, white men of privilege with the kind of personal and familial resources that made the prospect of serious prison time vanish into thin air every day. Reddick had seen it happen too many times to pretend otherwise.

147

There was another, more salient reason he couldn't turn Baumhower's three surviving partners in to the police, of course – he'd just shot Baumhower to death – but Reddick couldn't share this with Dana without taking the chance she'd call the authorities herself, just to keep him from killing anyone else. Even though they had a tacit understanding that murder had been his intent all along, hearing that he'd actually taken someone's life – and the life of an unarmed man, at that – would probably undermine what will she had left to serve as his silent accomplice.

'But maybe this time—' Dana started to say.

'I've gotta go,' Reddick said, anxious to get off the phone.

'Joe...'

'I didn't ask for any of this to happen, Dana. Whatever I have to do to keep you and Jake safe from these fuckers, they brought upon themselves. Remember?'

In the hush that followed, he could picture his wife softly nodding her head. Afraid to say anything more.

FIFTEEN

Shortly after one a.m. Sunday morning, Andy Baumhower's cell phone rang atop the bedside table of a twenty-eight-year-old commercial carpenter named Tony Ortiz. Roused from a deep sleep, Ortiz reached a hand out in the dark to grab the phone, then stopped, remembering the instructions he'd been given earlier that evening. He sat up, yawning, pulled a tube sock he'd placed on the nightstand before turning in over his right hand, and then used that hand to answer the phone.

'Yeah?'

He got to his feet and took the phone into the kitchen, not wanting his wife Maria to hear the ensuing conversation.

'Reddick?' the caller asked.

He hadn't been told anything about him, but if Ortiz had been forced to guess, he would have said the guy was a big, red-faced white boy.

'Who?'

'Reddick. Joe Reddick. Cut the bullshit, asshole.'

Ortiz had to chuckle. 'Sorry, home, but there ain't no "Reddix" here.'

'What, you think tryin' to sound like some stupid *vato* from the 'hood is supposed to fool

149

me? How dumb do you think I am?'

Now Ortiz openly laughed. 'I don't know how dumb you are,' he said, 'and I don't give a fuck. *Buenos noches, pendejo.*'

He hung up and turned Baumhower's phone off, then went back to bed, chortling himself to sleep.

From behind the wheel of an emerald green BMW flying south along the 405 through the Sepulveda Pass, Ben Clarke tried Andy Baumhower's number two more times before giving up. It had been a long shot, seeing if somebody would be dumb enough to actually answer the dead man's phone, but the payoff in relief was immeasurable. Back at Baumhower's crib, before the police had shown up, Cross had almost convinced Clarke that Joe Reddick was behind Andy's murder, but now Clarke knew for certain the story they'd told the cops instead was true. Whoever the idiot was he'd just spoken to over the phone, he wasn't Reddick. Man of many talents or no, there was no way a white bread like Reddick could have mimicked a younger, Spanish-speaking, East LA homeboy – and likely burglar and murderer – to such perfection.

No fucking way.

It was a load off Clarke's mind. With Baumhower dead, their task of scraping together Ruben's money before he came looking for it had just become more difficult than ever. Clarke didn't need to be worrying about Reddick, too. Cross had given him implicit orders to kill

150

Reddick back at Baumhower's place, thinking he was an immediate threat, but now that could wait; Reddick hadn't killed Andy Baumhower, so there was no rush to do away with him. Clarke would get around to wasting the fool once all their business with Ruben was over and done with.

Assuming it ever would be.

Sunday morning around eight, Reddick walked across the street from his Echo Park apartment to see his neighbor Toni Ortiz. The two men had met months before on the day Reddick moved in, Ortiz sprinting over from his front porch, a lit cigarette pinched between his lips, to catch a floor lamp that was about to fall off the U-Haul trailer Reddick had rented for the afternoon. Ortiz helped Reddick and the day laborer he had hired finish the unloading for the price of all the beer he could drink, and he and Reddick had been friends ever since.

'Well?' Reddick asked.

Ortiz placed Andy Baumhower's iPhone, wrapped up in an old blue washcloth, into Reddick's open palm, grinning like a man about to tell an offhand joke. 'It rang just like you said. I think it was about one a.m., maybe a little later, I'm not sure.'

'And?'

'Man asked for you. I tol' 'im to go fuck hisself.'

Reddick requested details and was pleased to hear there weren't many. Ortiz's conversation with Clarke – and it almost certainly had to have

151

been Clarke – had been short and sweet, exactly as Reddick had hoped. Whether the ruse had worked or not, only time would tell, but he had at least given Clarke and his two friends one more reason to think he had had nothing to do with Andy Baumhower's death. He had big plans for the trio today and taking them by surprise was essential to his success.

Reddick thanked Ortiz for his time and paid him the fifty dollar fee they'd agreed upon. Ortiz took the money, shook Reddick's hand warmly, and watched his neighbor get into his car and drive off before going back to bed himself, having asked not a single question about Andy Baumhower's phone or the pissed off white man who had placed a call to it hours earlier. He'd been happy to do Reddick the midnight-hour favor, but he didn't want to know any more about the white man's private affairs than was absolutely necessary.

He just had the feeling it'd be easier to go on liking Reddick that way.

Iris Mitchell had recognized her mistake the moment she went to get out of the car Saturday night. Her purse wasn't there. She'd left it back at Perry's.

It had taken all the courage she could muster just to spend the night in her own home, rather than at her parents'. Her father would have been happy to have her, no questions asked, but her mother would have grilled her like an auditor for the IRS. And what explanation could Iris have given her that wouldn't have made her sound like she'd lost her mind? Her parents loved Perry Cross; they knew nothing about his gambling and propensity to lie because she'd gone to great lengths to maintain their ignorance of such things. Now, all of a sudden, their future son-in-law was not only a thief and a liar, but a murderer, too?

They'd never believe it. They'd tell her what she'd overheard Perry and Will say back at Perry's condo was part of something much more innocent than a murder conspiracy, just bits and pieces of a harmless conversation she'd completely misconstrued in the heat of a lovers' quarrel. And they would convince her they were right. Before she knew it, they'd have her talking to Perry on the phone, accepting his explanations for everything and apologizing for having been such a tempestuous, impressionable fool.

As it was, one long, sleepless night later, she had almost brought herself to this point on her own. But not quite. Doubt was creeping in as memory began to lose its finer edges – had Will said 'a *murder* that we committed' or simply 'a crime'? – but she was still confident enough in her interpretation of what she'd overheard the day before to be afraid. Too afraid to see or talk to Perry until she'd had sufficient time to think things through. They were finished, in any case; his forgery alone had sealed that deal. The only thing left to be determined was how dangerous it was to be around him now.

It was a question she would have put off answering indefinitely, given a choice. But her wallet was at Perry's and she had to get it back.

Her ID and her checkbook were in it, and Perry had already proven that such things could not be entrusted to him for long.

It was Sunday. He could loaf around the house all day on Saturdays, but on Sundays Perry liked to go out, either to the gym, the beach, or – prior to his oath of abstinence, anyway – one of those sleazy card casinos in Gardena. Iris still had her keys. If she timed it right, she could slip into his condo while he was gone, retrieve her wallet, and leave, avoiding any contact with Perry altogether.

She just needed to be a little lucky.

SIXTEEN

The first sign Finola Winn had that something wasn't quite right at Gillis Rainey's West Hollywood home was the unlocked front door; she turned the knob and the door just swung open in her hand. Inside, a number of other things struck her as odd: lights on throughout both floors, a full set of keys on a table in the alcove, a Black-Berry smartphone and wallet atop a dresser in the master bedroom. Rainey's car – a late model Lincoln Navigator – was sitting in the garage.

Winn was here alone, having not been up to the fight she knew she'd have to wage to get her partner to start their Sunday shift by tagging along, working a case that seemed to deserve the smallest share of their time. Still, she could guess what Norm would have said without actually having to hear him say it: *So what?*

People left the lights on in their homes all the time, and walked out of the house without their keys with similar regularity. A diabetic like Rainey, off his meds for one reason or another, could have strolled outside one early evening a week ago, perhaps to retrieve the trash bins from the curb, and forgotten where he was going and why he was going there before he even reached the end of the driveway. How he could have

155

gotten from there to Atwater Village and the Los Angeles River would be harder to figure, but not impossible. To a skeptic like Norm Lerner, there was always a way to explain the presence of a stiff that did not involve criminal activity.

Winn, on the other hand, could detect the mark of foul play in the most innocuous of things, which was why she could see nothing at every turn in Gillis Rainey's home now but the evidence of ... what? A kidnapping, maybe? There was a full glass of white wine on a coffee table in the living room and the stereo was on but silent, as if Rainey had been listening to a CD before he left – or was taken from – the house. The dead man's insulin kit, complete with insulin, lay open on the counter of the master bath.

Winn pictured her partner in the foyer, looking this way and that, sniffing the air like a blood-hound trying desperately to catch the scent of something that wasn't there. 'I don't see any signs of a struggle. Do you?'

No, Winn would have had to admit. She didn't. Which didn't prove that Rainey hadn't been forcibly removed from the premises, but it did make such a scenario more difficult to envision.

'You put a gun in somebody's face at the front door, there quite often *isn't* any struggle,' she said, actually sparring with a man who was only standing there beside her in her mind.

Norm would tell her she was reaching, allowing all the conclusions she'd jumped to follow-ing their conversation with Rainey's mother to color her judgment, and he'd probably be right.

The house was a cornucopia of incongruities, maybe, but as a crime scene it was sorely lacking. If Gillis Rainey had left the place in a curious state of flux, there was nothing here to indicate he'd been forced to do so against his will.

She and Norm had other cases on their docket. Bigger cases, more pressing cases, and most importantly, cases that required no imagination to be classified as homicides. It was time to do the responsible thing and move on.

Which was not the same thing as giving up. When she eventually left Rainey's home, it was exactly as Winn had found it, with one small exception: She took the dead man's cell phone with her. Inside the car out front, she turned the BlackBerry on, hoping to scan through Rainey's contact list, only to find the device was password protected. No computer geek herself, she'd have to get one of the department's tech guys to open the phone up for her. Calling in a favor might get it done as early as tomorrow.

In the meantime, she'd work her other cases with Norm and wait. Then, once she had access to Rainey's data, she'd check it for one associate of his in particular: his 'little friend Perry,' as Lorraine Rainey had called him. If the man was there, she and Norm would run him down and pay him a visit.

Just to see how hard he'd take the news that his dancing and business partner, Gillis Rainey, was dead.

SEVENTEEN

Reddick chose to take Perry Cross down first.

Ben Clarke was the man he wanted dead most in all the world, but the plan he'd come up with for dealing with Andy Baumhower's three friends made starting with either Cross or Will Sinnott a wiser choice. He'd decided to kill all three at once, in one place, rather than individually, and so his first mark had to be someone capable of drawing the other two into a trap at Reddick's behest just to save his own skin. Based upon what he'd already seen of the big man, Reddick didn't think Clarke would fit the bill. Baumhower had described Cross as Class Act's unofficial leader and intimated Sinnott was a drunk. Between the two, Cross seemed better suited for Reddick's purposes.

He had gone over the files on Baumhower's laptop thoroughly that morning and compiled several pages of notes; he felt like he knew his three targets as well as anyone working on such short notice could. He knew where each man lived and conducted business; their marital status and line of work. Photos on Baumhower's MacBook had given him some idea of what each man looked like and email exchanges between the trio had established their hierarchy as clearly as a PowerPoint presentation. If any one of them could call a Sunday morning emergency meeting the other two would feel compelled to attend, it was Perry Cross.

Cross's condo in Venice was on the second floor of a converted apartment building on Abbot Kinney that featured no form of security Reddick could ascertain. The main entrance was unlocked and the open carport out back had no gate to discourage theft. Maybe if Cross had been the equal of his partners he'd have been able to afford a more impregnable home, but Reddick had read enough about him on Baumhower's MacBook to know that he was the financial runt of the Class Act litter.

After spending thirty minutes surveying the territory, Reddick left his car and went to the building's entrance, a small black gym bag in hand. It was a little after nine o'clock. He paused to study the names on some of the mailboxes, then went inside and climbed the stairs to the second floor, encountering no one on the way. At the landing, he drew a pay-as-you-go cell phone he had purchased the day before from his bag and called Cross's home number. An answering machine picked up after the fourth ring and Reddick, trying to sound several years older and considerably less composed, left Cross a message:

'Oh, hey, I'm calling for Perry Cross? Are you there? Mr Cross, this is Brad Dunphy in unit one-oh-five downstairs. Listen, I'm really sorry, but I just scratched up the side of your car pretty badly down here in the carport. I was going to leave you a note, but—'

'Hello? Who's this?'

Somebody had picked up the phone. Bent out of shape, big time.

'Mr Cross? Oh, you are there, good. Well, yes, like I said, this is Brad Dunphy, your neighbor down in unit one-oh-five, and—'

'You said something about scratching my car?'

'It's more than a scratch, really. That's why I thought I'd better call. I feel terrible about this, really awful, and I'm down here with the car right now if you'd like to come take a look for yourself.'

Reddick heard a loud click, indicating the man on the other end of the line had hung up.

Stifling a grin, he raced down the hall to the door to Cross's unit and caught him just as he was about to fly through it, car keys in hand. He was still dressed for bed in a silkscreened gray T-shirt and green flannel pajama bottoms.

Reddick jammed the nose of his .40 caliber Smith & Wesson hard into his gut, stopping him cold in the open doorway.

'Uh-uh. Back inside, Mr Cross. Hurry up.'

The younger man's mouth opened to speak, but then realization dawned, common sense took over, and he backpedaled into his condo, Reddick following and closing the door right behind him.

'Make a sound and your life ends right here,' Reddick said. 'Try me and see.'

Cross just looked at him. Unsettled, but not yet afraid. Reddick made a note-to-self: This was a different animal than Andy Baumhower.

160

'Anyone else here?' Reddick asked.

'No.'

'You're sure?'

'Yes. You must be Joe Reddick,' Cross said.

'That's right. So now you know what time it is and why you don't want to give me any fucking trouble. Don't you?'

'I think so.'

Reddick dropped his bag to the floor and slammed a fist into the other man's abdomen, just under his ribcage, bringing Cross, coughing and gasping for breath, to his knees.

'When I ask a question, I need you to be a bit more affirmative than that, Mr Cross.'

'Yes! Yes, I know,' Cross managed, down on all fours now, eyes fixed on the floor.

'When you're ready, we're gonna find a phone and you're gonna call your boys Ben and Will, tell them they need to come over right away.'

Reddick waited for Cross to respond. Cross sucked air into his lungs, pushed himself up to his feet again, the air of defiance he'd shown Reddick moments earlier already making a comeback.

'And why should I do that? You're going to kill me anyway,' he said.

'Am I?'

'You murdered Andy, didn't you?'

'Maybe I murdered Andy because he ran his fucking mouth instead of doing what I told him to do. You ever think of that?'

Cross didn't answer, weighing the chances that Reddick was telling him the truth, that maybe he wanted more out of all this than just Cross's

161

head, and those of his friends Clarke and Sinnott, on a stick.

'You've only got two choices, asshole,' Reddick said. 'You can play along and live long enough to see what I've got in mind for you, or don't and join your pal Baumhower right now. What's it gonna be?'

Cross looked first at Reddick, then at the gun that was now pointed directly at his chest. One seemed to promise death just as much as the other. He didn't know who Reddick was or what his ultimate intentions were, but he decided what Reddick had just told him was indisputable: If he didn't follow the man's orders, at least for the moment, he was as good as dead.

'OK,' Cross said.

They wound up in the playroom, Cross on the couch, Reddick in a chair only inches away, the little gym bag sitting on the floor at his left hand. Reddick had the other man's cell phone, Cross having led him to it in the bedroom upon being asked. The Smith & Wesson forty was sitting in Reddick's lap, aimed with almost casual indifference in Cross's general direction. Still, Cross wasn't fooled into thinking his visitor couldn't kill him with one shot if he tried something stupid. The more he saw of Reddick, the surer he became of his capacity for mayhem.

'OK, listen up,' Reddick said. 'You're gonna call Sinnott first, then Clarke. On speaker, so we can both listen in. In twenty words or less, you're gonna give your friends a reason to get their asses over here ASAP. Don't answer any questions and don't take no for an answer. Tell 'em anything you want, but keep it brief and get the job done.' He leaned forward in his chair to give Cross a closer look at his face. 'And understand this: I know coded language when I hear it, and I know more about the three of you than you could imagine. You try dropping any secret messages on either of your friends, your call's gonna end with a bang. You catch my drift?'

Cross just glared at him.

'I don't hear you.'

'Yes,' Cross said.

Reddick dialed both numbers for him, having committed each to memory as part of the info he'd taken off Baumhower's laptop. He was not at all surprised to learn that Cross was an expert liar; at the point of a gun, the younger man made a case for needing to see Clarke and Sinnott right away that sounded both plausible and unforced. He said the cops had called him that morning with some follow-up questions regarding Andy Baumhower's murder and he wanted to make sure they all had their stories straight, before Clarke and Sinnott could be questioned next. Sinnott bought in right away, keeping Cross on the phone no longer than a minute or two, but Clarke, as Reddick might have predicted, was a harder sell.

The big man's voice, even heard over Cross's speakerphone, was instantly familiar; the memories it brought back for Reddick chilled him to the bone, and he had to fight the urge to kill Cross right now, without comment or provocation, in his stead. As he listened in, Cross was

163

forced to do some fast talking to deflect all of Clarke's demands for elaboration, rephrasing his request for a meeting as a direct order so that Clarke would accept it as non-negotiable. Cross was crimson with anger when he handed the phone back to Reddick, embarrassed to have had his authority over his partners so openly tested.

Reddick sat back in his chair again, digging in for a long wait. There was an extended silence as Cross studied him, trying to determine the exact nature of the adversary he was facing.

'What exactly do you want?' he asked.

'For starters? I want you to shut the fuck up,' Reddick said. But there'd been nothing about the way he'd said it to suggest he hadn't meant it at least partly in jest.

'What Ben did was a mistake,' Cross said. 'It was stupid and wholly unnecessary.'

'And he was acting entirely on his own, I suppose.'

'Yes. He was. Didn't Andy tell you that?'

'Andy told me a lot of things.'

'Including...?'

'How your friend Gillis Rainey wound up dead in the LA River?' Reddick nodded. 'I'm afraid so.'

Cross took the news incredibly well; the twinge of disappointment that flashed across his face had almost been too small for Reddick to catch.

'Did you have any idea Andy had put him there before he told you? I'm betting you didn't.'

'And if I didn't?'

164

'Then you must know what I'm telling you is the truth. Only an idiot like Ben would think blackmailing a man to keep him silent about something he doesn't even know he knows could ever be a good idea. I mean, do I look that stupid to you?'

'You look plenty stupid to me,' Reddick said. 'But so what? What's done is done. I don't give a rat's ass now who or what made Clarke do what he did.'

'You think we're all equally culpable.'

'Damn straight.'

'So what happens after you get us all together? Surely you don't intend to do to us what you did to Andy?'

Reddick ignored the question.

Cross let out a small chuckle, incredulous. 'You can't be serious. You'd kill four people just because one of them broke into your house and shook your wife and kid up a little?'

Reddick bristled, incensed to hear a smarmy little weasel like Cross describe Dana and Jake's ordeal in such blasé terms. 'I know,' he said. 'Doesn't seem fair, does it?' His eyes turned black and his jaw grew taut, giving Cross his first real look at the madman he was facing. 'But that's life. Sometimes, the shit end of the stick is all you get.'

165

EIGHTEEN

Cross could see Reddick was all done talking, but Cross went on talking anyway, finally understanding the full extent of the danger he was in.

'If you know as much about us as you say you do, you must know what we're worth. What we could pay you to let us go and just forget about all this.'

'Shut up, Cross,' Reddick said, and this time there was no questioning his sincerity.

Cross took the hint and fell silent, putting his mind to work immediately on the problem at hand. A smarter man than Andy Baumhower, he didn't need Reddick to tell him what he had to lose by trying something foolish. He knew Reddick could make his death either quick and painless, or slow and agonizing, and between the two, Cross had a definite preference. But that wasn't his only reason to be cooperative. There was also hope; the possibility, however remote, that between now and the time Will Sinnott and Ben Clarke arrived at the condo, something for Reddick would go wrong. He'd make a mistake or lose his nerve, or Clarke would take the initiative and do something reckless to disarm him.

Reddick sat there eyeing Cross with mild amusement, reading his mind as easily as he might were he actually inside it. Cross was neither a hero nor a fool; he would wait things out and see what developed. Still, Reddick knew, he bore watching. Pragmatist or no, the closer a man came to the hour of his own death, the more likely he was to try anything – *any-thing* – to save his skin.

Reddick expected this to be especially true of Clarke. The big man was the first to heed Cross's call, roughly twenty minutes after receiving it. Reddick and Cross went to answer his knock at the door together, Reddick hiding behind it until Clarke had stepped across the threshold and into the spider's web. Reddick gave him a split second to see what was coming, just to twist the knife a little, then greeted him the same way he had greeted Reddick at Dana's two days before, with a blow to the head that carried the weight of an oil tanker. Or so it must have seemed to Clarke, having been hit with the two-fold force of the heel of Reddick's gun and the thirst for Clarke's blood Reddick had been choking on since the two had last met.

Your boy over there breathes a word about the accident to anybody, you're all dead.

Clarke crumbled to the floor like a windblown house of cards, Cross stepping out of the way to let gravity do with him what it would. His face came to earth first and the rest followed, his landing making a sound not unlike a baby grand falling off the back of a speeding truck. He blinked once or twice, not fully out, and Reddick helped him along with a kick to the jaw that left him drooling blood and teeth all over Cross's carpet. That should have been the end of it, the big man having absorbed enough punishment to kill a man half his size, but Clarke's voice was still booming in Reddick's ears.

I'll start with the kid and leave you for last.

Reddick kicked him again, once, twice, three more times, all in the chest and midsection now, as Cross stood at a distance and watched, his face alight with both fascination and terror. After the third kick, Reddick spun around abruptly to face Cross, sucking wind, sweating buckets, and it became obvious to Cross that, for several seconds at least, Reddick had completely forgotten there was someone else in the room.

A landline phone somewhere in the condo chose this moment to ring. It had rung once before fifteen minutes ago, not long after Cross had made his calls to Sinnott and Clarke demanding a meeting, but Reddick had ignored it then, just as he intended to ignore it now. Even if the caller was Sinnott, he could see nothing to be gained by letting Cross answer it.

This time, however, the incessant ringing was harder to shut out. The sight of Clarke had turned something loose inside Reddick and his head was pounding, crawling with voices and images from out of his near and distant past. Little Joe's sheet-enshrouded body on a gurney. *If anything happens to me, your wife and little boy are dead.* The white of Dana's eyes as Clarke flashed the blade of a knife directly in front of her face. Donovan Sykes standing in room number 10-G of the Palm Beach County Courthouse, smiling at the inside joke of a life sentence for having

168

slaughtered Reddick's entire family.

Cross's phone rang once more and stopped. Reddick shook his head to clear it, wincing, and told Cross to take Clarke back to the playroom.

'What? He outweighs me by forty pounds!'

'Grab him by the ankles and drag him!' Reddick snapped. 'Now!'

Cross did as he was told, Reddick trailing behind. Leaving a smear of blood along the floor as he went, Clarke looked for all the world like dead weight in the most literal sense, a thought that brought Reddick little grief. When they reached the playroom, Cross huffing and puffing like he'd just scaled a high wall, Reddick took a roll of duct tape from his gym bag and tossed it to him.

'Bind his hands behind his back and his ankles together,' he said. 'Then cover his mouth. Hurry the hell up.'

Again, Cross complied without argument, though Reddick could tell he was watching him now with a different level of interest, perhaps looking for a weakness that hadn't been there before. It was for certain that Reddick *felt* more vulnerable; being this close to relief from his greatest fear, to putting the threat of Clarke and his friends bringing harm to Dana and Jake behind him forever, had him feeling anxious and lightheaded. His skull was still throbbing and his legs were weak. He wasn't so far gone that he couldn't drop Cross with a single shot if pushed, but he knew he had to appear diminished enough to give Cross reason to wonder.

Once Clarke was trussed up to his satisfaction,

169

emitting a baleful moan or two that no dead man could utter, Reddick returned to his chair and ordered Cross to do likewise on the couch, where both men took up the waiting game anew.

Reddick wanted this thing over with. He *needed* it over with. He checked his watch, the effort of focusing his eyes on the dial almost more than he could bear, and saw that nearly forty minutes had passed since Cross had gotten off the phone with Sinnott.

'Where the fuck is he?' he asked.

Cross shrugged, the expression on his face falling just short of a smirk. It seemed he was starting to feel like his old, arrogant self again, an observation that only heightened Reddick's mounting anxiety.

Seven more minutes passed and Reddick was contemplating the unthinkable, killing Cross and Clarke while leaving Sinnott for later, when somebody knocked on the door. Reddick got to his feet and glanced at Clarke, who once again resembled nothing so much as a corpse; alive or dead, he wouldn't be going anywhere. Reddick gestured for Cross to rise and the two of them went to the door, where they took the same positions they had upon Clarke's arrival.

Cross let Sinnott in and Reddick stepped forward, into Sinnott's view, to close the door behind him. He felt no need to welcome Sinnott as he had Clarke, and he could see at a glance that it would have been overkill if he had. Sinnott wasn't the sorry sister Baumhower had been, but he was surely only one rung up the ladder from it; true to the photos Reddick had seen on Baumhower's laptop, he was a pudgy doughboy with bloodshot eyes who reacted to the sight of Reddick and his gun like someone who'd just found a scorpion in a dresser drawer. Had he squealed aloud, Reddick wouldn't have been surprised.

But he didn't squeal. All he did was exchange a glance with Cross, whose face told him everything he could have possibly wanted to know.

'Oh, Jesus...'

'Shut it,' Reddick said. 'Into the other room. Let's go.'

Cross led the way back into his playroom, Reddick taking up the rear. Sinnott's eyes fell to the trail of Clarke's blood they were following and his knees buckled once, almost giving way altogether. In the playroom, they found Clarke exactly as Reddick and Cross had left him, eyes closed and body motionless. Sinnott took one look at him and collapsed into a chair, unable to obey Reddick's first order a moment longer.

'Oh, Jesus,' he said again.

'Check to see if he's still breathing,' Reddick told Cross.

'Check him yourself,' Cross said. He understood that the moment had come for Reddick to either put up or shut up – the three men he wanted dead were all here now, ripe for the slaughter – and doing Reddick's bidding no longer offered any discernible payoff. If he wished to torture them before killing them, he would; continuing to kiss his ass wasn't going to change that.

Reddick knew he was being tested and wasn't

171

happy about it, but neither was he ready to start shooting. His idea all along had been to waste Cross and his three friends with a single shot each, in rapid succession, and then beat a hasty retreat. If he started with Cross now, he would have to do them all, and he realized with some consternation that he wasn't prepared to do Clarke in his present state. They were all here because of him; Reddick needed Clarke awake and cognizant when he pulled the trigger. Putting one in the back of his head while he lay on the floor like a wet sack of grain just wasn't going to be good enough.

'Back up,' Reddick told Cross.

Cross complied after taking great pains to be slow about it.

Reddick closed in on Clarke, crouched down to probe his wrist for a pulse, careful to keep sight of Cross all the while. It took a few seconds to find one, but a pulse was there, though it could only have been more faint had it been absent altogether. Reddick slapped him once, twice across the cheeks, trying to bring him around. The big man's eyes had fluttered open, then closed again, when someone behind Reddick said, 'Drop the gun, Mr Reddick, and turn around very slowly.'

It was Sinnott's voice.

Reddick turned his head, saw Sinnott standing in front of the chair he'd been sitting in only moments before, what Reddick judged from this distance to be a nine millimeter Beretta clutched tightly in his right hand. 'Please. Drop the gun. I'll shoot you if you don't, I promise you.'

172

Reddick had every reason not to believe him except for the way he was holding the weapon. Sinnott didn't look like a stranger to it. Rather, he appeared to barely notice it was there, exhibiting a nonchalance about firearms Reddick had seen only in people who owned guns and had no shortage of experience in using them.

Reddick assessed his options, concluded there was really only one that wasn't likely to prove fatal. If only to live to fight another day for Dana and Jake, he dropped the Smith & Wesson to the floor, drew himself upright again, and turned around to face Sinnott directly.

'I can imagine what you must be thinking,' Cross said, easing over to retrieve Reddick's gun. 'He doesn't much look the type, does he? But old Will's a former army reservist who's quite the gunslinger on the shooting range. He took me out with him once, and I could barely believe it myself.'

'Shut up, Perry,' Sinnott said.

'Shut up? Or what? You'll shoot me, too?'

Reddick felt like a fool. He should have checked Sinnott for weapons at the door; he'd done that much to Clarke before ordering Cross to drag him in here. He hadn't seen anything about Sinnott's military background on Baumhower's MacBook, but that was no excuse. Judging the man's threat potential by his benign appearance alone had been an amateur's mistake, and by right, Reddick deserved to pay for it with his life.

'I saw Ben open his eyes. He isn't dead but he's hurt bad,' Sinnott said. 'We've gotta call nine-one-one.'

'And bring the paramedics here?' Cross asked. 'Now? Are you nuts?'

'No, but ... Look at him! He's gonna die if we don't get him to a doctor!'

'So we'll take him to the emergency room ourselves.' Cross bent down to pull the tape from Clarke's mouth, nodded his head at Reddick. 'Just as soon as we figure out what to do with *him*.'

'There's only one thing you *can* do with me,' Reddick said. 'The only question is, which one of you little bitches has the balls to do it?'

Cross stood up, aimed Reddick's own forty at his left temple. 'Actually, I'll be more than up to the task when the time comes, Mr Reddick, but I'd rather not do you here in my own home. You've made quite a mess of the place already, don't you think?'

'It's not too late to make a deal. Maybe we won't have to kill you at all,' Sinnott said.

Cross looked over at him, incensed. 'What are you talking about?'

'I know who he is and why he's doing this, Perry.' He turned his gaze on Reddick. 'You know why I had this gun on me today? Because I Googled your name last night. I read all the news stories about what happened to you and your first family back in Florida.'

Reddick didn't want to flinch, but he did. Somehow, having these fuckers know his history felt like the greatest gut-punch of all.

'What news stories?' Cross asked.

'It's none of your fucking business,' Reddick

said.

'He was a cop in West Palm Beach,' Sinnott said. 'Nine years ago, some sick fuck broke into his home and murdered his wife and kids. Papers called it the worst multiple homicide in the city's history.'

Reddick took a step toward him, found the will to freeze only when Sinnott raised the gun in his hand. 'I'll do it, Mr Reddick. I don't want to, but I will, believe me.'

He waited to see if Reddick's compliance was going to hold. Reddick glowered at him with a heat Sinnott could practically feel, but he didn't move an inch.

'Sit down. On the couch, on your hands,' Sinnott said.

Reddick did.

'Of all the people in the goddamn world, Ben threatens to kill this poor devil's family,' Sinnott said to Cross. 'Is it any wonder he's come after all of us?'

Cross gave Reddick a lingering look, appraising him anew. 'All the more reason to get him the hell out of here and kill him,' he said. 'And fast.'

'No. We've done enough killing.' To Reddick, Sinnott said, 'We never meant to hurt anybody. We aren't murderers. No matter what Ben may have told you, the rest of us would have never allowed him to harm you or your family.'

'Will...'

'How much does he know?' Sinnott asked Cross.

'Everything. Andy told him everything.'

'Then he knows we're responsible for Gillis's death and we know he's responsible for Andy's. Unless I miss my guess, we've even got the gun now that could prove it.' Sinnott addressed Reddick again. 'What Ben did to you was wrong, Mr Reddick, and maybe you think all four of us should pay for it. But the way I see it, between what you've done to Ben and Andy, you've had your pound of flesh and then some. Walk away. Give us your word you'll leave things as they are and we'll let you go.'

'My ass we will!' Cross said.

'It's the only way, Perry. Because I won't be part of any more killing unless it's forced upon me. Unless *he* forces it upon me.'

'You crazy fuck. You think we can trust him not to come after us again?'

'We can if he cares for his family as much as I think he does.' To Reddick: 'I'm trying to give you one last chance to clear the slate. To go back to your wife and son and forget you ever met Andy Baumhower. All you have to do is walk away and promise never to bother any of us again.' He added, 'But you have to decide now. Ben may be dying. I need an answer.'

Reddick was amazed to find himself actually thinking it over. Since Friday afternoon, he'd all but given up any hope of returning to the life he once had with Dana and Jake; every effort he'd made to cover his tracks, both here and at Baumhower's last night, had been more a product of instinct than any real belief he could get away with murder. And yet here was Sinnott offering him an out, a third fork in the road of his

176

probable future that did not lead to death or incarceration. It sounded tempting.

If only it were real.

'This is bullshit!' Cross said, and again he brought the nose of Reddick's Smith & Wesson an inch from the side of his head. 'Either you kill this sonofabitch right now, or I will!'

If it was a bluff, it was a good one. Sinnott took the threat seriously enough to be visibly shaken by it and Reddick braced himself to die. Silence took over the room, Cross and Sinnott locked in a standoff, Reddick trying to decide which armed man he should lunge toward in a last ditch – and almost certainly futile – effort to save himself.

Then they all heard a small sound at the front door. A key scratching around in the lock.

'Shit!' Sinnott said.

Cross brought a finger to his lips to silence him. They heard the door open and someone step inside, trying to be quiet about it. Cross realized who it must be immediately. He shoved Reddick's forty into the back of his waistband and gestured for Sinnott to stay where he was, with Reddick, then went out into the hall alone.

Iris was standing at the door when Cross found her, as stock still as a statuette, her eyes glued to the trail of blood on the floor.

'Oh, my God. Is that blood?'

Cross closed fast upon her, doing his best to block her view. 'Ben had a little accident. It's no big deal, but it's ugly. I thought you were gone for good?'

'I was. I am. But...' She knelt down, plucked something white from a puddle of crimson on the floor at her feet: a chunk of shattered tooth. She looked to Cross for some explanation, but all he did was offer a blank stare in return.

Now Iris remembered to be afraid, the reason she'd called ahead twice to make sure the condo was empty before coming back to retrieve her ID. But her fear wasn't enough to staunch the need she suddenly had to know what lay beyond the red streak someone – Ben? – had laid down on Cross's carpet for her to follow. She tried to push past Cross but he took her by the arm and held fast.

'I'm sorry, Iris, but you have to leave,' he said.

She ripped her arm free and was down the hall before he could stop her. He caught up to her at the playroom door, but by then it was too late; the door was open in her hand and she was peering in, transfixed. Horrified. Will Sinnott was holding a gun on a man she'd never seen before and a beaten and bloody Ben Clarke lay on his side on the floor, hands and feet bound with what looked like duct tape.

'This sonofabitch killed Andy and tried to kill Ben,' Sinnott stammered.

'Andy? Andy's dead?' Iris hadn't yet heard about Baumhower's death.

'Your friends have got it all backwards,' Reddick said. 'Actually, they were just about to kill *me*.'

'Shut up!' Sinnott snapped.

'He's crazy, Iris,' Cross said, stepping around her into the room to bar her further entrance.

178

'We don't know who he is or what he wants, but he broke into Andy's home last night and killed him, just like Will says, and this morning he broke in here and attacked Ben.'

Again she pushed past Cross, this time to stand over Clarke, seeking a better look at his injuries. The big man was semiconscious now but not making a sound. 'Have you called nine-one-one? Ben needs an ambulance!'

'We were just about to do that when you showed up.'

'So do it! What are you waiting for?' She flipped open her own phone, started to make the call herself.

Sinnott gave Cross a look, panic-stricken: Stop her.

Cross snatched the phone from Iris's hand and took her by the arm again, intending to steer her from the room back out into the hall. 'No! We can handle this ourselves. In the meantime, you have to leave. It's for your own protection.'

He tried to move her toward the door but she wouldn't budge. 'No! I don't believe you!'

A tussle ensued between them. Sinnott stood there slack-jawed, watching, barely cognizant of the gun he was supposed to be training on Reddick. In all the excitement, he failed to notice that Reddick was no longer sitting on his hands, and paid no heed to the fact that Reddick's Smith & Wesson forty, equally forgotten by Cross, remained holstered at the rear waistband of Cross's pants, right where Reddick could see it.

Reddick was up off the couch and holding the

179

gun at Cross's head before either Cross or Sinnott could blink. Reflexively, Sinnott made to shoot him, but he couldn't pull the trigger. Nothing short of a bloodbath with Iris in the middle would follow if he did, and he knew it.

Reddick tossed Cross aside to exchange him for Iris, too fast for Sinnott to do anything about it. Everything was coming apart at the seams now and Reddick was improvising, barely able to think straight.

'If you scream, little lady, all hell's gonna break loose,' he said. Then, to Sinnott: 'Put the gun down.'

'Fuck that, Will,' Cross said. 'You put that gun down and we're all dead!'

Sinnott didn't need Cross to explain his meaning. Reddick had come here to kill Sinnott and his two friends, and the only thing standing in his way now was the .9 millimeter Beretta Sinnott had pointed in his direction.

'Let the woman go,' Cross told Reddick. 'You aren't really going to hurt her, anyway.'

'You believe that, asshole, come ahead,' Reddick said. 'But when all the shooting stops and she's dead, that's gonna be on *you*, not me.'

He started backing out of the room, dragging Iris with him.

'No, please!' she cried.

Neither Cross nor Sinnott moved.

'First man through this door after I close it had better have Kevlar balls,' Reddick said. And then, just like that, he and Iris were out of the room and gone, the playroom door slammed shut behind them.

180

Cross waited for Sinnott to give chase, said, 'Well? Don't just stand there, you dumbass – go after them!'

'Me? You heard what he said! The first man out that door—'

Cross stepped forward to tear the Beretta from his hands and the two of them inched slowly toward the door, pausing at the threshold to listen for any sounds out in the hall. Hearing nothing, Cross gingerly opened the door and poked his head out...

The hallway was empty. Beyond it, the condo's front door sat wide open.

'Shit!' Cross spun on Sinnott, blue eyes ablaze. 'Why the fuck didn't you shoot him while you had the chance?'

Sinnott opened his mouth to answer, outraged, only to stop at the sound of gravel being shaken in an iron drum behind him. He and Cross both turned to find Clarke laughing as best he could, down on his right side, eyes half-open, wheezing into the carpet through a mouth full of blood and broken teeth.

'Pussies,' he said.

NINETEEN

Iris never screamed on their way out to Reddick's car. He'd warned her against it before they'd exited Cross's building, breathing hard into her ear while pressing his gun to the base of her spine where no one could easily see it, and she chose not to try him. She didn't know who this man was or what he was capable of, but it was his animal-like desperation, more than his projected menace, that frightened her just enough to keep her silent.

A couple on beach cruiser bicycles rolled past as they crossed the street, but neither rider gave them so much as a glance. Reddick guided Iris into the black Mustang's driver's seat, hurried around the front of the car to get in on the passenger side, and tossed her the keys. 'You drive,' he said. When she made to ask where, he cut her off: 'Just move!'

She got the Mustang started and drove off, Reddick peering anxiously behind them all the while, watching to see if Cross or Sinnott would appear in pursuit. He was holding the forty loose in his lap, a threat he had apparently forgotten he was supposed to be leveling against her.

Iris drove in silence for three blocks, then Reddick said, 'Turn right at the next signal. I'll

182

tell you where to stop.'

'Who are you?'

'Nobody you need to worry about. I'm not going to hurt you. I just needed you to get out of there in one piece, that's all.'

'They said you killed Andy.'

Reddick's eyes narrowed. 'Andy killed himself,' he said.

'What about Gillis Rainey?'

'Shut up and drive.'

A moment passed, then Iris gathered her nerve and asked, 'Did Gillis kill himself, too?'

'Pull over here and stop the car.'

Iris did as instructed. They were now on a quiet and narrow residential street just north of Abbot Kinney, where a kid on a skateboard or an old woman towing a shopping cart were the only ones likely to bear passing witness to their presence.

'I need you to do me a favor,' Reddick said.

'A favor?'

'I need you to give me at least twenty-four hours before going to the police.'

'You're letting me go?'

Reddick could barely believe it himself. 'Yes.'

'But you haven't answered my question yet.'

'Look—'

'Did Gillis kill himself, too?'

Reddick studied her, saw that beneath all the surface beauty was a bulldog that was never easily moved, once it had sunk its teeth into something. 'No. Your friends did that.'

Iris closed her eyes and held her breath for just an instant. It was true. Goddamnit, it was true.

183

'Who are you?' she asked Reddick again.

'I don't have time for this, sister. If Cross and his pals don't send the police out looking for me, they'll be out here looking for me themselves.'

Iris still didn't move. It was gradually becoming obvious to her that the desperation she sensed in Reddick was behind all of this; he was dangerous, yes, but only in the way an abused woman can sometimes become dangerous, finally tortured one too many times. 'Perry's my fiancé,' she said. 'I need to know what kind of man I'm about to marry. You said they were trying to kill you. Why?'

Too weary to resist any longer, Reddick surrendered, said, 'Baumhower and I had a car accident last weekend near the LA River. He'd just dumped Rainey's body there and they were afraid I'd report it to the police. So Clarke broke into my home, tied my wife up at knifepoint and drugged my little boy, said he'd kill us all if I didn't keep my mouth shut.' Reddick let Iris take this all in, then added wryly, 'I think I'd reconsider that engagement, if I were you.'

Iris didn't speak for a long moment. She'd been fearing the worst but this went beyond any nightmare she could have possibly imagined.

'So you killed Andy and tried to kill Ben.'

'Get out of the car.' He was pointing the gun at her again.

'Why didn't you just go to the police?'

'I had my reasons. Open the goddamn door and get out before I shoot you!'

She finally opened the door and stepped out, but only stood there watching as Reddick climbed over the car's center console to take the wheel. 'We can go to the police together. You and me, right now,' she said.

Reddick laughed. 'Why? Because you can prove that anything I've just told you is true? Thanks but no thanks.'

He started the engine but Iris, refusing to take the hint, wouldn't budge. 'If I do what you ask – wait twenty-four hours before calling the police – what are you going to do?'

'What I have to do.'

'I don't want Perry hurt.'

'Yeah? That's too fucking bad.' He grabbed the door with his free hand, waited for her to step out of the way before slamming it shut. He rolled his window down and said, 'You wanna make the call, make the call. I don't give a damn. But do yourself a favor and stay away from Cross. I'm not the killer here, he is.'

He threw the Mustang into gear and left her standing in the middle of the street.

TWENTY

On Cross's orders, Sinnott took Ben Clarke to the emergency room at St John's Hospital in Santa Monica. Clarke was fully conscious now and fit to argue, but in too much pain not to know better than to go. He and Sinnott had instructions to tell the doctors that he had incurred his injuries clowning around on a skateboard and tumbling down a long flight of stairs, and to stick with that story no matter how much skepticism it received.

Cross, meanwhile, stayed behind to clean up his condo and try to make contact with Iris, hoping Reddick had let her go once his escape from Cross's place had been complete. Getting hold of Iris in any case wouldn't be easy, however, because she didn't have her phone; Cross had taken it away from her when she'd tried to call 911 for Clarke and it was still in his possession. He tried her at home and only got voicemail.

He knew he should call the police for her sake alone but couldn't bring himself to do it. Reddick in police custody was the last thing he needed. As accomplished a liar as he was, Cross couldn't imagine how he and the others might spin a lie for the authorities that could explain away everything Reddick would tell them. Rainey's kidnapping and death, Andy's dumping of his body, Clarke's assault upon Reddick's family – all would be revealed if the police got involved and found Reddick alive and conversant. Better to let them find out about Iris's kidnapping either on their own, or with Iris's help if she was still alive, than make the call himself. And it would be better still if they never found out about it at all.

If he could contact Iris before she filed a report, he might be able to keep a lid on things, but he couldn't reach her. He tried her at home three times, then gave up. He had no choice now but to plan for the worst. He went to work scrubbing every trace of Clarke's blood from his condo and tried to think of a story to tell the authorities that could counter anything Iris might choose to offer.

It took him about twenty minutes to come up with something suitable.

Iris was a mess.

She'd just been kidnapped and released by a stranger with a gun who'd all but admitted to murdering Andy Baumhower. The man who'd been her fiancé only two days before, along with his two closest friends, were very possibly murderers themselves. Her car was parked less than a block from Perry's home, her wallet and ID were still somewhere inside, and now Perry had her cell phone and – unless she'd lost them somewhere else – her car keys, too.

Walking on shaky legs in the general direction

of Perry's condo, she knew intellectually that calling the police was a no-brainer. In spite of her kidnapper's request that she do otherwise, it seemed like the only sane thing to do. Guns were being waved around, Ben Clarke had been badly beaten, and two other people, ostensibly, were dead. But she was afraid to make the call. She had the feeling doing so would prove to be a terrible mistake, the catalyst for a host of unintended and irreversible consequences, and try as she might, she couldn't shake it.

What could she tell the police, in any case, that would make any sense?

Only Perry knew what the hell was really going on, and she wanted to understand it all herself before she did anything that couldn't be undone. She wondered if Perry, given the chance, could put everything that had happened today and yesterday in some kind of order that would prove none of it was as sinister as it seemed. He wasn't a murderer and the man in the Mustang was simply delusional; Gillis Rainey had died of natural causes and so had Andy Baumhower.

No. She knew better than to hold out such a hope.

Whatever the truth was, Iris was sure it was ugly and terrifying, and nothing Perry could say would convince her otherwise. She had come to see her ex-fiancé in an entirely different light since discovering the check he'd forged two days ago in her name, and he scared her now. More so, even, than the man who had dragged her out of his condo at gunpoint this morning and abandoned her in the middle of the street.

That man was a total stranger to her, yet, much to her amazement, she found herself believing everything he had told her. Rather than 'crazy' – Perry's word – he had struck her as wounded and enraged, two things any man would be had his family been physically abused and threatened with death by a mindless thug like Ben Clarke, as the stranger had claimed was the case. He was far from harmless, to be sure; she wasn't so confused as to be blind to the damage he could do to others, given the proper motivation. But he wasn't a mindless killer, either. The fact that he had let her go, unharmed, when killing her would have guaranteed him the twenty-four hours of freedom he'd simply asked her for, seemed proof enough of that.

Iris didn't owe the man anything. She had promised him nothing. If she called the police now and, in the end, he was the only one to get hurt, she would have little reason to feel guilty about it.

And yet she knew she would just the same.

Cross joined Clarke and Sinnott at St John's Hospital just as Clarke was being released. The big man looked like shit and, when he tried to speak, sounded worse. His mouth was full of gauze and his head was wrapped in a skull-cap of white. Even sitting in one of the waiting room chairs, he moved as if every breath incurred more pain than he could bear.

The first thing he said to Cross was, 'That fucker's dead.'

Same old Ben Clarke.

Sinnott ran down the official list of his injuries for Cross's edification: moderate concussion, four broken teeth, one cracked rib, and multiple upper body contusions. The doctors had wanted to hold him overnight for observation but were assured Clarke would only crawl out of bed and flee at his first opportunity if they pressed the issue, so they reluctantly let him go instead, a fistful of pain meds in hand.

The short walk to Cross's car out in the carport seemed to take forever, he and Sinnott guiding Clarke along like a blind man with one foot in a cast. Cross drove the three of them into the parking structure where they sat for a while in a space next to Sinnott's Acura. The building was dark and cool and made for an ideal placc to bring Clarke up to speed and discuss their next move.

'Do you think she'll go to the police?' Sinnott asked from the back seat of Cross's Escalade, referring to Iris.

'If she isn't dead? I can't imagine why she wouldn't,' Cross said. 'Assuming he's let her go, anyway.'

'He must have let her go. We're the ones he wants dead, not her.'

'True. But this fucker Joe Reddick's pretty sharp. He might get the bright idea to hold on to her as leverage, something to offer us – or me, anyway – in exchange for a meeting.'

'Except it's been, what? Almost three hours since he took her? Surely we would have heard from him by now if that was what he was going to do.'

Cross shrugged. 'Maybe.'

'Christ,' Sinnott said, burying his face in his hands. 'I need a drink. If he does let her go and she runs to the cops—'

'Don't worry about it. I've already figured that part out.'

'How?'

'By coming up with a story that will be better than hers. Because think about it: What can she can tell them that will make an ounce of sense? And she won't be able to prove a word of it, in any case.'

'Unless the asshole's told her everything,' Clarke said. Up to now he'd remained silent, either content to let Cross and Sinnott go at it alone, or in too much pain to intervene.

'Everything?' Cross turned to look at him.

'Gillis, Andy, what I did to his bitch and little kid – *everything*.'

In truth, Cross had wondered about this himself, and the prospect secretly terrified him. All he said to Clarke, however, was, 'Why would he? She's his hostage, not his fucking shrink.'

'We need to find him,' Sinnott said, starting to unravel. 'Without Reddick to back her up, it won't matter what Iris tells the police. Did you check his bag again? Maybe—'

'I checked it,' Cross said, referring to the little black gym bag Reddick had left behind at his condo. 'What there was the first time we looked is all there is: a disposable cell phone and a second roll of duct tape, that's it. Nothing to tell us where he might be now, with or without Iris.'

'You fucking dickwads,' Clarke said. 'We don't need to know where he's at. All we gotta do is sit tight and wait.'

'Wait?' Sinnott asked. 'For what?'

'For Reddick to call or try us again.' He took a deep breath, grimacing, then mumbled on. 'Or are you dumb enough to think he's all done fucking with us?'

Sinnott had no answer.

'We could go out lookin' for him, sure. I know where both he and his old lady live and I know where he works. But why go to him when it's just a matter of time before the asshole comes to us?'

'Ben's right,' Cross said, only now realizing it himself. 'Chasing Reddick's tail is probably exactly what he wants us to do. If we wait for him to chase ours instead, and we're ready for him when he shows, the advantage will be ours, not his.'

'Unless he's still got Iris,' Sinnott said.

He wasn't expecting Clarke to agree with him, especially in his present state, but when Cross didn't reply either, he was stunned.

'Wait a minute. As long as he's got Iris, he's holding all the cards. Right?'

'That all depends on ... how much she knows,' Clarke said, barely getting the words out. He'd already popped a dose of Vicodin since getting in the car and he was starting to fade. 'Don't matter if she's his shrink or not. Longer she and Reddick are together, the more time he's gonna have to tell her his side of things. And if he does that—'

192

'It might be better for us if he kills her,' Cross said.

Sinnott studied the only side of his face he could see from where he sat, looking for some inkling of regret, but he may as well have been searching for a tear in a porcelain doll's eye. He'd known Cross now for going on four years, and every time he thought he could no longer be surprised by his utter lack of compassion, the man did or said something to prove him wrong.

'You don't really mean that?'

Cross met his gaze evenly in the car's rearview mirror. 'I like Iris quite a lot, Will, but as you well know, she broke off our engagement yesterday. So dead or alive, it makes no difference. Either way, she's lost to me.'

Sinnott, words failing him, fell back in his seat and asked no more questions.

Reddick drove down to Irvine to see Dana and Jake. He didn't know what else to do. He needed time to think and getting out of Los Angeles for a while seemed like a good idea.

During the drive down, he wondered what Cross's girlfriend was going to do. Asking her not to call the police had been a longshot, at best, but it was a longshot worth taking. He'd been so pathetic – fleeing Cross's condo with his tail between his legs, taking a hostage he had no intention of holding or harming – she might have felt sorry enough for him to want to help. And there was no love lost between her and Cross, that much seemed obvious. If he was lucky, she'd buy in, give him until at least the

193

next morning to finish the job he'd started.

If not, he was probably fucked.

The police would be looking for him now and it would just be a matter of time before they found him. Cross, Clarke and Sinnott would have a lot of questions to answer, and they might even be charged with Gillis Rainey's murder, but this was small consolation to Reddick. Seeing Clarke and his friends behind bars had never been the objective. These punks had money and families with considerable influence, and if they wanted to exact payback for Reddick's failure to play ball with Clarke, they could just as easily arrange it from a prison cell as a poolside lounge at home. So nothing at all had changed; Reddick still needed them dead. The grave was the only place for them where Dana and Jake would forever be beyond their reach.

Killing Baumhower had been the first step; he had three more to go. Or possibly only two if the beating he'd given Clarke today proved fatal. Jesus, he hoped that was the case. Because he was already tired; murder cut hard against his grain. He'd shot or killed his fair share of bad guys back in West Palm Beach, so pulling the trigger on assholes who had it coming was nothing new to him. But what he was doing now was something entirely different; this was premeditated assassination, and it required a level of emotional detachment he had never plumbed before.

Clarke and, to a lesser degree, Cross, would be easy to kill. He'd seen enough of both men now to know that they *needed* killing, that they were

194

narcissistic, baby-faced little animals who, if they hadn't murdered Gillis Rainey, would have simply murdered someone else, somewhere, some day. Their kind always found a victim, eventually. But Sinnott was just a sop, as greedy and selfish as the other two, perhaps, but nowhere near as inhumane. He'd actually offered Reddick a deal, not merely out of desperation but as a matter of conscience. He'd believed it was the right thing to do. The idea of putting a gun to the fat boy's head and blowing a hole through it brought Reddick little joy. In fact, he was far from certain he could manage it when and if the time came. He could only hope Sinnott would make things easier for him the way Baumhower had, by saying or doing something incendiary to nudge Reddick over the edge.

He arrived at the motel a few minutes after noon, not fully satisfied he hadn't been tailed until he killed the Mustang's ignition in the parking lot. Dana and Jake's room was empty. He hadn't called ahead to let them know he was coming and now he regretted it. He gave in to an irrational rush of fear for as long as it took to get Dana on the phone and hear that they were just down the street having ice cream. He got back in the car to pick them up and they found a public park where Jake could play while he and Dana sat at a bench under a shade tree, away from the other parents, and talked.

Dana picked up on his mood right away.

'What's happened?' she asked.

'A lot. Far more than you want to know. Suffice it to say, this thing's fully in motion now and the chances of it ending well are nil.'

'Did you...'

'I killed Baumhower yesterday and maybe one of the others. Clarke, the one with the knife and the mask.'

There, he'd said it, in plain English so there could be no misunderstanding: He'd murdered one man and possibly a second. They'd been skirting around the obvious for almost two days now and there wasn't any point to the charade anymore. Killing Baumhower and his friends had been his intent all along and, now that Baumhower was dead, there was no turning back from it. To pretend otherwise was just a sham.

He watched Dana's face fall, her last shred of hope for his salvation gone, and said, 'It is what it is. I'm sorry.'

She was silent for a long time. Their son was racing through the sand on the playground without a care in the world, laughing like a little madman, and in the sight she slowly gained a new, unexpected appreciation for what her husband had done and his rationale for doing it. Jake was theirs and no one had the right to take him away from them. The law was supposed to exist to protect them from monsters like Clarke and his friends but it was too haphazard to trust. Reddick described them as people with money and power, and those were the kinds of people who often rendered the law a mirthless joke, slipping between the cracks of the judicial system to get away with every crime imaginable – rape, theft, assault – and yes, even murder.

Reddick had risked everything for her and Jake, and up to now she'd been acting like he didn't have to, like the course of action he had chosen to take was an unnecessary concession to his own, intractable paranoia. But she was wrong. She had no doubts about that anymore. Reddick was doing what he had to do to spare her a life of always wondering if this was the night Baumhower's people would have their revenge against the three of them, or the next. He was fighting the fight that Clarke had brought to *him*, not the other way around. And that didn't make him crazy – it just made him uncompromising in his duties as husband and father.

Dana decided he'd been fighting alone long enough.

'Tell me everything,' she said.

He studied her, unsure of her meaning.

'You've already told me the worst. You may as well tell me the rest. I think I deserve to know.'

She had that look on her face she always got when anger had turned to resignation, and getting in her way was akin to throwing yourself in front of a moving train.

So Reddick told her everything.

197

TWENTY-ONE

The first thing Dana said after Reddick finished his tale of woe was, 'You can't do this all by yourself.'

And he didn't need to ask her what she meant because he'd been thinking the same thing for hours. When he'd first committed to the insane mission he was on, it seemed simple enough: Kill Baumhower and his big friend in the mask. As far as he knew, Baumhower was just a weak-kneed punk with something to hide and his accomplice an overgrown bully who liked to play with knives. But once he discovered Baumhower actually had three accomplices, not just one, and that all four men had the far-reaching power of big money behind them, the task at hand took on a new and far more daunting dimension.

He had pressed on fueled by the faint hope that speed and the element of surprise could even the odds against him, but any chance of that had been lost this morning at Cross's condo, where everything that could have gone wrong did. Now Cross and his friends knew he was gunning for them and would use every tool at their disposal to flee, defend themselves, or worst of all, go on the offensive.

There was nothing supernatural about wealth, but its range was always unpredictable; it could set things in motion or stop them cold, in places near and far, big and small. Judges' chambers, corporate offices, police headquarters, military bases, crackhouse motels – wealth could infiltrate them all, and leave its mark behind. It wasn't paranoia to think so; it was just facing facts. The right phone call from Sinnott's father, or a golf buddy of Clarke's, and Reddick could be in the crosshairs of a scope within an hour. The game had changed, it was that simple, and trying to play it alone the rest of the way seemed to Reddick like a surefire recipe for defeat.

He needed help.

Figuring out what kind of help he needed, and to whom he could turn to ask for it, wasn't going to be easy. He didn't want to involve anyone he was close to and few people had the skill set or pedigree the job was likely to require. Who could he ask to risk their life on his behalf, and what could he offer them in return?

Throughout the drive north back to Los Angeles late Sunday afternoon, Reddick put his mind to work on the problem and came up with a list of possibilities.

It was a very *short* list.

'Iris, baby, are you OK? Did he hurt you?'

'Cut the bullshit, Perry. You don't care if he hurt me or not and we both know it. If you did, our names would be all over the news by now.'

Iris could hear Perry breathing on the other end of the line.

199

'If you're asking why I didn't call the police...'

'I'm not asking you anything. I only called because I need my things. My wallet and my keys.'

'Hold on a minute. Are you saying Reddick let you go? You're safe?'

'Safe is a relative term. I'm free and physically unharmed, if that's what you're asking. But I need my ID and my car keys, and you've got them both.'

'Sure, sure. Where are you? I'll come get you right now. We can talk and I can explain what the hell happened this morning. I mean, you must be wondering, right?'

'I don't want to hear any explanations. I just want my things. And I don't want you to pick me up, either. Frankly, Perry, I don't feel safe being alone with you right now, so I was going to suggest we meet somewhere in public. The food court in Farmer's Market, say in forty minutes?'

Cross snickered. 'Are you kidding? You're afraid of being alone with *me*? That fucking wackjob Reddick's the one who put a gun to your head and dragged you off, not me!'

'Is that his name? Reddick?'

'What the hell did he say to you? He's crazy, Iris, I told you that. Whatever it was that's got you acting like this, it was a lie. A goddamn lie!'

'Fine. If you don't want to come—'

'OK, OK. Take it easy, shit. Where will you be in the food court?'

'In the west patio, near the ice cream place. "Gill's," I think it's called. My car's still parked on the street outside your condo. You can use my keys to drive it up so I won't have to come get it later.'

'But I'm not at home right now, I'm at Ben's. It would take me at least an hour to get the car and then drive it out to West LA.'

'So I'll give you an hour. But that's all. Just one hour.'

'And then how will I get back to my place?'

'I don't know. Take a taxi, maybe? You stole seventy-five hundred dollars from me only three days ago. You should be good for the fare.'

Cross was in the process of stammering a rejoinder when she hung up.

'Well?' Sinnott asked, as Cross angrily snapped the lid closed on his cell phone.

'You heard it. She wants me to bring her car and her wallet to her at the fucking Farmer's Market in an hour.'

'Then Reddick just let her go?'

'So she says. Or, maybe, so Reddick would have us believe.'

Following his inference, Sinnott's face, incredibly, grew paler still.

They were sitting in the living room of Clarke's Culver City home, where they could watch for any unwanted visitors through the big picture window that faced the street. It was a few minutes past four o'clock. Clarke was upstairs in the bedroom asleep, a snoring giant dosed to oblivion with prescription painkillers. Cross had a drink in his hand, his first of the day, and Sinnott was nursing his third just since they'd arrived, counting on alcohol to do for his fear what Clarke's meds had done for his pain. His Beretta lay out in the open on the arm of his chair; the right one, near his gun hand.

'Are you going to go?' Sinnott asked.

Cross got to his feet. 'Of course. We both are.'

'Me? But Ben—'

'Fuck Ben. He can take care of himself. I'm going out to Farmer's Market and you're going with me as backup.'

'You think it's a trap?'

'I don't know. But it'd be a lucky break for us if it is.'

'How the hell do you figure that?'

'Because that would mean Ben was right: Reddick's come to us. If it's a trap, he's going to be there somewhere for you to find and take care of, like you should have done this morning. Won't he?'

Cross glared at him, waiting for an argument. Sinnott just nodded his head and took another swig of his drink.

'Christ, what a nightmare. Every time you think it can't get any worse...'

'Shut up, Will, and let's go.'

'Ruben will be here in five days to get his money, Andy's dead, Ben's a cripple, and we're running around worried about fucking Reddick.'

Cross snatched the gun off Sinnott's chair and aimed it at his left eye. 'Shut the fuck up and get on your feet or I swear to God I'll kill you myself!'

Sinnott stood up slowly, wobbly but unflinching. 'You or Reddick. Today or tomorrow.' He wrenched the gun from Cross's limp hand.

202

'What the fuck's the difference?'

He made his way to the door and went out to the car, showing no signs of caring whether Cross was following or not.

TWENTY-TWO

The landmark Farmer's Market in Los Angeles
was a contradiction in time. Much of the 200-
acre, ranch-style shopping and dining complex
in the heart of the city's Fairfax district still
appeared as it had at its opening in 1934 – the
white clapboard walls and green tiled roofs, the
open patios crammed with folding chairs and
umbrella-festooned tables, the lush green land-
scaping ringing its exterior. But counterpoint to
all these things were intrusions of a less fanciful
present: franchise coffee shops and ATM
machines, menu boards that didn't list a single
item priced under a dollar, a trolley line in the
parking lot that connected the market to the
towering mega-mall adjacent.

Still, for all its incongruities, Farmer's Market
remained the popular social hub it had been
almost from the beginning, when Angelenos
were first moved to say about it, without the
irony such a comical tagline would demand
today: 'Meet me at Third and Fairfax.' It was
quaint and comfortable, and it bustled and hum-
med with a heavy, multicultural crowd, day or
night.

It was the crowd and the open layout of the
place Iris was thinking about when she chose the

market as the site for her rendezvous with Cross. She wanted lots of people around and a dozen different points of exit to choose from should she feel the need to bolt, and this location offered her both, even this late on a Sunday afternoon.

Waiting for Cross at a table in a corner of the agreed-upon west patio, she went over her reasons for suggesting this meeting for what felt like the hundredth time, and again had to wonder if they weren't the work of a woman who'd lost her mind. She did indeed need her keys, car, and wallet, and she sure as hell wasn't going alone to Cross's place to get them, but that was just a pretense. After six hours of holding back, she had finally decided to call the police, unable to go on refusing to do so simply because a wild man with a gun had asked her not to, and she couldn't bring herself to make the call until she'd talked to Cross. She felt she owed him that much.

Her kidnapper this morning – Cross had called him 'Reddick' – had accused Cross of being nothing less than a murderer, a suspicion she herself had been living with for over twenty-four hours, and she was reluctant to bring the authorities down upon Cross without giving him a chance to answer such a serious charge to her face. Maybe he could convince her that he had played no major role in either the killing of Gillis Rainey or Ben Clarke's alleged assault upon Reddick's family. Ben was both a thug and a pea-brained asshole, Iris had always despised him with a passion, so it wasn't hard for her to imagine him being solely responsible for both offenses. If Cross could persuade her that such was the case, she might be willing to do nothing, at least for a while. But if he couldn't – if all his words of self-defense rang hollow and false – she could call the police almost gladly, her conscience clear. Still conflicted about Reddick, perhaps, but ready to let her ex-fiancé suffer whatever consequences came his way.

It wasn't that long ago she had loved him without reservation. His lies alone had made it impossible for her to go on doing so, but she still cared for him enough to wish him no ill. She wanted his side of the story to relieve her of the notion that she had come within months of marrying a man she had never really known at all.

Cross and Sinnott were late getting to the market by several minutes. Cross had visited the market's website on his smartphone before leaving Clarke's home and found a layout of the complex, so he and Sinnott arrived with a detailed plan of attack firmly in place: where to park the cars, what individual entrance each would use to enter the food court, what position Sinnott would take inside that offered the clearest possible view of the west patio and all its surrounding points of access and egress.

Cross entered first, leaving Sinnott with instructions to lag behind for a minute or two. He scanned the milling crowd, as much looking for Reddick as Iris, and found the latter sitting at a table across the way, near an ice cream stand called 'Gill's,' as promised. As near as he could tell, she was alone. He watched her for several seconds, testing her behavior for indications of conspiracy, and seeing none, started slowly toward her.

She saw him coming before he got there but didn't smile. In fact, if he was able to detect anything in her reaction to seeing him, it was dread. Not a good sign.

He stood over her before taking a seat, said, 'Are you alone?'

'Of course. Who else—' She stopped, catching on. 'Oh. No. Reddick isn't here.'

Cross sat down across from her, laid her wallet and keys on the table. 'You're sure he didn't hurt you? He didn't lay a hand on you at all?'

'No. I'm fine.' She reached out, grabbed her things. 'Where did you park my car?'

'I'll walk you out and show you. After we've had a chance to talk.'

'I told you, Perry. I'm not interested in hearing any more of your lies.'

'Lies? What lies? You mean about the check?'

Iris didn't answer him.

'What did he tell you, Iris? Why are you acting like this?'

She looked around to make sure they couldn't be overheard, then lowered her voice to say, 'He told me you and your boys killed Gillis Rainey and threatened to do the same to his wife and child. That's what he told me.'

'That's insane.'

'Is it? I heard you and Will talking about Gillis in the playroom yesterday, just before I left. You said Andy had dumped his body in the LA River.'

Now it was Cross's turn to fall silent. Will had been right: Just when you thought things couldn't get any worse...

'We never laid a hand on Gillis. His death was an accident, I swear to you.'

'What kind of accident?'

He could get up and just walk away without saying another word, but Cross knew that would only send Iris straight to the police. And she knew too much for him to let her do that now. 'He owed us money. A lot of it, and he kept refusing to pay it back. So we grabbed him and told him we weren't letting him go until he paid up. We were only trying to scare him, Iris.'

'You kidnapped him?'

'That would be the legal term for it, yes. But he was a fucking diabetic, can you believe that? I'd only heard him mention it once, I'd completely forgotten about it until we found him where we'd locked him up, dead, his mouth all frothed over like a goddamn dog, or something.'

Iris turned her eyes away from him, shaking her head from side to side. 'Oh, Perry...'

'It was a goddamn accident. An incredible stroke of bad luck. But to the police, it would have been murder. We'd have all ended up in prison for life. So we did what we had to do to protect ourselves. We had Andy get rid of the body.' A small, sad smile crossed his face. 'And naturally, the dumbshit made a complete mess of it.'

'He ran into Reddick's car trying to get away.'

208

'Yes. Jesus, why bother with all these questions if you already know all the answers?'

'Because I don't know *why*, Perry. Why would you do these things? How could you?'

'You haven't been listening. Everything I've done I *had* to do.'

'Including what you did to Reddick?'

'That was Ben's idea, not mine. And needless to say, it was a mistake. Reddick really is crazy you know. He murdered Andy in cold blood and tried to do the same to me, Will, and Ben. If anybody's a murderer in all this, it's him.'

'If that were true, he would have killed me. Don't you think?'

'Look, I don't want to argue with you. You can believe what you want to believe. But I need to know what you're going to do. Have you called the police?'

'No. But I will if you don't.'

Cross had to laugh at the suggestion. 'Me? I just told you—'

'That Gillis's death was an accident and that you had nothing to do with what Ben did to Reddick.'

'That's right.'

'In that case, the best thing you could possibly do for yourself is turn yourself in, before the police come looking for you and find you. Let Ben and Will fend for themselves. You can afford to hire a good attorney, Perry, and a really great one could probably fix all this so you do next to no time at all. Maybe even get you off completely.'

'Really? Next to no time at all, huh?' Cross

209

leaned in close across the table, hissed, 'Fuck that. And fuck you.'

Iris had been expecting this reaction; she would have been a fool to think Cross would respond any other way. But it still stung. Somewhere deep down inside, in a corner of her being he had somehow not yet managed to scorch black, she still had feelings for this man.

But not enough to take another minute of his bullshit.

'Suit yourself,' she said with a little shrug, and started to push away from the table.

'Wait. Wait!' Cross grabbed her wrists with both hands to stop her cold, a naked desperation he had heretofore kept hidden rising to the surface. He despised himself for the show of weakness he knew he was putting on, aware that Sinnott – and possibly even Reddick – was watching, but try as he might, short of strangling Iris right there at the table, he could see no way around what he was about to do next: beg.

'Let me go,' Iris said. They were making a small scene and she could feel the eyes of several people upon her.

'I'm sorry. Please, wait. There's ... something I haven't told you yet,' Cross said.

He hadn't meant it as a carrot on a stick, but that was how she took it. Just another goddamn trick. And yet, Iris couldn't help but wonder: Dear God, could there really be anything more to hear?

'What is it?'

'Sit back down and I'll tell you. Please.'

Having had to say 'please' twice in the span of

210

fifteen seconds, it was all Cross could do not to gag on his own shame. Iris glanced at his hands on her wrists, stating a condition for surrender, and he released her. She sat back down. Waited.

'It isn't just Reddick and the police I have to worry about,' Cross said. 'There's someone else. Someone way more sick and dangerous than Reddick.'

'Who?'

'I can't tell you who. All I can say is, he's the reason we needed Gillis to pay us what he owed us so badly. This guy loaned us a big chunk of change a while back and the debt comes due at the end of the week. Trouble is, we don't have the scratch, and if we don't come up with it, we're all dead. And I don't just mean "dead," Iris. I mean with a red-hot coathanger wire running through our fucking ears "dead." That's the kind of animal this guy is.'

'Jesus.'

'Yeah. So going to the police is not an option for any of us. That might get Reddick and the law off our backs over the long haul, but it won't do anything to appease our psychotic little friend. This guy will get payback, no matter how long he has to wait for it, and I don't mind telling you, thinking about what he might do to get it is a little disconcerting.'

Iris didn't know what to think. It sounded so incredible, as if everything Cross had told her before hadn't already been improbable enough. But she believed him. After years of practice, she had finally learned to tell the difference between what a lie sounded like coming out of his mouth and the truth.

'And this is why you forged a check from me for seventy-five hundred dollars?'

'Of course. If I'd thought I could get away with it, I would have made it out for more. It was a lousy thing to do, I know, but I was desperate. And I couldn't just ask you for the money without your demanding to know what it was for, so...'

'You should still go to the police. They can protect you,' Iris said.

'The hell they can. Maybe I'm not making myself clear. The man I'm talking about can't be touched by the police. He's got connections everywhere, in and out of law enforcement. If we don't pay him, nothing's going to save us from this asshole, Iris. *Nothing*.'

Whether it was true or not, Iris could see Cross believed it, too much to make arguing with him worth the energy it would take to change his mind. 'So what are you asking me to do?'

'Nothing. I'm asking you not to do anything, or call anybody or talk to anybody about any of what I've just told you, for at least a couple of days, or until Ben and Will and I can figure out a way to pay this guy off. Once that's done, if you want to drop a dime on us, I'll dial nine-one-one myself and hand you the phone, I swear to God.'

Cross didn't believe in God, so the promise meant nothing to Iris; she recognized it as his first flatout lie of the afternoon, in any case. If she were to remain silent the way he was asking her to – the same way Reddick had asked earlier that day, if for different reasons entirely – the minute Cross felt he was safe from the maniac he'd just described, he'd be actively avoiding any contact with the police, back in full denial mode. Iris had no illusions about this. But if she turned him over to the authorities now and he ended up dead as a result, his body mutilated in some grotesque fashion, she knew she would never be able to shake the idea that she had been responsible. Damning Reddick to whatever fate the police were sure to subject him to was going to be hard enough to live with; setting Cross up to be tortured and killed by some sadistic madman would only make matters infinitely worse.

'What about Reddick?' she asked.

'Reddick's a non-factor,' Cross said. 'He caught us by surprise this morning, but that's all over. Now that we know he's gunning for us, we'll be ready for him next time.'

'And if there is no "next time"? If he decides killing Andy was revenge enough for what the four of you did to him, and leaves the rest up to the police?'

'Did he say that?' Cross asked hopefully. 'Is that what he said he intends to do?'

'Not in so many words. Answer the question, Perry.'

'Well, first of all, "the four of us" didn't do anything to him. I keep telling you that. But if Reddick wants to let bygones be bygones, hey, I'd be happy to do the same, of course. That would make just one less thing for us to worry about.'

He was lying again and this time, Iris called

him on it. 'I don't want him hurt, Perry. None of this was his fault. If the poor bastard killed Andy like you say, he'll probably do time for it, and that's punishment enough, as far as I'm concerned.'

'Maybe. Maybe not. Let's not forget what he did to Ben.'

'Ben had that coming, and more. To hell with Ben. If you want me to help you, those are my terms, take it or leave it. I don't want Reddick hurt.'

Cross would have liked nothing better than to tell this fool bitch again to go fuck herself and walk away. Who the hell did she think she was, Reddick's *mother*? But his present circumstances did not allow for such indulgences; Iris was the rock and Ruben was the hard place, and between the two, he had no room to do anything but bend over and capitulate.

'OK. You've got my word that as long as he doesn't fuck with us, we won't fuck with him,' he said. 'Fair enough?'

Hell no, it wasn't fair enough, Iris thought. Not to Reddick and certainly not to Gillis Rainey. But it was the closest thing to a square deal she was ever likely to get out of Perry Cross and she'd just be wasting her breath trying to negotiate something better out of him.

'I'll give you two days,' she said.

'I need to the end of the week.'

'Two days. No more and no less. After that, I go the police alone and let whatever happens happen.'

Cross hesitated, conflicted. 'I don't suppose...'

'No way in hell. I'll let the seventy-five hundred you've already stolen from me ride, but that's it. The rest you're going to have to raise on your own.'

Perry looked at her as if seeing her for the first time. Had she always been this fucking hard, or was this change in her something new, just one more unintended consequence of his own recent stupidity?

'Fine. Two days.'

She rose from the table again, making sure this time to be too quick for him to stop her. 'I don't know what happened to you, Perry. Maybe you were always this way and I just didn't see it. But you need help, and I hope you live long enough to get it. I really do.'

He had a comeback ready on his tongue, but she was gone before he could open his mouth.

TWENTY-THREE

The melody was familiar. Clarke was sure he had heard it a thousand times before. Still, he couldn't place it.

It came and went, long stretches of silence sandwiched between iterations, a tinny chime over dime-store speakers nagging him for attention. Finally, he gave in and opened his eyes, blinked through a haze of pain into a dark room turned on its side: his bedroom.

He peered into the shadowy void, tried to remember what he was doing here, on his stomach in his bed, aching from head to foot. The incessant jingle persisted. At last, he recognized it for what it was: the theme music from *Rocky*, clipped and denuded down to the flat-note triviality of a cell phone ringtone. *His* cell phone.

Where the hell the instrument was in the room, Clarke couldn't begin to guess, but he knew he lacked the will to ignore it for another second. To anyone else, it would have been a minor irritant at most, but to him, at this moment, the sound of the phone held all the aural power of a running leaf blower strapped to the side of his skull. And there was no point in shouting out for Cross or Sinnott to put an end to it; his throat was as dry as soot and the effort of raising his

216

voice loud enough to be heard beyond the bedroom walls was likely beyond his means.

Slowly, he rolled to one side on the bed, encountering pain so intense he thought for sure it would prove fatal. His head felt like a block of iron wedged in a vise and his ribcage cried out in agony with every intake of breath. Even the tips of his fingers hurt.

Reddick.

He used the man's name as fuel to continue his ascent, pulling himself all the way upright while envisioning their next meeting, and the myriad ways he might end it: with a knife or a sawed-off baseball bat, or a fireplace poker glowing white with heat.

Still half-blind in the dark, Clarke glanced about for the ringing phone, took a guess it was on the nightstand nearby, where a digital clock announced to the world that the time was 6:42 p.m. He'd been asleep for over three hours. Summoning all his strength and tolerance for pain, Clarke pushed a hand forward, groping, and found the phone. He thumbed the answer button to silence it and gingerly brought it up to his bandaged head.

'Yeah?'

The caller made him wait a few seconds for a response. 'So you pulled through. Guess I should have tried a little harder.'

Clarke recognized the voice immediately, stomach churning like a cauldron brimming with acid. 'You motherfucker! You cocksucking son-ofabitch—'

'Take it easy, Mr Clarke. I didn't call to get

your feathers up. I just wanted to know where to send the flowers, that's all.'

'You're all dead, Reddick. You, the bitch and ... and your little boy – you're all fuckin' ... dead, I swear to God!'

'Yeah, I remember you saying that once before. Your pal Baumhower made me the same promise last night – and we all know how unlikely he is to make good now, don't we?'

'You wanna try me again ... asshole?' Clarke sputtered, a spiraling rage sapping what little strength he had left. 'Just name ... the time and place.'

Again, the man on the other end of the line fell silent. Then: 'No problem. The time is now.' Reddick lowered his voice to a mere whisper. 'The place is *here*.'

He hung up.

Here and now. Clarke tossed the phone to one side on the bed, feeling lightheaded and nauseated. What the fuck did Reddick mean? Could he be here now, somewhere outside, waiting? Maybe even inside the house, in the very next room? Was that possible?

'Perry! Will!'

He was screaming at the top of his lungs, but it was a pointless waste of energy; in his present state, he couldn't muster the volume of a Chihuahua choking on a bone. He decided Cross and Sinnott were gone, in any case; were either man still here, playing nursemaid, he surely would have saved Clarke the trouble of answering the goddamn phone.

Clarke was on his own.

218

He was sick to his stomach and wracked with pain, as close to the doorstep of death as a man could come and not cross it, but he had to move. If Reddick was here and coming for him, he wasn't going to find Clarke laying helpless on the bed, just waiting to die. Clarke had made it that easy for him once already, and he wasn't going to do it again. This time, he was going to be ready when Reddick showed his face, and the outcome of their next meeting was going to be significantly different from their last.

Anticipating this moment, he'd made a point of leaving a loaded Glock on the nightstand near his phone before taking to his bed. Remembering the weapon now, he reached out to take it into his right hand, then pushed himself to his feet, stifling a war cry of agony to block out the pain.

Taking one humiliating, baby step after another, he slowly made his way out of the bedroom.

Reddick didn't know whether to laugh or cry. Ben Clarke was still alive.

It was good to know he wasn't a patient in a hospital somewhere, however. By answering his own cell phone, the big man had all but ruled that possibility out. Cell phones weren't allowed in ICUs. So Reddick didn't have to worry about getting to Clarke again without creeping down hospital hallways and stairwells, trying to evade security guards and medical staff.

Though he'd led Clarke to believe otherwise, that he was somewhere outside of a hospital room was all Reddick actually knew about the big man. Sitting in a strip-mall Mexican restaurant in Manhattan Beach, miles from Clarke's Culver City home address, Reddick had only made the call to Clarke's cell phone to find out if he was still breathing and, if he was, how hard it might be to finish him off. He hadn't planned to speak a word into the phone until he'd heard Clarke's voice on the other end of the line, sounding all hurt and pathetic, and the temptation to put the fear of God in the asshole became too great to ignore. Reddick was the angel of death and he wanted Clarke to know it, and he liked the idea of the big fuck pissing his pants wondering if Reddick wasn't right there with him somewhere, waiting just around the next corner to put him out of his misery.

That moment was coming, of course, for Clarke as well as his two friends Perry Cross and Will Sinnott, but for now Reddick was content to bide his time. He was a walking wreck, emotionally spent and sleep deprived, and he desperately needed some rest. While the clock was still ticking on the twenty-four hours he had asked Cross's girlfriend to give him before calling the cops, he thought it better to back off and regroup than push ahead and risk making a fatal mistake. Wherever Clarke was, he could wait.

But he wouldn't have to wait long.

TWENTY-FOUR

Given explicit instructions by Cross to go straight back to Culver City to watch over Clarke, Will Sinnott had gone looking for Iris Mitchell instead.

When he rang the doorbell at the Brentwood home of Lester and Ellen Mitchell, Iris's parents, a few minutes after seven p.m. Sunday night, it was Iris herself who answered the door. He thought she might slam it right back in his face, so obvious was her impulse to do so. But she didn't.

'How did you know where to find me?'

Sinnott shrugged. 'I'm a lush. Not an idiot. You weren't at home, so...'

He'd been here once before, at a Christmas party last year, and it wasn't the kind of home one could easily forget. Set far back from a curbless street off San Vicente, at the end of a driveway that seemed to go on forever past walls of hibiscus and azaleas, the Mitchell estate was a single-story monument to postmodern architecture, turrets and columns intermingling with gabled roofs and oversized windows. It had every right to be an eyesore, but the overall effect was stunning, especially in the muted light of early evening.

'What do you want?' Iris asked. She was thankful now that she'd decided to hide out with her parents for a while; she hadn't told them anything about her reasons for coming, but her father was upstairs in his study and could be counted on to help if Sinnott made any attempt to lay a hand on her.

'May I come in?'

'You haven't answered my question.'

'I'm not going to hurt you, Iris. Jesus. I just need to talk to you, that's all.'

She surveyed the dark carport behind him. 'Are you alone?'

'Of course. And no, if you're wondering, Perry doesn't know I'm here.'

She gave him a lingering look, then nodded her head and ushered him in.

They settled in a living room as spotless and beautiful as a furniture ad in a magazine, burning logs snapping and popping discreetly in the fireplace. Iris didn't bother offering Sinnott anything to drink.

'Well?'

He just sat there for a moment, trying to convince himself all over again that this was the right thing to do, and not an act of cowardice he would long regret. 'Are we alone?'

'Mother's out, but my father's upstairs. If I were to scream, he'd be down here in three seconds with the loaded gun he always keeps in a desk drawer.'

'Have you—'

'No. I haven't told either of them anything. Hurry up and get to the point, Will.'

Sinnott nodded. 'I know you told Perry you wouldn't go to the police until we're sure we can pay Ruben off. But I wanted to hear you say it for myself. I need to know you intend to keep your word.'

He didn't care if he was being paranoid. Once Cross had told him how his meeting with Iris at Farmer's Market had gone down, that he'd been forced to tell her everything there was to tell about Gillis Rainey's death and Clarke's attack upon Joe Reddick's family, Sinnott had been consumed by fear. Despite all of Cross's assurances, he simply couldn't believe Iris would make good on her promise to remain silent, even if for only forty-eight hours.

And he had good reason to be concerned, because Iris herself was indeed having similar doubts. In the two hours-plus since her rendezvous with Cross, she had picked up the phone more than once with the intention of calling the police, convinced she'd been a fool not to do so sooner. But she had yet to follow through. Each time she tried, she thought of Reddick, and remembered the crazy man Cross had said he and his friends were in debt to, and what he was likely to do to them if they were unable to pay him off. It sounded absurd, yes, like just the kind of oversized lie Cross might tell to save his ass, but there was no way to test its validity without risking the unthinkable, having to live with the knowledge that some maniac had skinned three men alive – or worse – because she'd made a simple phone call.

Still, with every passing minute, her resolve to

keep silent had been wavering more and more, just as Sinnott feared it might – until now. The look on Sinnott's face, and the terrible apprehension his inebriation couldn't hide, seemed to erase any doubt that what Cross had told her was true.

'I haven't called the police yet, and I have no immediate plans to do so,' Iris said. 'Is that good enough for you?'

'I'm sorry,' Sinnott said, 'but I had to be sure. You don't know this guy, Iris. What kind of animal he is.'

'You just said his name was "Ruben"? Is that right?'

'Ruben Lizama. Yes.'

'So tell me. Who is he? And what kind of "animal" is he, exactly?'

'Perry didn't say? I thought—'

'He only gave me a rough outline. But since you're here, Will, you may as well enlighten me further. If I'm going to continue to be an accessory to kidnapping and murder for you boys, that's the least you could do in return, don't you think?'

Sinnott hesitated. If Cross had been vague with her in regards to Ruben, he must have had his reasons. Still, Iris was right: In exchange for what they were asking of her, telling her what little of the truth she didn't already know seemed a small price to pay.

'You can never repeat what I'm about to tell you,' he said, 'most especially to the police. You can tell them everything else, but not this. Your life, as well as ours, may depend on it. Swear to

224

me, Iris.'

Her life might depend on it? This was something Iris hadn't been prepared to hear. Still, she nodded in agreement.

'His full name is Ruben Lizama, like I said. He's a friend of Ben's. His father is Jorge Lizama, head of one of the largest and most powerful drug families in Mexico. Ever hear of him?'

Iris shook her head. A Mexican drug family. God in heaven, was there no end to how bad this nightmare could get?

'These are the people leaving notes for the federal *policia* on headless bodies all over Michoacan. The ones who walk into drug rehab centers in broad daylight and kill everybody inside just to make a point, women and children included. Ruben does the worst of their dirty work and he does it because he *likes* it.'

He told her all the rest: How Ben had talked them into agreeing to launder a quarter million dollars of Lizama family money, just so the moron could say he was in business with a criminal he admired; how one crazy thing after another had conspired to prevent them from paying Ruben off on time. First, Cross had made the insane decision to feed his pathetic gambling habit with Ruben's money, then Gillis Rainey refused to return the $100,000 they'd foolishly entrusted to him, money they could have used to make up for Cross's losses. Their botched kidnapping of Rainey, resulting in his death; Andy making a possible witness out of Joe Reddick after disposing of Rainey's body; Ben unilaterally attempting to ensure Reddick's silence by threatening to kill him and his entire family; Reddick responding to Ben's threat by seeking to kill them all. Sinnott left out nothing, telling Iris the whole, sordid story in intricate detail, unable to see how holding back now could serve any possible purpose.

He was pleading for mercy, hoping once she'd heard just how badly fate had fucked them over, how the most innocent of their intentions had led to a disaster beyond their control, she'd have no choice but to empathize and cut them some slack. Andy having a fender bender with Joe Reddick, the worst possible person to run into that night, was just one example of how doomed they'd been from the start.

'What do you mean?' Iris asked.

Sinnott told her what he'd read about Reddick on the Internet, about the family he'd lost nine years ago in Florida to a maniac not that far removed from Ruben Lizama.

'He was probably already insane. God knows I would have been. Starting all over again here in LA just to have Ben put a knife to his wife and son's throats must have been all the excuse he needed to lose it completely.'

Iris was struck dumb. Her inclination to take Reddick's side over Cross's had been a mystery to her, but now she understood what it was about him she had found so deserving of her sympathy. For once, the pain and vulnerability she'd sensed in a man she barely knew had actually been real, and not just a figment of her imagination.

'Perry says he let you go without hurting you,'

226

Sinnott said. 'Is that true?'

Iris nodded.

'But he didn't tell you anything about his intentions. What he plans to do about me, Ben and Perry now, I mean.'

'No.'

'You think he might just let it go? Is there any chance of that?'

'I don't know. Maybe.' She actually doubted there was any chance whatsoever of Reddick letting it go, but she couldn't bring herself to say it. 'And you?'

'Me?'

'You and Ben. Perry promised you'd all leave Reddick be if I waited two days before going to the police, but maybe he was only speaking for himself. You say Reddick killed Andy and tried to kill Ben. Are you and Ben willing to forget that?'

After a pause, Sinnott said, 'Andy was my friend, and I'm not fond of the idea of his killer going scot-free. But he and Ben were the ones responsible for making an enemy of Reddick, not me, so I couldn't care less what happens to Reddick after this. Right now, my only concern in life is Ruben Lizama, and doing whatever I have to do to keep him from sticking me feet first into a goddamn wood chipper or something.'

It was the same argument for leniency Cross had made earlier, only coming from Will Sinnott, it sounded more pitiful and genuinely desperate. Iris had never cared much for any of Cross's three friends-slash-business partners,

227

but Will was the one she distrusted the least. Clarke was an asshole from the ground up and Andy Baumhower had been a spineless weasel; Sinnott, on the other hand, was just a walking cocktail glass so intent on impressing his parents, he could be talked into anything that might help him build a fortune of his own.

'Do you know where I could find Reddick?' Iris asked.

'What?'

'If Ben went to his home, you must have an address for him. I want it.'

Sinnott shook his head from side to side, said, 'No way. Forget about it.'

'I don't want to see the man suffer any more than he already has, Will, and one of you is going to kill him if he keeps coming after you. It's just a matter of time.'

'And you think you can stop him?'

'I can try.'

Sinnott laughed. 'You're crazy. This guy's as psychotic as Ruben is, only different. You got near him once and lived to tell about it, but next time—'

'I'm willing to take my chances. I want that address, Will. If his little boy ends up an orphan over this, I'm going to hold you just as responsible as anyone else. Is that what you want?'

He should hardly have cared what the lady thought of him at this point, but he did. Over the last few months, thanks to Ben and Perry, he had become somebody he barely recognized, and his sense of self-loathing was almost overpowering. He wasn't just an unscrupulous momma's boy stinking of gin anymore – he was a kidnapper and an accessory to murder. The level of disgrace he had brought to his family was something he would never be able to live down. And yet Iris could still see some good in him, some sliver of decency that separated him from real assholes like Ben Clarke and Perry Cross. It wasn't much, but it was something worth holding on to.

He pulled his cell phone from his pocket, navigated to the notes he'd taken from his online research on Reddick.

'Get a pen and something to write on,' he said.

TWENTY-FIVE

'Where the fuck are you?' Cross asked. 'Ben says he's still at the house all alone.'

'I was hungry and stopped to get something to eat. I'm on my way over to his place right now.'

It was going on two hours since Cross had sent Sinnott off to keep Clarke company, so he knew there was more to Sinnott's delay than he was telling. But Cross let it go, because their goddamn cell connection was bad and he didn't have the patience to ask the other man to repeat everything he had to say twice.

'Well, hurry the hell up and get over there. Fucking Reddick called him on his cell phone and Ben's about to lose his goddamn mind.'

'Reddick called him?' Sinnott asked in a panic.

'You heard me. He thinks Reddick's right outside his door and needs somebody to hold his hand before he has an aneurism.' Sinnott said something else but static broke his voice into a dozen unintelligible pieces. 'You're breaking up, Will, I gotta let you go,' Cross said. 'Just get over to Ben's right away and call me the minute you get there.'

He ended the call without waiting for Sinnott to respond.

* * *

Clarke was waiting for Reddick in the dark, sitting in his living room in a plush leather chair that offered a clear view of the front door. His Glock was still clutched in his right hand, dangling precipitously over the edge of the chair's armrest.

From time to time, his head bobbed forward and his eyes fluttered closed, then opened again, though he was only barely aware that this was happening. Several minutes ago, he'd succumbed to the rising discomfort of his injuries and washed four Vicodin tablets down with a shot of Johnny Walker Black, paying no heed to the 'two tablets every eight hours' directions on the bottle, and now the blessed fog of anesthesia was gradually closing around him.

He caught himself nodding off, snapped to attention. Reddick was coming for him first, he was sure of it, and there was no fucking way Clarke wasn't going to have a warm, full clip of 115- grain hollowpoints ready and waiting for his ass when he got here. Cross was sending Sinnott over to help him defend the fort, and that was fine, but Reddick belonged to Clarke and nobody else. If Will even thought about popping a cap in him before Clarke could have his fun with him, he'd be the next one to die. That was no bullshit.

The gun started to slide from Clarke's grasp and he closed his fist to catch it, damn near firing off a round into the floor. He brought his arm up, set the Glock down in his lap, finger still on the trigger. He squinted in the direction of the door and mumbled an invitation under his

231

breath: 'Come on, motherfucker. Come on.'

His chin fell toward his chest, his eyes slid closed, and the dark of the living room slowly dissolved to full black.

A half-block away, crouched down in the back seat of Dana's Ford sedan where he was all but invisible behind heavily tinted rear windows and the sunshade he'd propped up against the windshield, Reddick watched Clarke's house and wondered what to make of it. He hadn't seen a light glow from within in fifteen minutes, nor any motion at any of the windows. He was beginning to think that maybe he'd chosen the wrong place to look for Clarke and the others.

Or that they were better at playing possum than he would have suspected.

The latter was his best-case scenario, all three of the men he was after gathered inside, in one place together, having been spooked by Reddick's call to Clarke earlier into huddling up like a pack of startled hens in a coop. It could all be over tonight, one way or another.

But if they were back at Cross's crib instead, or at Sinnott's out in Encino, or scattered across the goddamn universe at some combination of all three locations, the hunt would have to go on, until every one of them was dead or the police, finally alerted to his mission by Cross's lady friend, found Reddick and locked him up.

Or worse.

Searching Clarke's place for signs of life was like watching a mausoleum; there was nothing there to see. Reddick was edging up in his seat, about to take his surveillance efforts to Sinnott's home in the San Fernando Valley, when an Acura coupe cruised silently past his window and parked directly in front of Clarke's address. A man Reddick recognized as Will Sinnott got out, stopped to survey the street, then went up to the front door as Reddick reached for his binoculars. The porch, like the rest of the house, was pitch black, so it was impossible to be sure, but it looked to Reddick like Sinnott was ringing the bell.

Something he wasn't likely to do, Reddick thought, unless he was expecting Clarke to be home.

Sinnott didn't like it. Clarke wasn't answering his phone or the doorbell and his house was as dark as a pool of ink. He was in no shape to go out and had called Perry less than an hour ago to ask what the hell was taking Sinnott so long to get there, so he had to be somewhere inside. The only thing Sinnott could figure was that the big man had taken another dose of his meds and fallen asleep again. Or had Reddick dropped by and...?

Sinnott tried the bell one more time, knocked, and shouted Clarke's name. Nothing. He'd wondered why Cross had told him to grab Clarke's spare house keys before they'd left him here earlier that afternoon, but now the move made perfect sense. Cross's capacity to anticipate the unexpected never ceased to amaze him.

With the trepidation of a diver entering a shark

cage, he put the key in the lock and carefully opened the door.

From the farthest reaches of the cold, black sleep he had plunged into, the last note of a ringing doorbell having broken it, Clarke became vaguely aware of something pounding on his skull. Then someone called his name. A scratching, metal on metal, followed by ... what? A footstep?

Shit!

He raised his head, opened his eyes just in time to see the silhouette of a man, caught in relief against the open front door, easing catlike into his home. His reflexes were shot, dulled by drugs and sleep, but adrenaline made up the difference as he raised his right arm, aimed the Glock at Reddick – who else would it fucking be? – and fired: once, twice, three times.

He heard the man let out a low grunt, saw him drop to the floor on his face, no effort made to brace his fall, and grow still.

Adios, Joe.

Relief and something else – Clarke thought it might be pride – washed over him, and suddenly the combined forces of Vicodin and exhaustion were drawing him back down to sleep again, dimming the lights on the world faster than he could gather the strength to fight it.

Reddick had been rushing across the front lawn, intending to catch Sinnott at the door before he could close it behind himself, when he heard the shots and saw Sinnott fall. He realized what had happened immediately: Clarke or Cross, or maybe even both, had mistaken Sinnott for him and cut him down in error. One down, two more to go, he thought. Smith & Wesson .40 out and at his side, he inched his way up to the porch, to one side of the door, and waited.

Nothing happened. The door stayed open, and no one appeared to drag Sinnott inside.

Reddick let a few more seconds go by, feeling increasingly conspicuous standing there on the porch with a gun in his hand, then crab-walked over to the door and, in a crouch, peeked inside the house.

In the dark, nothing stirred nor made a sound. Reddick sucked in a deep breath, dove across the threshold over Sinnott's body and rolled up into a firing position...

Silence.

His eyes scanned the house for movement, any kind of movement, gradually adjusting to the dark. Breathing hard, heart pounding, he was finally able to make out the shape of a large man slumped over in a chair in what he assumed was the living room. Clarke. From all appearances, no more alive than Sinnott.

Reddick closed the front door and, with one eye on Clarke, checked Sinnott's wrist for a pulse, afraid to leave anything more to chance. He didn't find one. He slowly made his way over to the man in the chair, gun at the ready, heard him snoring before he reached him. He noted the Glock in the big man's right hand and eased it from his grasp, encountering no resistance.

His first thought was to put a single round at the back of Clarke's head, finish him quick and clean and get the hell out; his second was to check Sinnott's body for the weapon he'd flashed at Cross's condo earlier that day and, if he found it, use that gun to kill Clarke, work the room afterwards to make it look like the two men had shot each other.

But then Reddick spotted the bottle of prescription meds and a fifth of scotch on a coffee table next to Clarke's chair, and two things immediately became clear to him: the cause of Clarke's unshakable stupor, and the most efficient way possible to end his miserable life.

Between courses at *Ago*, where he was having dinner alone, it occurred to Cross that Ben Clarke might have been right all along.

Joe Reddick was a do-gooder and an ex-cop, not the kind of guy who would have heard about Gillis Rainey's body being found in the LA River near the site of his accident with Andy Baumhower, put the two things together, and then remained silent about it. He would have gone to the police, sooner or later, and the only reason he hadn't yet was Clarke's intervention, as badly executed as it was. Reddick's soft spot was his family, more so than Clarke could have ever suspected, and maybe it could still be used against him. Maybe, if they could get him to take Clarke's original threat against his wife and son seriously again, they could stop him in his tracks or, failing that, at least slow him down long enough for them to deal with the more pressing problem that was Ruben Lizama.

They would need to find Reddick's wife and kid and put them back under Clarke's knife, let Reddick know their lives really and truly depended on him backing off *now*. But that wasn't likely to be easy; Reddick almost certainly had them hidden away somewhere safe. He was far too smart to have them both just sitting there at home, waiting for Clarke to come back, while he was out running around all over the city trying to kill Clarke and his friends.

So where could they be?

Cross couldn't begin to guess, but he thought he might know someone capable of finding out: Frank Blake. Blake was Iris Mitchell's brother-in-law, an insurance investigator with whom Cross had partied on several occasions. He was a poseur and a prematurely balding windbag who was constantly trying to impress people with the access to information his profession afforded him, and Cross could only barely tolerate his company. But unless all his talk about his powers of investigative research was bullshit, tracking down Reddick's family would be no problem for him.

Praying word of his messy break-up with Iris hadn't already muddied the waters between them, Cross called Blake from the restaurant and posed the favor, making up a story on the spot about Reddick being a disgruntled ex-employee he wanted to keep tabs on in preparation for a baseless wrongful termination suit. In particular, Cross said, he wanted to know where Reddick might be spending his nights lately outside of his

Los Angeles home.

Without sounding entirely sold on Cross's reasons for asking, Blake said he'd see what he could do and would get back to him sometime the next day.

One night stands weren't usually Cross's thing, but later that night, a gift fell into his lap that he wasn't about to turn down.

He'd gone to Primo Joe's, Clarke's nightclub in Century City, after dinner, just looking for a few drinks on the house and the diversion of a crowd in which to get lost, and without having to try, he'd made a friend at the bar within fifteen minutes. She was the raven-haired standout of a trio, falling all out of a black dress neither of her two girlfriends would have done half as much justice to. She caught a comment Cross made to the bartender that had the ring of authority to it and, surmising he was more than a mere regular here, proceeded to chat him up. Ordinarily, Cross would have only been interested in the banter – he had moved beyond half-drunk college co-eds in high heels and push-up bras long ago – but in the wake of being dumped, shit on, and blackmailed by Iris Mitchell, the timing seemed right for a little mindless fornication with a perfect stranger.

When they got around to deciding where they should go to do the deed, Cross offered to get them a room at the nearby Hyatt Regency, telling the girl – her name was actually 'Danni' – he couldn't take her home because it was under the rubble of renovation, a lie she both mistook and

238

appreciated as creative code for his being a married man.

At the Hyatt now, up in the suite he and Danni had just tumbled around in, Cross tried for the second time in almost two hours to reach Sinnott, not having spoken to him since dinner, when he'd told the fool to get over to Clarke's place right away. Sinnott never called back to say he made it, nor responded to the voicemail message Cross left for him later, before Cross had left Primo Joe's.

Lying naked in a sweat-soaked bed at the Hyatt, his date puttering around in the bathroom getting ready for Round Two, Cross found himself once again listening to Sinnott's outgoing voicemail message instead of to Sinnott himself. He dialed Clarke's number and netted similar results. This last was no real surprise; Clarke was probably asleep, up to his eyeballs in booze and painkillers. But even accounting for the annoying habit he had of choosing cell phone ringtones he could only hear half the time, Sinnott's silence was disturbing, and Cross finally had to wonder if something were indeed amiss. Could Reddick have followed up his phone call to Clarke with a visit to his home?

Given time to think about it, wonder would have no doubt turned to concern, and concern on to apprehension. But Danni was out of the bathroom and on top of him again before Cross could even turn off his phone, and he couldn't find the wherewithal to discourage her. Rather than the moderately amusing fuck he'd been expecting, the girl had turned out to be an extraordinary one, patient and generous and full of surprises, and once she started in on him, disarmed by alcohol as he was, the will to slow her down was not in his possession. So he gave himself up to the moment, telling himself he deserved this respite from the madness of the past week, and let Danni have her way with him, tossing his phone to the floor with all his clothes.

He couldn't forget them completely, but for a while at least, Sinnott and Clarke and Joe Reddick were filed away in Cross's mind under the heading of things he could worry about later.

TWENTY-SIX

Now there was only Cross.

With Clarke and Sinnott's deaths tonight, Reddick's original hit list of four people had been reduced to one, and that one man was Perry Cross. Reddick could see nothing else standing between himself and long-term peace of mind.

For a while, he toyed with the idea of leaving Cross to the authorities. From all appearances, he wasn't half the thug Clarke had been, and even Sinnott had seemed more capable of engaging in physical violence. But Cross was the mastermind of the crew, the head of the serpent that had Reddick so terrified, and at his condo in Venice he had demonstrated a bent for cruelty that neither Sinnott nor Baumhower had shown. Clarke may have been the quartet's most willing killer, but Reddick suspected Cross would prove to be its most persistent. Left alive for the law to do with him what it would, Cross would neither forget the debt he owed Reddick, nor act impulsively to repay it, as any of his three partners might have in his place. He would remember, and he would plan, and as soon as he was able, he would strike.

So like his friends, he had to die.

He wasn't going to make himself an easy

target, however. Reddick knew that. Which was why he wasn't surprised when Cross never showed up at any of the three places he looked for him that night. He would have been a fool to go home, of course, but Reddick had hoped Cross would at least try crashing at either Clarke's home or Sinnott's instead. When midnight came and went and he had failed to appear at either residence, nor his own, Reddick reluctantly decided to postpone the hunt for him until morning, realizing he might be waiting for a man who had jumped on a plane and fled Los Angeles – if not the continental United States – hours ago.

Unlike Cross, Reddick had no compunction about sleeping in his own bed that night. He had avoided this luxury long enough, and the thought of Cross coming to look for him at home was hardly a deterrent. If he couldn't defend himself in his own abode against an amateur like Cross, Reddick thought, he deserved to die.

He parked Dana's sedan on the street, a full block west of the house and not far from where he'd left his Mustang earlier in the day, then sat there behind the wheel for a moment, looking for incongruities. Nothing immediately jumped out at him. His home was dark and quiet and the sidewalks were deserted. He didn't know what Cross owned, but only a few of the unfamiliar vehicles on the street resembled anything Reddick could picture him driving, even on an impromptu stakeout mission: a green BMW, a black Lexus, and a silver Audi TT. All three cars appeared to be cold and vacant – until the taillights on the Audi flickered on for a moment and someone inside lowered the driver's side window to let in some air.

Reddick snatched his binoculars off the passenger seat and focused them on the Audi's side mirror. He couldn't see much of the driver but what he could see ruled out Cross, unless Andy Baumhower's friend thought a blonde wig and red lipstick would make for a clever disguise. Reddick found the hooded sweatshirt he'd thrown in the back seat, slipped it on and got out of the car. He pulled the hood up over his head to bury his face deep in shadow, shoved his hands and his forty inside the sweatshirt's pockets, and started walking.

Cross's girlfriend never saw him coming. She'd let the car's windows fog over with her breath before cracking the side one and the rear hadn't cleared in time for her to catch his approach in it.

'What the hell are you doing here?'

She turned at the sound of Reddick's voice, found him standing in the street only inches from her face, and nearly jumped through the Audi's headliner. She clumsily turned the car's ignition to the accessories position, rolled her window all the way down, and cried, 'Jesus! You scared the shit out of me!'

'I asked you a question.' Reddick's head turned this way and that, his eyes scanning the street for any sign of Cross.

'I need to talk to you.'

'Forget it. Go home.'

'I spoke to Will Sinnott a few hours ago. He

told me something I think you'd be interested to know.'

'Bullshit. If this is some kind of trick——'

'It's not a trick. Nobody knows I'm here, I came here on my own.'

'Great. Then you can get the hell out of here on your own. Right now, before you get hurt.'

'You may not need to do any more killing, Mr Reddick,' the blonde said, spitting the words out before he could silence her. 'Because you aren't the only one who might like to see Perry and his friends dead.'

That gave Reddick reason to pause. 'What are you talking about?'

'Can we go inside?'

'No, goddamnit! What the fuck are you talking about?'

Cross's girlfriend opened her door, stepped out of the car to look him straight in the eye.

'Inside,' she said.

Iris told Reddick everything about Ruben Lizama she'd learned from Cross and Sinnott. They sat at his dining room table, the whole house dark except for the tiny light over the stove in the kitchen nearby. The gun he'd pointed at her head that morning lay atop the table, right in front of him where he could reach it in a flash if he found the need to use it. At some point, he had asked for her name and she gave it to him: 'Iris Mitchell.'

'OK. So Cross and his pals are in hock to some psycho with the Mexican mafia,' Reddick said. 'What is that to me?'

'I told you. It means you can stop worrying about killing Perry, Will, and Ben because Ruben, if he's half the killer they say he is, will probably do the job for you. You've already got Andy's blood on your hands – why hurt anybody else if you don't have to?'

'Because I'm not interested in playing the percentages, that's why,' Reddick said, not bothering to correct Iris's false belief that Sinnott and Clarke were still alive. 'I've got a zero-tolerance policy where my family's welfare is concerned, and I'm not going to count on Ruben Lizama or anyone else to guarantee it. That's *my* job.'

'And the only way to do your job is to kill Perry and the others yourself.'

'That's the only way, yeah.'

'Because you don't want what happened to you in Florida to happen here.'

Reddick recoiled. First Sinnott, now Iris Mitchell – why couldn't they leave Kaye and the children in peace? 'What, did you fucking Google my name, too?'

'No. But Will told me what he discovered about you when *he* did.'

'My past is *my* business, not yours or anyone else's. And that's all the conversation we're going to have on the subject.'

'Or else what? You'll kill me, too?'

Reddick glared at her, feeling his powers of restraint giving way to the overwhelming need to vent, to give voice to his outrage and pain he'd been fighting for days. 'You weren't there, lady,' he said, seething. 'You think I'm being unreasonable, letting something that happened nine years ago turn me into the very thing I used to despise. But you weren't there to see the blood and the bodies, to buy the caskets, to stand next to three open graves and watch your world – your *whole fucking world* – go down into the earth for the worms to feed on like so much shit.

'Yeah, I'm crazy. You're goddamn right, I'm crazy.' Reddick leaned across the table toward her, hissed, 'But I'd be crazier still to let it happen again.'

He fell back into his chair and grew still. The house descended into silence. Iris did nothing to disturb it, afraid to push him past the point of no return.

'If you don't stop now, they'll put you away for life,' she said finally. 'Your wife and son will be alive, yes, but they won't have you. Is that what you want?'

'What I want, I used to have. Twice. But I'm living proof that the things we want aren't meant to last. Something or someone always fucks it up. So I've learned it's better to make do with the next best thing.'

'And what is that?'

'A clear conscience.'

'I don't understand.'

'Of course you don't. But I'll try to explain it to you anyway.'

As she waited for him to go on, Reddick wondered why in the hell he was doing this, peeling the sheet off the cold, dark corpse of his past just to try and justify his actions to this woman, a woman he didn't know and had no real reason to trust. And yet he did trust her. She

246

was Cross's girlfriend, pretty and young and accustomed to money just like him, but whereas little more could be said about Cross, Reddick had the sense that Iris was a different animal, one far more human and grounded in reality. The fact that she could have turned him over to the police hours ago and hadn't only reinforced the idea that her empathy for him might actually be genuine.

'When Kaye and the kids died...' he began.

'Your family in Florida.'

Reddick nodded. 'I blamed myself for years afterward, convinced they'd still be alive if I'd only done something, *anything*, differently. Come home from work sooner that day or put better locks on the doors. I didn't even know the crazy fuck who killed them, and he didn't know me – I'd never heard his name until they found his prints in the house – and yet I thought, if I'd been a better cop, I would have found him and put him away before he could do what he did. It didn't matter that I'd never worked a case in which he was involved. I should have found him and stopped him.

'It was insane, of course. I'd had no role whatsoever in what happened to Kaye and the kids, and eventually I figured that out. But it took years to get wise, and in the meantime I lived with the guilt of being complicit in their murders, of not having done enough to defend my wife and my children from the monsters I knew first-hand are lurking around every corner of this shithole world we live in.'

Reddick paused, recognizing the need to slow

247

down and catch his breath. He hadn't talked about any of this for over a year, since his last few sessions with Howard Elkins, the shrink he used to see here in Los Angeles, and he knew how hard and deep he could fall if he let this train get away from him. When he started up again, it was with a greater focus on control, his voice a laser light piercing the dark.

'You learn to get over the loss. If I lost Dana and Jake, either to your friend Cross or by some other means, there's a chance I could survive it. I've done it before, maybe I could do it again. But not the guilt. The guilt's another matter. This time, there *is* something I can do to protect what's mine, to change the script before it gets written, and there's no way in hell I'm not going to do it. No way. The price I have to pay, that's fucking immaterial. As long as I know in the end I did everything I could do to keep Dana and Jake safe and sound – *everything* – that's all that matters.'

He waited for Iris to offer some rebuttal, but she just sat there looking at him, her eyes shimmering with tears. There were a million things she could say to dispute his reasoning, but none she could voice and actually believe. She had heard all the evidence and the only conclusion she could reach was the same one Reddick himself had come to long ago: Murder was the only guarantee. And nothing less than a guarantee would do. Maybe it was fair to ask others to count on an imperfect criminal justice system to protect their loved ones from harm, but not Reddick. Reddick deserved to know, with absolute,

248

unqualified certainty, that Perry and his friends would never threaten his family again.

And Iris didn't know how to deny him that.

'I won't help you,' she said.

'I didn't ask you to. All I need from you is what you've already promised me: another twelve hours without police interference.'

Iris remained silent.

'Say it.'

'There has to be another way. They're just stupid little boys who like to pretend they're more badass than they are. Ben might be a little dangerous, but Will wouldn't hurt a fly, and Perry—'

'You're wasting your breath, lady.'

'Perry's just a bully who likes to talk tough. He's no killer. Please.'

Reddick stared back at her, trying to give her one last chance to change her mind.

'Please,' Iris said again. And now the tears she'd been managing to hold at bay for the last several minutes were flowing freely. Not because Perry and his friends deserved to be mourned, but because she knew they were already as good as dead.

And she wanted to be able to tell herself later she'd made every possible effort to plead for their lives.

TWENTY-SEVEN

'Shit!'

Cross reared up in the bed, waited for his eyes to fully focus on the hotel alarm clock he'd just glanced at. There'd been no mistake: It was 7:28 a.m.

He leapt to his feet, snatched his pants off the floor and began throwing on his clothes. The girl named Danni stirred behind him, face down atop the sheets and slobbering all over a pillow, but she did not awaken. There were purple marks on the cheeks of her ass Cross could not remember making.

He'd had too much to drink and exhausted himself trying to match his partner climax for climax, allowing what should have been a two-hour party to turn into an allnighter he couldn't afford. Cursing his stupidity, he checked his phone while slipping on his shoes and, much to his horror, saw no messages waiting for him. This being Monday, Sinnott, if not Clarke, should have been up by now and made at least one attempt to return Cross's calls from the night before. That he hadn't erased all doubt in Cross's mind that something was wrong.

Very wrong.

He left the room without a word to the girl and

250

called both Sinnott and Clarke on his way down to his car, knowing he'd only get their voice-mails again before he actually did. He didn't bother leaving any more messages, just hauled ass over to Clarke's home as fast as rush-hour traffic would permit.

The first thing he noticed upon reaching the house was Sinnott's Acura, parked right in front where it couldn't be missed. It was the worst of all possible signs, dashing the faint hope Cross had been holding on to that one or both of his friends was elsewhere. With Clarke's car still back at Cross's condo, the Acura's presence here made it highly likely that both Clarke and Sinnott were here, as well.

So why weren't they answering their goddamn phones?

Cross parked his own car and went up to Clarke's door, walking like a man being escorted to the gallows. He looked for indications of a break-in, a shattered door jamb or a broken win-dow, but everything about the house appeared normal. He rang the bell once, twice, and cursed himself for letting Sinnott take Clarke's spare set of keys instead of holding on to to them himself. Nobody came to the door, nor made a sound on the other side.

'Ben! Will! Open the goddamn door!'

Now he pounded on the door with a fist, changing nothing. The house remained silent. A picture of what might lay inside formed in his mind and, for the first time in his adult life, fear took hold of him with a grip he couldn't break. He started to go back to his car, then stopped, inspired by a sudden thought. He produced his cell phone, dialed Sinnott's number. He pressed his ear to the ice-cold surface of the door...

... and heard Sinnott's phone faintly chime from somewhere inside the house.

How he got to his car and behind the wheel, he would never be able to recall. His next conscious thought found him on the freeway, driving like a wild man eastbound on the 10, destination unknown. Sinnott was dead, and probably Clarke, as well. There was nothing else for him to believe. Reddick had killed them both, and now the crazy sonofabitch would be coming after Cross.

Unless he could be stopped.

But how? Reporting him to the police, even as a triple murderer, was still a move guaranteed to cause Cross more problems than it would solve. His life over the last two weeks had become a whisper-thin scaffolding of felonies and lies that Reddick, alive and conversant, could bring down in thirty seconds. A dead Joe Reddick, on the other hand, would make the perfect patsy, somebody Cross could blame for damn near everything the police would expect Cross himself to explain – the deaths of his three friends and, maybe, even that of Gillis Rainey, as well. It wouldn't be easy, but Cross was sure that, given time, he'd be able to tie Reddick to all of it to the satisfaction of the authorities. With Reddick dead, who would remain among the living to tell a different story?

Iris.

Iris would have to be dealt with, of course. Her

252

perpetual silence either purchased or forced upon her, one or the other. But that was something else Cross was confident he could accomplish, given an hour or two of unfettered thought to consider the problem. He had experience handling Iris; putting her in check for good would be a piece of cake. All he had to do was figure out how to make a dead man out of Reddick before Reddick made a dead man out of him.

Cross slowed the car, steadied his breathing, and eased his grip on the steering wheel, willing himself down from the state of all-out panic he'd allowed to overtake him. He had to start thinking clearly again if he wanted to survive. What to do first?

Make sure Will Sinnott and Ben Clarke were really dead, he decided. Assuming that was the case when it wasn't would be foolish and counterproductive. Sinnott had a gun and knew how to use it, but if Clarke were still alive, fucked up as he was, he would make for a better ally. Clarke knew people Cross and Sinnott did not, the kind of people who'd be willing and able to either shut Reddick down themselves or help Cross and Clarke do it on their own. They would not work for free, but that was OK.

Cross began driving with a purpose now, doubling back on the freeway to head for Clarke's office at Nightshades, his nightclub in Santa Monica. Finding his friend there would be nothing short of a miracle, one that defied all logic, but he didn't care. Hoping for miracles was what he was down to at this point and

253

shooting his brains out, just to save Reddick the trouble, was his only other alternative.

There was a lone car he didn't recognize in the club's parking lot when he arrived, a white GMC Yukon in nondescript trim, and his heart soared with relief. It had to be Clarke's, he thought, something the big man had rented or borrowed to throw Reddick off the scent. Reddick himself would have never parked a car here so conspicuously and, this early in the morning, it was unlikely to belong to one of Clarke's employees. Cross parked his Escalade in an adjacent space, jumped out, and went to the Yukon's side glass to peer into its interior.

The man in the passenger seat, beside a beefy driver with dark brown skin, rolled his window down and showed Cross a warm smile.

'Perry, what's up? Come, get in. We can wait for our friend Ben together,' Ruben Lizama said.

TWENTY-EIGHT

Today was the day it would all be over. Reddick had no more need for patience or stealth. His plan now was simple: Find Cross and kill him. Lay his weapon down immediately thereafter and wait for the police to cuff him. No muss, no fuss.

He couldn't trust Iris Mitchell to stay out of his way, so he'd left her this morning at his place, bound and gagged in his bedroom as she had been for most of the night. If the two of them were lucky, she wouldn't be there much longer. Cross would be dead by noon and, at Reddick's urging, the cops would show up to rescue her soon thereafter.

Reddick's first stop today had been Cross's condo in Santa Monica. He'd arrived just after eight a.m. and departed less than ten minutes later, having completed a seek and destroy mission that was a model of speed and efficiency: He blasted his way into Cross's building, searched every room of his unit, and got out as soon as it became obvious Cross wasn't there, fleeing the scene in Dana's sedan almost too quickly for more than a pair of potential witnesses to take note of him.

Now he was sitting in the waiting area of

Cross's office in Century City, flipping through the pages of a magazine while listening to every word Cross's receptionist – a short, zaftig Asian with braces on her teeth – spoke into the phone. He'd flashed an old private security badge at her when he walked in, told her he was here to see Cross regarding the matter of the burglary at Andy Baumhower's residence over the weekend. Mr Cross wasn't in, she'd said, but Reddick was welcome to wait for him if he cared to. Reddick, satisfied she wasn't feeding him a line, accepted the offer and sat down.

He was taking a calculated risk, setting a trap for Cross he might see right through should he call in and hear that a 'cop' was there waiting for him, but Reddick simply lacked the will to do anything else. This was his last stand. The havoc he'd wreaked at Cross's condo, the callous disregard he'd shown for anyone who might have had the misfortune of getting in his way, had taken something out of him. Maybe for the first time in days, he was able to see the sick, rabid dog he had become, the murderer of unarmed men, and the realization left him too spent to go on chasing Cross forever. He still wanted Cross dead, he still *needed* him dead, but the blind, white hot rage that had made his killing of Andy Baumhower and Ben Clarke possible was something Reddick no longer possessed.

Cross had to come to *him* now. Either inadvertently or by way of deception, it didn't matter which. And he had to do it fast, before Reddick lost the courage altogether to kill him.

Twenty minutes went by, then thirty. The girl

behind the receptionist's desk answered three incoming calls as he listened, advising the person on the other end of the line each time that Mr Cross wasn't in. Reddick began to get antsy. He picked up another magazine, nearly tore its cover off peeling it open. He could see the LAPD uniforms now, poring over the wreckage of Cross's condominium, calling in a general description of the armed man one of Cross's neighbors had seen running down the hall on his way out of the building...

The door opened behind him and Reddick looked up, saw two people enter the room and approach the receptionist: a black woman and a white man, both middle-aged, the former dressed like a well-heeled attorney, the latter a used car salesman on the skids. The guy gave Reddick a brief glance, then turned back around. Reddick had never laid eyes on either him or his friend before, but he knew who – or *what* – they were in an instant.

'May I help you?' the receptionist asked.

Finola Winn showed her the contents of a brown leather ID folio, said, 'I'm Detective Winn, this is Detective Lerner. We're here to see Perry Cross.'

The girl behind the desk made a face, pinned between the twin forces of confusion and surprise. 'Is Mr Cross in some kind of trouble?' she asked.

Winn and Norm Lerner traded a glance.

'Not necessarily. We just need to ask him a few questions, that's all,' Winn said. 'Is he in?'

'You mean questions about the burglary at Mr Baumhower's place?'

'Who?'

'Mr Baumhower. I thought ... Well, aren't you all here about the same thing?'

She craned her neck to see past the two detectives, and turning around to follow her gaze, they saw that the man who'd been sitting there earlier was suddenly gone.

TWENTY-NINE

For the first time in his life, Cross didn't trust himself to tell a lie. He was sure that a lie would get stuck in his throat, and that Ruben would kill him on the spot, right there in the car in the parking lot of Ben's club. So he did the next best thing and offered Ruben a highly modified version of the truth, laying the blame for everything that had gone wrong over the last thirteen days at the feet of Joe Reddick.

'Who the fuck is Joe Reddick?' Ruben asked.

Cross said Reddick was some crazy Andy Baumhower had once done business with who'd been trying to extort money from him for months, and when Baumhower wouldn't pay him off, the asshole went ballistic. First he'd killed Baumhower, then gone after his three Class Act partners, possibly killing Ben Clarke and Will Sinnott as well, Cross wasn't sure. He described the visit he'd just paid to Clarke's home and how the test call he'd made to Sinnott's cell phone had all but convinced him that both men were inside the house, dead.

Ruben listened intently to all of this, mild curiosity turning into something far more incendiary right before Cross's eyes as he began to suspect what Cross was leading up to.

'This is all terrible news,' he said. 'I like Ben, and I hope you're wrong about him being dead. But none of this has anything to do with me, does it? Or the money you're going to pay me Friday, as agreed?'

Cross tried to make his mouth move, failed, and tried again. 'No. No, of course not,' he stammered. 'It's just...'

'Yes?'

'Reddick. Goddamn Reddick. His interference has made it damn near impossible for us to function. We've got your money, Ruben, that's not a problem, but it's not all in one place, and we were in the process of gathering it all together when Reddick started fucking with us. If not for him, I'd be handing you what we owe you right now, I swear to God.'

'I don't care about "right now." What I care about is what you intend to give me four days from now. If Ben and Andy and your other friend – Will? – are all dead like you say—'

'I can still get the money for you. All by myself, every penny of it. But I can't do it and worry about Reddick, too. I need him out of the way so I can work without having to look over my fucking shoulder every five seconds.'

'I don't understand. You've reported this man to the police, yes? After he killed Andy? So why haven't they found him by now?'

'I don't know,' Cross lied, unable to see where he had any alternative. Their reasons for having never turned the police on to Reddick were all related to their catastrophic kidnapping of Gillis Rainey, and that was something Cross had already decided to withhold from Ruben, lest he realize how desperate they'd been, only two weeks ago, to raise his quarter million dollars. 'The guy's smart. He knows things. If he were easy to find, we would have found him and killed him ourselves.'

'You know what I think? I think this is all bullshit,' Ruben said, finally showing a flash of anger. 'I think you can't pay me, and Ben and the others have all run away and left you – what is the expression? – "holding on to the bag." So you tell me this ridiculous story about Joe Reddick so I'll give you enough time to maybe run away, too.'

'No! *No!*' Cross cried. 'I'm telling you the truth, I swear it!'

'Perhaps you do not understand how great an insult it will be if, on Friday, you cannot keep the promise you all made to me. I trusted you and Ben; I believed you when you told me you could take dirty money and make it clean. If I have to go back to my family now and tell them it was a mistake to do business with you...'

'Please. You have to believe me. I can still get you your money. I just need the rest of the week to work on it. Without any more distractions from Reddick.'

'Reddick, Reddick. Joe Reddick! *Fuck* this Joe Reddick!'

Ruben turned to his man Poeto, who could have been a mustachioed, oversized test dummy propped behind the car's wheel for all the interest he'd shown to this point in their conversation.

'¿Qué piensas, Poeto? ¿Será mierda, ó no? Debo de creer lo que me dice esta perrita gringa, o será que le clavo mi pinche cuchillo en su ojo.'

The driver gave Cross a disinterested look, as if examining a spoiled piece of meat. *'Patrón, yo no creo que él tenga los huevos para mentírle. Pero tal vez él tenga demasiado miedo para no intentarlo. Quizá deberíamos ir a la casa del Señor Clarke y ahi nos darémos cuenta sí sus amigos estan muertos como él dice.'*

As Cross watched, his inability to understand a word of the exchange he had just heard magnifying his sense of doom, Ruben nodded, the driver's answer to his questions apparently meeting his approval. Ruben turned back to Cross, said, 'You will take us to Ben's house now. If there are two dead men inside like you say, I will give you four more days to meet your obligations to me. And I will personally see to it that this *puta* "Joe Reddick" – if there really is such a person – doesn't bother you anymore.'

Cross started to exhale with relief, until he saw Ruben reach into a jacket pocket and withdraw a small, military-style folding knife. Opening the stubby, curved blade, Ruben said, 'But first, I must ask you to convince me that this will not all be a waste of my time. If you want me to believe that everything you are telling me is true, you need to offer me some token of your good intentions. Otherwise...'

Cross broke into a cold sweat, unable to turn his eyes away from the razor-like weapon Ruben was rolling around in his hand like a toy. 'I don't

... What do you want me to do?'

Ruben smiled. 'There is this thing gangsters do in Japan. It is called *"Yubitsume."* When they have fucked something up very badly, to show the members of their clan how sorry they are, they cut a finger off. Sometimes, more than one. I saw it in a movie once. It was *sick.*'

By the grin on his face, it was clear to Cross that Ruben's use of the word 'sick' was as a euphemism for something that had excited him to the point of orgasm.

'And you *are* sorry, right, Perry? That I must kill a man I do not know, and wait four more days for you to pay me what you owe me, because you have made it necessary for me to do so?'

Cross could feel the contents of his stomach grow instantly rancid, and if his life had not depended on his doing nothing to upset Ruben further, he would have given in to the urge to vomit all over the man's rental car. He wasn't ready to mutilate himself, but he wasn't ready to die, either. And yet Ruben was waiting for him to choose between the two.

Cross nodded his head and put a quavering hand out for the knife.

After Winn commandeered a freight elevator, flashing her badge and barking orders at a maintenance man she found standing in an open utility closet, she and Lerner caught the guy they'd seen up in Cross's office down in the lobby, just as he was about to exit the building. Lerner kept asking his partner all the way down what they were doing, chasing after somebody who wasn't the man they'd come here to see, but if Winn knew the answer, she was keeping it to herself.

Sucking wind, Winn introduced herself and Lerner, displaying her badge yet again, and the guy just looked at them like two kids trying to sell magazine subscriptions for the annual school fundraiser.

'How can I help you, detectives?'

'We just saw you upstairs in the offices of Class Act Productions,' Winn said. 'You seemed to leave in quite a hurry when we showed up.'

'Well, I am in a hurry,' the guy said, unfazed by the accusation, 'but that's got nothing to do with you. I've got a ten o'clock meeting in Burbank I'm not gonna make if I don't get out of here pretty quick. What's this all about?'

'Would you mind if we asked to see some ID, Mister...'

'Reddick. Joe Reddick.' He handed Winn his wallet, open to his driver's license. They were all standing just inside the lobby entrance and a heavy flow of foot traffic was swarming all around them. Lerner wasn't sure, but he thought he caught Reddick – if that was really his name – give the doors a brief glance, as if measuring his distance from the nearest one.

Winn looked Reddick's ID over, held on to his wallet after she was done. 'What line of work are you in, Mr Reddick?'

'I'm a field investigator for the City Attorney's office. Look—'

Lerner nodded his head to no one, suspicions

confirmed. Not every ex-cop in the world looked like one, but the mark of the Job on Reddick was as hard to miss as a full-body tattoo.

'And your interest in Class Act is?' Lerner asked, cutting in on his partner's line of questioning. Something about Reddick had his interest now and he was anxious to figure out what it was.

'Their CEO was witness to an accident a couple months back involving an MTA bus and a pedestrian who's now suing the city. I was here to get a statement from him, but the asshole stood me up.'

'Are you referring to Perry Cross?' Winn asked.

'That's him. Let me ask you guys again, in case you missed the question the first time: What's this all about? What do you want with me?'

'The girl upstairs seems to think you're one of us. She said something about a burglary at "Mr Baumhower's" place. Any idea what she was talking about?'

'None.'

'You didn't tell her you were a police officer investigating a burglary?'

'Impersonating a police officer would be a criminal offense. Why would I do something like that?'

'You tell us, Mr Reddick,' Lerner said. 'Why *would* you do something like that?'

He smiled in lieu of crossing his arms and setting his feet, just to let Reddick know he could take all the time he wanted to answer;

Lerner and Winn weren't going anywhere.

'OK, so maybe I did misrepresent myself a little up there,' Reddick said, clearly more pained by the confession than shamed by it. 'It's like I said: I've been chasing this jackass Cross for days now and getting nowhere. He's ducking me. So I thought, this morning we'll try something different. See if he'd be more receptive to a call from Detective Reddick than Joe from the City Attorney's office. It was a dumb move, but I was desperate. I don't get a statement from this clown soon, I'm gonna be out of a job.'

He looked to the cops for some reaction and got very little in return. Lerner still couldn't figure it out. There was something oddly familiar about Reddick – his name, his face? – but Lerner couldn't put his finger on what it was.

'The name "Gillis Rainey" mean anything to you?' Winn asked, breaking the short silence.

'Rainey? No.' Reddick shook his head.

Winn finally handed his wallet back to him. 'OK. Thanks for the help. If we need to talk to you again, we'll be in touch.'

Reddick nodded, slipped his wallet back into his coat pocket.

'And no more playing policeman, Mr Reddick. No matter how "desperate" you get. Understand?'

'Sure thing. Thanks for the pass.'

He slipped away. Winn waited until he was out of sight to turn to Lerner and ask, 'Well? What do you think?'

'I don't know. He had no reaction to Rainey's name that I could see. Still...'

'He wants more from Perry Cross than just a statement.'

'Yeah. That's the feeling I got, too. Along with something else.'

Winn waited for him to go on.

'I know the guy from somewhere. His name or his face is familiar to me, maybe both.'

'Well, he used to be a member of the club he only pretends to be in now, that much is obvious. Yes?'

'Oh, yeah. No doubt about it.'

'So maybe you ran across him when he was on the Job?'

Lerner shrugged. 'Maybe. But I don't think so.' He'd met a lot of cops in his time with the LAPD, some with other agencies and others in various divisions within the department, so it was hard to say for sure that Reddick hadn't been one of them. But that just wasn't the feeling Lerner had about him.

He gave himself a few more seconds to think about it, then shook his head, said, 'Aw, what the hell. Whoever he is, he's probably got nothing to do with Rainey. And that's all we're supposed to be interested in here, right?'

'Right,' Winn said, though she sounded less than convinced.

Boarding a regular elevator this time, the two cops went back upstairs to have another talk with Cross's receptionist.

THIRTY

If Reddick didn't know before that his time for killing Cross was running out, he knew it now. He'd bought himself, at best, a few more hours of freedom, bullshitting detectives Winn and Lerner of the LAPD into letting him go, but that was it. Any minute now, the pair – who he imagined were investigating the death of Gillis Rainey, since they'd dropped the dead man's name – would connect him to the break-in at Cross's condo and have every uniform in the city watching out for him.

He had to find Cross fast.

He sat in Dana's car, having parked it not far from Cross's office building, just south of Century City, and tried to think. He couldn't afford to keep chasing Cross's tail. That was a loser's game. He still had to find a way to bring Cross to him, laughable as such an idea was, considering what Cross knew about his intentions.

He'd had the asshole's phone number, just as he'd had Clarke's and Sinnott's, since he pulled it off Andy Baumhower's laptop Saturday night, but he'd been loath to use it before now. He hadn't worried that calling Clarke would send him running because Clarke hadn't been smart enough to run, but Sinnott and Cross were a different matter. He thought both men could be easily spooked into taking flight, possibly disappearing for good, so he'd resisted the temptation to contact either just for the sake of scaring them shitless.

By now, however, Cross probably knew that Clarke and Sinnott were dead and was already inclined to run, so Reddick had little to lose by giving him a call. He just couldn't imagine what he could say to the little prick over the phone to coerce him into a meeting.

Reddick was tired of the hunt and Cross had to be even more so. Maybe he'd agree to a meet just for the chance to put an end to it, once and for all, if Reddick could convince him the odds of his survival would all be in his favor.

'Bring all the friends you want, I don't give a shit. Just show up.' Would Cross take that kind of bait?

Reddick doubted it. And he didn't want to give him that much of an advantage, in any case. What he wanted was him and Cross in a room, alone, no friends and no witnesses. Five minutes, that's all he needed. But how to get the sonofabitch in that room? What besides the promise of closure did Reddick have to offer Cross as a lure?

Iris. He'd forgotten all about Iris.

Unless she'd found a way to free herself, she should still be back in the bedroom of his home where he'd left her, bound and gagged. Threatening to kill her for Cross's benefit would be pointless, he knew, because Cross wouldn't take such a threat from him seriously and wouldn't give a shit if he did. Reddick had already put a gun to the girl's head once in Cross's presence and seen what he would do about it, which was nothing. But if Iris called Cross instead of Reddick, under some false pretense, maybe she could do what Reddick couldn't, talk Cross into a rendezvous of some kind where Reddick would be waiting for him in her stead.

Of course, Iris would want no part of such a plan. She'd know she was leading Cross to his death and would refuse to make the call. But Reddick would have to convince her to do it regardless. Her status as an innocent bystander in this war between him and Cross notwithstanding, if he had to hurt her, he would. He would do whatever was necessary. He was too desperate now to keep making allowances for decency and fair play, and his goal of ensuring Dana and Jake's long-term safety, by killing the last man who could threaten it, was too close at hand.

He would try to scare Iris into calling Cross first. If that didn't work, he would find the will somewhere to win her cooperation by other means.

The stub that had once been the pinky finger on Cross's left hand hurt like a sonofabitch. Ruben had wrapped a tourniquet around it, using a strip of cloth torn from Cross's shirt sleeve, so it wasn't bleeding much anymore, but the pain was still damn near unbearable.

And yet the finger was the least of Cross's problems. They all knew now that Clarke and

270

Sinnott were indeed dead. They knew it because, right after Cross had completed the twisted self-surgery Ruben had forced upon him, Ruben's driver had driven them out to Clarke's place and, following his employer's instructions, broken into the house to find the bodies. He'd just sauntered around back, acting as cool and entitled to be there as a man from the gas company, and forced his way into the home, in broad fucking daylight, Cross had no idea how. When the big man had reappeared a few minutes later, strolling back to the car the same way he'd left it, Cross could tell by the look on his face that what he'd seen inside the house wasn't good. No translation of his all-*Espanol* report to Ruben had been necessary.

'Well? I was right, wasn't I?' he asked. 'They're dead, aren't they?'

'Yes,' Ruben said. 'They're dead.' His rage was beyond his power to completely conceal, but he was holding it in check well, demonstrating more self-control than Cross would have thought the man possessed. 'But it is strange.'

'What's strange?'

'Poeto says it doesn't look like this man Reddick was the one who killed them. He says it looks like Ben killed the other man and then died of other causes. A drug overdose, perhaps.'

'What? That's crazy!' Cross cried.

'Your friend Will was shot, yes, but with Ben's gun, and he is the only one with any visible wounds. Poeto says Ben's body is sitting in a chair and that there is a liquor bottle and pills nearby. He says there is no sign that anyone else

271

was ever there.'

Cross's head began to reel. Ruben was looking at him with open distrust now. 'Listen to me,' he said. 'I don't care what it looks like to fucking "Poeto." Reddick killed them both, just like he killed Andy. He's an ex-cop, he knows how to fix things so they appear to be something else.'

'An ex-cop? Now this Joe Reddick of yours is an ex-policeman?'

It was a detail Cross had previously neglected to mention, and not accidentally.

'Yeah. What, didn't I tell you that?'

Ruben didn't answer him right away, searching his face for the deceit he was certain had to be there. 'I think I've heard enough about this man, Perry. I want to meet him, face-to-face. You will take us to him. *Now.*'

Cross shook his head, swallowing air as if it were a horse pill. 'I can't. I don't know where he lives. But I can find out. All I need—'

Ruben lunged across the seat to slap him across the face with the back of his right hand, hard enough that Cross's butchered pinky finger was momentarily forgotten. 'Enough of this bullshit! I am out of patience with you! You will tell me where I can find this imaginary friend of yours or I will cut your lying tongue out of your mouth and make you fucking *eat it*!'

Cross was too terrified, and now in too much pain, to do much more than babble. 'I don't...'

Of his three partners, he was the only one who had never found a use for Reddick's address; Andy had taken it from Reddick himself after their accident, Ben had gotten it from Andy, and

Will had almost certainly collected this piece of data when he'd researched Reddick online. Given time, Cross could get it, too, but he had no more time. The fury on Ruben's face said his time had all run out.

Ruben closed the space between them in one pounce, locked Cross's wounded hand in a vise-like grip and said, 'Last chance, *pendejo*. Where is this Joe Reddick?'

His bloody stump of a finger clamped tight within Ruben's fist, pain searing a hole in his brain, Cross came to the very edge of blacking out. He was doomed. But then:

'Wait. Wait!'

He had remembered the call he'd placed to Iris's brother-in-law, Frank Blake, the night before, and the favor he'd asked of him.

Ruben was still leaning in to breathe into his face, eyes as bright as white flame, but he eased his grip on Cross's hand almost imperceptibly. 'Yes?'

'One call. There's a man who might know,' Cross said, gasping for air. 'Please. Let me make just one call.'

Ruben didn't move, or speak. He looked into Cross's eyes as if he were trying to light his very soul on fire. The knife had reappeared in his right hand, a silver promise of death hovering only inches from Cross's throat.

'OK.' Ruben released Cross's left hand, slid back across the car's rear seat to give him room. 'One call. No more. Go.'

Cross found his cell phone and dialed Blake's number. He was without faith and had never said a prayer in his life, but that didn't stop him now from begging Jesus Christ himself to intervene on his behalf and put Blake on the other end of the line.

Both Ruben and his driver watched intently as Cross listened to the phone ring in his ear, sounding as if it might never stop.

'Please,' Cross said out loud.

He counted seven rings, then eight.

'Hello?'

It was Blake. Cross closed his eyes and exhaled with relief. 'Frank, it's Perry. I'm calling to see if you got that info I asked for last night. On Joe Reddick?'

'Oh. Hey, Perry. Yeah, I've got it,' Blake said, his voice devoid of all enthusiasm. 'But here's the thing...'

'Blake, I'm kind of in a hurry here. I just need you to give me the guy's address right now and email me anything else you might have, ASAP.'

'I'd like to do that, Perry, but I don't know if I should. Something about this just doesn't seem kosher to me. I've been trying to reach Iris to ask her about it, but—'

'Iris? Iris has nothing to do with this, what the hell are you trying to call *her* for?' Cross wanted desperately to scream into the phone – this mindless jackass was going to get him fucking killed! – but he knew he didn't dare. If Blake hung up on him before giving up Reddick's address, Ruben might not give Cross another chance to call the asshole back.

'I just want to be sure she's OK with my doing this for you, that's all,' Blake said. 'No offense,

274

man, but I get the feeling there's more going on here than you're telling me.'

'You're right. There is. And as soon as I get a chance to breathe, I'll tell you all about it. But right now, Frank, all I can tell you is, I need you to give me the man's address and email me whatever else you've got on him, *this second*, or so help me God, brother, me and Iris both are gonna be in a world of hurt. A *world* of fucking hurt.'

'Then this does involve Iris. She's in some kind of trouble?'

'Frank, for Chrissake! I'm begging you!'

Cross began to weep, Ruben and the big man behind the Yukon's wheel staring at him, as Iris's brother-in-law took forever to make up his mind.

'OK. Fuck it,' Blake said at last. 'I'll do it. But if I find out later you've been punking me, man, I'm not gonna be happy.'

'I know that name. "Joe Reddick." Why the hell do I know that name?'

Lerner and Winn were riding a crowded elevator down from Cross's office and Lerner was talking as if they were the only two people in the car. He kept saying the same thing, more or less, over and over again, and it was starting to get on his partner's nerves.

Winn didn't respond to him, however, until the car emptied out into the lobby and they were standing at some remove from anyone else, waiting for another elevator to take them down to the building's parking lot. 'He couldn't be

275

somebody you busted once? Or a person of interest in a case you caught?'

Lerner shook his head. 'I don't think so. At least, I don't remember him as a bad guy. It's something else.'

'What else is there? If you don't know him from the Job, and you didn't meet him through Sandy...'

Sandy was Lerner's wife. He shook his head again, totally baffled. 'I dunno.'

'Tell you what. Why don't we wait 'til we get to the car and see what the computer turns up. Maybe you'll figure it out then.'

'You think he's in the system?'

'If he isn't, it sure sounds like he ought to be. He tells the girl upstairs he wants to see Cross about a burglary at the home of one of his partners over the weekend, only minutes after she takes a call from the police regarding a similar break-in at Cross's place this morning. What, you think that's just a coincidence?'

'No. I don't,' Lerner conceded. 'But—'

'First thing we're gonna do when we get to the car is check to see if there are any open warrants on Mr Reddick. Then we're gonna look for an open ticket on either of the break-ins the girl described.'

'And if we find one?'

'If we find one, we're gonna run Reddick down and ask him a few more questions. Starting with why he lied to us about his interest in Cross and ending with how he knew there'd been a burglary at the home of this guy – "Baumhower," was it? – if he wasn't the one who committed it.'

Lerner nodded. 'OK. I like it. Assuming...'

'Assuming any of this turns out to have something to do with Gillis Rainey and the case we're supposed to be working.'

'Yeah. Asuming that,' Lerner said, just as a parking lot elevator opened its doors for them and Winn stepped inside.

THIRTY-ONE

Reddick knew he'd walked into a trap the moment he passed through the door. Nobody put his lights out this time, as Ben Clarke had at Dana's three days earlier, but a similar, unpleasant surprise was waiting for him, nonetheless.

The first sign of trouble was Iris, sitting in a chair in his living room, still bound and gagged exactly as he'd left her. Other signs quickly followed: two men standing on either side of Iris, one of them Perry Cross, the other a stranger – dark-skinned and wild-eyed, smiling like Reddick was an answer to a prayer. And then there was a third man, Hispanic like Cross's friend but larger, a suited hulk stepping in from Reddick's right to jam a gun to the side of his head the second he entered the house.

Reddick's right hand instinctively flinched, his own weapon calling it to the waistband of his pants, but he stopped it cold even before the young guy with the grin said, 'Oh, no, no, no. Please, don't do that. We need to talk first.'

Ruben Lizama, Reddick thought. This had to be Ruben Lizama.

The big guy in the suit found Reddick's .40, took it away from him without a word, then practically threw him to the center of the room.

278

The smaller Hispanic turned to Cross. 'This is him? Joe Reddick?'

Cross nodded, flashing Reddick a little smile of his own. In the chair beside him, Iris whined into the gag over her mouth and squirmed, eyes begging Reddick's forgiveness.

'And I guess you must be the piece of shit known as Ruben Lizama,' Reddick said.

The grin on Cross's face fell away as the big man with the gun used it to club Reddick on the back of the head, dropping him to his knees.

'You know about me?' Still feigning good cheer, Ruben turned to Cross. 'How does he know about me?'

'I don't know. I swear,' Cross said. 'Unless...' He cast a glance in the direction of his former fiancée.

'Don't blame the lady, dickhead,' Reddick said through clenched teeth. 'If she'd wanted to sell you out, you think I would have had to leave her here all hogtied like that? She was trying to *help* your sorry ass.'

Ruben stepped forward to hover over him, no longer finding it necessary to smile. 'Perry says you are a dangerous man. That you are responsible for the deaths of three of our friends. Ben Clarke, Andy Baumhower and...' He turned back to Cross, seeking assistance.

'Will Sinnott,' Cross said.

'Yes. Will Sinnott. Is this true?'

Reddick could hear the words but he wasn't listening. His mind was on Dana and Jake, and how all the destruction he'd leveled against the earth over the last four days to protect them was

279

about to prove thoroughly meaningless.

Off a raised eyebrow from Ruben, the giant with the gun kicked Reddick in the ribs from behind, taking the wind right out of him. He toppled forward at Ruben's feet, hands barely bracing his fall before his face hit the floor. Iris was trying to scream now.

'You will answer my questions, please,' Ruben said.

His associate lifted Reddick back up by his hair, stuck his gun in Reddick's right ear. Nothing about surrender appealed to Reddick, but any move he might make to save himself now would be suicide. Stringing this asshole Lizama along, biding his time until a greater opening for taking the offensive presented itself, seemed his only immediate option for survival, and he owed it to Dana and Jake to swallow his pride and take it.

'Yeah, I wasted the fuckers,' he said. 'What else do you wanna know?'

'There. Did I tell you?' Cross said. 'Kill the sonofabitch already!'

He was a bundle of nerves, rocking on the balls of his feet as if the floor beneath them were white hot. Reddick noticed for the first time the blood-soaked bandage on his left hand.

'Man's in a hurry to shut me up,' Reddick said to Ruben. 'I were you, I'd wonder why.'

'Shut your fucking mouth!' To Ruben, Cross said, 'What is with all this talking? He's admitted he killed Ben and the others. What more do you need to know?'

'Let me see if I can guess what's going on

here,' Reddick said, still addressing Ruben. 'He told you I've got the money he owes you, or that I'm the reason he doesn't. That right?'

'I said—' Cross took a step toward him, then froze when Ruben turned his head, let his eyes alone issue a warning to back off.

To Reddick, Ruben said, 'Are you saying he's lying to me?'

'I'm saying he's full of shit. I've got nothing to do with your money and never did. He and his friends didn't have it to give you before any of us ever met.'

Unable to help himself, Cross lunged at him, lifting a leg to put a foot in his teeth. But Reddick, fully expecting the move, raised both arms to block the kick, then threw a short right hand into the younger man's groin, able to put enough behind the blow, even on his knees, to drop him like a little girl.

As Cross rolled around on the floor, moaning, hands pinned between his legs, Ruben gazed down upon him and said, 'You will tell me no more lies, Perry. Is it true, what he says? That he is not the reason you cannot pay me what I am owed?'

Cross didn't respond fast enough to suit him. Ruben kicked him in the buttocks, hard enough to bruise bone, screaming, 'Answer me!'

'Yes! Yes! We had a run of bad luck and suffered some ... some unexpected losses.' Cross sat up, glowered at Reddick. 'But we could have raised your money anyway if not for him! We would have had it days ago if he hadn't fucked things up!'

281

Reddick finally snapped, all his reasons for keeping still forgotten. He didn't give a shit what Ruben Lizama thought about him, or what Lizama held him responsible for, but hearing Cross portray him as the villain in this nightmare, rather than the victim of it, was too great an insult to bear. It had all begun with Cross, not Ben Clarke or Andy Baumhower, and the little prick and his friends had probably cost Reddick what little hope he'd ever had of living a normal life with the second family he'd built from the ashes of his first one. Hell if Reddick was going to listen to him pass the fucking buck a second longer.

Paying no heed to the gun at his head, he leapt across the floor on his hands and knees and took Cross by the throat. Cross went white, eyes bulging out of his head, mouth agape as his windpipe clamped shut beneath Reddick's iron grip. Reddick kept waiting for the big man behind him to put a bullet in his back, but the gunshot he was expecting never came. What came instead was a blow to the back of his head that filled his eyes with stars and loosened his hold on Cross's throat before the job of killing him was done.

After that, Reddick went flailing down an all-too-familiar black hole of unconsciousness.

'Why the fuck didn't you shoot him?' Cross screamed at Ruben's man Poeto, the minute he had enough breath in his lungs to speak.

Reddick lay face down on the floor, drooling into the carpet. Iris, still listing to one side in the

282

chair, was sobbing uncontrollably.

'That is not the question you should be asking, Perry,' Ruben said, opening his knife with a flourish. He reached down, grabbed Cross by the throat and yanked him to his feet. 'The question you should be asking is, why the fuck don't we shoot *you*?'

Cross didn't have an answer. He had run out of things to say in his own defense. Ruben was going to kill him, that was finally a foregone conclusion thanks to Reddick, and it was almost a relief to hear him imply that he might simply 'shoot' Cross to death, rather than carve him up like a pig in a slaughterhouse.

Cross shook his head from side to side, too weak to offer anything more in the way of a plea for mercy. Laughably, his cell phone chose this moment to chime, a new email message coming in, and the sound of it almost passed beneath his level of consciousness ... until it suddenly occurred to him who the sender might be, and what his message could contain.

He had found one more excuse for Ruben to spare his life, after all.

Detectives Winn and Lerner were caught in a traffic jam. Neither was surprised. The eastbound 10 leading into downtown was always a slog, almost never for any discernible reason, and today the backup was worse than usual, with cars limping to a brake-light crawl as far back as Western Avenue.

If they could have justified using their dash lights, they would have put them on just to see how many drivers ahead would notice and get out of their way. But they weren't sure that the mission they were on constituted an emergency of that magnitude. They were on their way to Joe Reddick's Echo Park address of record in the hope of finding him home, and how much of a danger he was to the general public they were sworn to protect was something they were still uncertain about.

They did, however, feel safe in assuming he was involved in the murder of at least one person, Perry Cross's business partner Andrew Baumhower. The computer in the car had verified that someone had indeed broken into both Baumhower's home two nights ago and Cross's residence this morning, and Baumhower had apparently been killed during the commission of the former crime. As Reddick had used the Baumhower burglary as an excuse to seek a meeting with Cross at his office, it didn't seem like much of a stretch to picture him being Baumhower's killer. Especially in light of the fact that Reddick fit the description witnesses gave the police of the crazed home invasion robber who had broken into Cross's place in Venice today.

And yet, this image of Reddick didn't particularly jibe with his lack of a criminal record, for one thing, nor his personal backstory, for another. Because what Lerner finally remembered about the man, his memory refreshed by Googling his name on the in-car computer and scanning the old news stories that came up, was that Reddick may have never before played the *perpetrator* of a violent crime, but he sure as hell had played the *victim*. Big time.

'Jesus,' Winn had said after Lerner read one of the stories about Reddick's experiences in Florida out loud to her.

'Yeah. No wonder his name was familiar to me. All the hours of Court-TV I watch every week, I must've seen a half-dozen shows about the poor bastard back then.'

'So what the hell does it mean? It's been nine years. What, he moves out to LA and waits 'til now to go off the deep end? And why go off on Cross and his partners? What's the connection?'

'I've got a far more salient question for you,' Lerner said.

'Yeah, I know: What's—'

'...any of this crap got to do with Gillis Rainey? Right. Sooner or later, No, we've got to figure it out. Otherwise...'

'Hey, you wanted a homicide to work, didn't you? Well, now we've got one.'

'Except it's not our homicide. The Baumhower case belongs to Valley, not us.'

Winn glanced over at him, flirting with a smile. 'So, you want to hand it over to them, let them talk to Mr Reddick, instead?'

Lerner just looked at her, irked once again by his partner's uncanny ability to use his own words against him.

Winn let her grin all the way out of the bag, said, 'No. I didn't think so.'

THIRTY-TWO

'Come on, Joe, wake up.' Cross slapped Reddick across the face again. 'Wake up, time's a wastin'!'

Reddick opened his eyes, saw Cross peering into them, their faces only inches apart. Reddick realized he was sitting in the chair Iris Mitchell had occupied earlier, his ankles tied together and his hands bound behind the chair's back. Iris was now laying on her side on the floor to his right, silent and motionless, leading Reddick to wonder if she hadn't just been shoved off the chair with the heel of someone's shoe.

Behind Cross, the big Mexican with the gun was still standing watch. There was no sign of Ruben Lizama in the room.

Reddick tested the tape on his wrists, rocking around on the chair with the effort, and didn't feel any give whatsoever.

'Forget it,' Cross said. 'You can't get loose. Poeto taped you up good.'

A thought suddenly occurred to Reddick: He was alive. Why was he still alive?

'I don't suppose I have to tell you what will happen if you start screaming,' Cross said. 'Or do I have to actually demonstrate?'

Reddick noticed now that he was holding a

286

knife in his one good hand. There was a renewed confidence about him; his eyes were still wild, but not with fear. This looked like madness.

'What you've gotta do is eat shit and die, asshole,' Reddick said. But his growing unease was obvious. He should be dead. Why the hell hadn't they killed him already?

'You're angry at me,' Cross said. 'Well, I can sort of see how you might be.' He leaned in to give Reddick a close-up look at the blade of the knife. 'But imagine how angry I am at *you*. How many reasons you've given me to do some really fucked up things to you before I kill you.' He laughed. 'And I *am* going to kill you. I think we can do away with any doubts you might have about that right now.'

So Ruben was going to let Cross do the honors, Reddick thought. But why? Shouldn't Cross be dead himself by now?

'What the fuck is this?' Reddick asked. 'Where's Lizama?'

'He had a little errand to run. He'll be back. In the meantime, you and I are going to have a little chat about money.'

None of this was making any sense. Reddick was beginning to feel queasy. 'What?'

'See, I got this idea while you were unconscious. I can't give Ruben the money I owe him, but maybe you can. You're a retired cop. Cops have pensions. If you've been a smart investor, you could be pretty well off. In fact, you could be loaded.'

The truth was, Reddick did have a decent nest egg socked away, built around his RBPD pension. But if Cross or Lizama were insane enough to think he was going to pull so much as a dime from it for either of *them*...

'You're dreaming,' he told Cross.

'Yeah. We figured you'd have that reaction. A badass like you isn't going to give up his life's savings – hell, his children's inheritance – just to save himself a little pain, right? You've gotta be properly motivated.'

Reddick was beginning to sense where this was going. He didn't know how it was possible, but he couldn't think of anything else Cross and his friends could possibly threaten him with and expect him to cave.

'Where's Lizama?' he asked again, voice rising to meet the level of his panic.

Cross smiled, confirming Reddick's worst fears. 'He's gone to get Dana and Jake,' he said.

Dana was losing her mind. Jake was going stir-crazy at the motel and she hadn't heard from Joe in almost twenty-four hours. Her calls just kept going straight to his voicemail.

He'd given her specific instructions to sit tight, but it was getting harder to do with each passing minute. The gravity of what she'd done – encouraged her husband to kill four people for the sake of their son – had finally begun to sink in. As had the depth of the love she had for Reddick, no matter how emotionally damaged he might be. She loved him, almost as much as she loved Jake, and yet she'd all but sent him to his death by granting him permission to go on this insane manhunt of his, in search of men who, by his estimation, had money enough to pay a small army to kill him if they couldn't kill him themselves.

If she could have thought of a way to stop him on her own, to undo the terrible mistake she'd made in letting him go in the first place, Dana would have done it. But she knew that anything she tried now would only run the risk of making things worse. Calling the police was out of the question. Reddick had already killed one man, maybe more, and the police would treat him accordingly. Would Joe just throw his hands up without a fight if they found him? Or was he too far gone to care whether he died an old man in a prison cell, or as the man he was today, in a hail of police gunfire?

Dana couldn't say.

And it was this uncertainty that ultimately resigned her to doing nothing. She and Jake would stay where they were, as Reddick had instructed, and hope – *pray* – for the best. They were safe here, at least that much she had no doubts about, and their safety was, after all, what her husband was out there risking everything for.

She just had to convince Jake to endure the motel a little longer. His boredom had the boy getting into everything. In the three days they'd been here, he'd opened all the dresser drawers and bathroom cabinets a dozen times, and at least once, he'd dumped the entire contents of her purse on the floor, including the gun Joe had given her for their protection. Luckily, Dana was in the room at the time and had snatched the weapon up before Jake could touch it, but the close call had scared her half to death, enough that she had pulled the clip from the gun once she was out of Jake's sight and hidden both where he could never reach them, between a blanket and extra pillow on a high rack in the closet.

Had she stopped to think about it, she would have realized how furious Joe would be to learn she'd done this, stored the semi-automatic, unloaded, where she couldn't possibly reach it quickly if she needed to. But it had been a long time since she'd stopped worrying about her and Jake being found here. How could they be? They were forty miles from home, registered in a motel none of them had ever been to before. Only Joe knew they were here.

She and Jake had nothing to fear.

Ruben had never spent much time in Orange County, but he knew how to get to Irvine. You just drove south from Los Angeles on the San Diego Freeway for about forty minutes, or until you could literally see the fortunes of the city shift from want to prosperity, shard-shaped, mirror-skinned skyscrapers rising up from the earth on every side.

Though he rarely drove himself anywhere, this was one trip Ruben was happy to make on his own. Even the impasses in traffic that intermittently slowed his progress couldn't dampen his mood. The more he thought about it, the more he had to admit Perry Cross was right: On some level, Joe Reddick was to blame for his troubles. And soon, Reddick would be made to pay for it.

With his blood, certainly, and if Ruben was lucky, many thousands of US dollars, as well, though this last remained a mere hope. It had been clever of Cross to think of it, keeping Reddick alive long enough to see if he had the resources to provide Ruben with the quarter million dollars he'd come here for. Many Americans had that kind of money saved for their retirement, why shouldn't Reddick? Still, Ruben wasn't making this drive to Irvine with the expectation it would result in his getting paid; that would have been foolish. No, he was driving down to Irvine, to find Reddick's wife and little boy, more to satisfy his growing need for vengeance than any desire to be compensated. What shape his vengeance would take he didn't yet know, and was in no hurry to consider. When the time came, his hostages in hand, he would let his black heart decide what to do with them, as he always did in such matters.

As for Cross, Ruben had already decided to rescind the deal he had struck with the *pendejo* only minutes ago: A quick, painless death if their efforts to extort $250,000 from Reddick paid off. Because a quick, painless death was unbefitting for the injuries Cross and his friends had inflicted upon Ruben. Whether he got paid now or not, Ruben had been cheated and lied to, taken for a fool and forced to expend time and energy to claim what he should have been freely given. Four days earlier than agreed or not, he should have been home by now, the money he'd entrusted to Ben Clarke laundered as promised and back in his possession. Instead, he was still

291

in Los Angeles, driving a goddamn rental car into Orange County, wrestling with his meager conscience over the damage he may soon feel compelled to do against a little boy he had yet to meet.

He was happy, yes, excited by the prospect of bringing Joe Reddick to his knees, because that was the rightful fate of anyone who ever crossed Ruben Lizama, however indirectly. But Ruben's happiness was like morning fog – it very quickly melted away – and now it was gone.

Leaving nothing but animal fury to take its place.

THIRTY-THREE

'What do you want me to do?' Reddick asked.

The words stuck in his throat like a nest of thorns, so much did capitulation turn his stomach. He was hanging by a mere thread of sanity, every ounce of his strength gone, and the only thing keeping him going now was the fear of what could happen to Dana and Jake if he didn't surrender, fully and unconditionally, to Cross and his friend Ruben Lizama.

'Do you have the money?' Cross asked.

'Yes. At least, I think so.'

A credit card. Dana's goddamn credit card, the one they'd had to use to get her registered into the motel, and the one she'd apparently used out there several times since. It shouldn't have been important, it would have been paranoia to even think of it, but Cross had gotten hold of their credit histories somehow, some friend of his had sent a copy of them to his cell phone, for Chrissake, and the charges in Irvine had pointed Cross to where Dana and Jake were hiding out just as surely as a neon sign.

Now Lizama was on his way to find them, a sadistic psychopath with a grudge to bear, and Reddick knew if he allowed himself to imagine what such a man might do to them for as long as a *second* ... he would snap for good. Give up the ghost of his sanity once and for all and seal everyone's fate. He had already come close to doing exactly that once, immediately after Cross had told him where Ruben Lizama was, and why. But after Cross had stuffed a rag in his mouth to stifle his screams and warned him to chill out, he'd found the strength to pull back. Breathe. Close his eyes and surrender.

Surrender.

'Can you get your hands on it?' Cross asked, ready to put the gag back in Reddick's mouth at any time. 'Electronically, I mean?'

Reddick tried to think. 'I don't know. I can try.'

'Try?' Cross laughed, a little boy finding mirth in the throes of an ant he was torching with a magnifying glass. 'Man, you'd better do more than that.'

It was clear to Reddick that Cross was mad; his mind had given way under the pressure Reddick and Ruben had separately exerted and his fear and desperation to survive had been supplanted by something else, something Reddick found far more disturbing: relief. He had to know that Ruben was going to kill him, that none of this was going to save him, and yet Cross was acting as if the two men had struck a bargain of some kind, like if Reddick came through with the money, he might still have something to gain from it. But what? What could Lizama have possibly promised him?

* * *

294

Escape.

Cross kept rolling the word around in his mind, over and over again, a goal to pursue like the gold ring on a merry-go-round.

Escape.

Fuck a painless death. There was no such thing. Death of any kind was defeat, the end to a story he had only begun to write, and Cross wasn't ready to just bend over and take it just because Ruben had promised him it wouldn't hurt. He could still run away. He had money enough for that. There were places in the world he could hide that neither Ruben nor Reddick would ever think to look for him, and, properly assimilated, he'd be impossible to find even if they cared to try. There'd be no honor in running, it would hurt his pride for years to come, but he'd be alive, and he would find a way to rebuild himself from the ground up and reclaim all that he'd lost. He could do it, he was sure of it.

But first he had to escape.

He thought he knew how he could do it. He dared not try to take on the gorilla Ruben had left here to watch over him on his own; all he had was a knife, and the big man had a gun, and even if he were unarmed, the giant Mexican could probably kill Cross with his bare hands, Ruben's knife stuck to the hilt in his fucking throat. But Reddick was another matter. Reddick might have a chance against Poeto and, more importantly, wouldn't hesitate to go after the big man regardless of the odds against him. All Reddick needed was an opportunity to try.

295

It wouldn't have to be much of a fight. Thirty seconds, perhaps even less. If the two assholes could just keep each other occupied for thirty seconds, it would be enough for Cross to hit the door running and never look back.

Cross took out his smartphone and opened up its online browser. 'We'll use my phone,' he said to Reddick. 'You tell me where the accounts are and how to log in, I'll do all the data entry.'

'That won't work,' Reddick said.

'What? Why the fuck not?'

'Because I don't remember the passwords. They're stored on my computer, I've never bothered to memorize them.'

'That's bullshit!' Cross said, though he was secretly overjoyed. Reddick was making this easier for him than he could have ever hoped. He needed an excuse to cut Reddick free and had been planning to pretend his phone had run out of battery power, ask if Reddick had another Internet-ready computer somewhere in the house. Now, no such feeble ploy on his part would be required.

Still, for Poeto's sake, he had to put on a show of outrage. 'You're stalling!'

'No. I'm not,' Reddick said forcefully. 'I can get into the accounts from my own machine, but that's the only way.'

Cross just stared at him.

'For Chrissake, it's the truth!'

Cross looked over his shoulder at Poeto, as if to say, 'Can you believe this shit?' And then, before the giant Mexican could misinterpret the gesture as a request for instructions – assuming he knew enough English to have followed a word of what had just been said – Cross turned back to Reddick and said, 'OK. Shit. Where is this computer of yours? And you'd better not fucking say "at the office."'

'No, it's here. In the bedroom.'

Cross looked at Poeto again, feigning great annoyance. 'We've gotta move him to the bedroom. He needs to use his own computer. *La computadora. ¿Comprende?*'

The big man shrugged his assent and took a step forward, seeking to give Reddick a better look at the gun in his hand in case he'd forgotten it was there.

'You try anything,' Cross said to Reddick, 'everybody dies. You, your wife, the boy – everybody. Got it?'

Reddick nodded.

Cross crouched down, used Ruben's knife to cut Reddick's legs free. Then he went around the chair behind Reddick to do the same for his hands. He leaned in, his face out of Poeto's view, and whispered something only Reddick could hear:

'Don't move.'

He quickly cut the tape from Reddick's wrists, using as little motion as possible in an effort to make the act imperceptible to the big man with the gun. As he'd hoped, confused though he had to be, Reddick followed his orders and remained still, doing nothing to suggest to the giant watching them that his hands were not still bound together behind the chair.

Now Cross pretended to hesitate, leaning in

and then back out again, as if he'd lost the nerve to use the knife at all. He finally straightened up, backed away from the chair, and looked to Poeto for help. A coward afraid of his own shadow.

'I can't. I don't trust him,' he said, holding the knife out for Ruben's driver to take.

Poeto didn't move.

'You do it!' Cross screamed, pushing the knife at the big man like it was something he could no longer stand to touch.

For a moment, Ruben's man still didn't move. Then, finally, he mumbled something under his breath, shook his head, and stepped forward to relieve Cross of the knife.

Reddick didn't waste any time trying to figure out what Cross was up to. That was something he decided he could worry about later. At the exact moment of exchange, while the big Mexican's attention was on almost everything else but him, Reddick leapt from the chair. He snatched at Poeto's gun with his left hand and threw a hard right to the big man's face, a punch he fully expected his survival to hinge upon. Had the giant known it was coming, the blow might have meant little to him, but the element of surprise lent it the power to stun Reddick was hoping for. As Cross clumsily stepped out of the way, Poeto staggered backward beneath Reddick's weight, nose gushing blood, and crashed to the floor with an audible grunt, Reddick taking pains to drive a knee into his diaphragm on impact. As the air flew out of him, Reddick threw two more rights at the big man's face, in rapid succession, and continued to fight for control of the gun with his left. In the struggle, the weapon went off once, twice, the rounds hitting nothing that Reddick could see.

He caught a blur of movement to one side: Cross, running for the door. Had Poeto given him time, Reddick would have next seen Iris – all but forgotten by the three men in the room – stick her bound legs out to trip Cross up, send him tumbling face first to the floor right beside her. But Reddick's attention was drawn elsewhere when Poeto tossed him off his chest like a toy he was tired of playing with, fighting back now, Reddick's moment of holding the upper hand having quickly come and gone.

Poeto was rearing up on one elbow, bringing his gun around to put a bullet in Reddick's face, when the front door burst open and two people with weapons of their own stormed into the room, a familiar black woman in a gray suit at the point.

'Police! Freeze!'

Ruben's man looked straight down the barrel of Finola Winn's gun, saw only an old female *mayate* he didn't think had the nerve to shoot. Winn let him make a quarter turn toward her before she put two rounds in his chest, not willing to trust that only one would have sufficed.

Now Lerner, gun held firmly out in front of him, played the same scene out with Cross, who had scrambled back to his feet just before the cops made their entrance. He was still holding Ruben Lizama's knife in his right hand.

'Drop it!' Lerner said.

'That's right, Cross. Drop it,' Reddick said,

slowly rising up from the floor. 'It's not his job to kill you, it's mine.'

'Shut up, Mr Reddick,' Winn ordered.

Lerner was still waiting for Cross to comply, his nerves visibly wearing thin. 'I'm not gonna tell you again,' he said. 'Put the knife down!'

'I'm not going to stop, Cross,' Reddick said. 'No matter where you go, no matter where you hide. You've got to know that by now.'

'I told you to shut up!' Winn snapped.

Cross glanced about the room, eyes flitting from one face to the next. He looked down at Iris, smiled, then turned the smile on Reddick. 'Fuck you,' he said.

He had the knife blade in his throat before either cop could stop him. His jugular spraying the room red, eyes rolling up in the back of his head, he drifted to the floor like a long length of ribbon, convulsed for several seconds, and grew still.

'Jesus,' Lerner said, as Iris broke out in muffled hysterics again.

While her partner checked Cross for a pulse, Winn turned to Reddick, her incredulity only barely contained. 'What the hell was going on here?' she demanded.

'I don't have time to answer that right now. There's a man on his way to Irvine to kill my wife and son!' Reddick put a hand in his trouser pocket for his phone.

Winn ordered him to halt, her service weapon trained right at his head, but Reddick paid her no heed. He dialed Dana's number instead and brought the phone up to his ear, mumbling a

300

prayer only God was meant to hear. How long had he been unconscious before Cross brought him to? Could Ruben already be in Irvine?

Please, Dana, he thought. Answer the phone. *Please.*

The TV was the only thing that could keep Jake still anymore, so it was on in their room almost constantly. Dana kept having to tell him to turn down the volume, and he had twice, but when she'd gone to the bathroom a moment ago, he'd cranked it up again and she had yet to notice, her mind on so many other things.

Had her phone been on vibrate, she might have seen it shudder across the room's only table when Reddick's call came in. But the ringer was on and the sound of it was buried hopelessly beneath the din of the clamorous cartoons Jake was watching. Sitting on the bed, Jake on the floor at its feet, she flipped through a new magazine she'd bought that morning and tried to pretend the television wasn't even on.

The SIG Sauer P220, still unloaded and banished to the closet, was far beyond her easy reach.

If he hadn't been in such a hurry, Ruben would have hung around the motel, watching people come and go until Reddick's wife and son revealed themselves to him. But he couldn't wait for that. He had to get back to Los Angeles and the mess he'd left in Poeto's lap before something went wrong, either the big man killed one of the three people in his charge or one of them

301

killed him. Any combination of various catastrophes was possible. So Ruben found the room he was looking for the fastest way he knew how: by asking the motel clerk.

She was alone in the empty lobby when he came in, just an overweight black woman in a ghastly green uniform who, at the sight of the knife in his hand – Ruben always liked to carry two – let him guide her into a back office without offering much more in the way of argument than a tiny squeal. At his instructions, she used the computer in the office to identify the room in which the 'Reddick' party was staying, then created a copy of the door key for him. Finding her unwavering cooperation more generous than pathetic, he thanked her for her time by killing her quickly, in a way far too clinical for him to derive any pleasure from it.

Reddick's wife and son were in room 108, at ground level, at the far end of the parking lot. It was the perfect location for Ruben's purposes: no stairs to climb and adjacent to only one room. He would be able to get in and get out easily, with just a minimal chance of encountering other motel guests. He waited for the only visible witnesses – an elderly couple inching to their parked car like snails in winter – to get in the vehicle and drive off, then hurriedly crossed the lot to room 108.

He stood at the door and listened for sounds of life on the other side. He heard a television playing, volume cranked up high, the silly voices and sound effects of what could only be a cartoon. He slipped the card key silently into its slot

302

with his left hand, held the knife at the ready with his right. He would kill the woman immediately, because he didn't need them both alive to get what he wanted out of Reddick, then render the child unconscious before loading him into his rental car and making a hasty escape. It was going to be easy.

He fully inserted the card, jerked down on the door handle with the lock's flash of green, and charged into the room.

It was empty.

The lights were on, the TV was blaring, but no one was here. Or so it appeared, until a black man larger than Poeto, with a mouth sprinkled with missing teeth and a scowl to rival that of any butcher Ruben had ever employed, stepped around a corner into his view, holding a cell phone up to his ear with one hand and a big-barreled revolver in the other.

'Yeah, he just showed up,' Orvis Andrews said calmly into the phone. 'Hold on.'

He raised the gun, shot Ruben dead-center in the face. Then he closed in, hovered over the dying man's body, and put one more in his chest, just to be on the safe side.

THIRTY-FOUR

It was over.

Reddick's relief was like a drug coursing through his veins, dissolving all fears, luring him toward sleep. What happened to him now held no importance. Dana and Jake were safe. Nothing else mattered, past, present, or future.

'I'm sorry,' Iris Mitchell said.

She was sitting across from him on his couch, uniformed cops and coroner's techs scurrying around the living room all about them. Reddick was right back where he'd started, in the same chair he'd been in when Cross had cut him loose, but this time his hands were bound behind his back by a pair of handcuffs, courtesy of one of the detectives who'd saved their lives; the male one, Lerner.

'For what?' Reddick asked. Lerner and his female partner, Winn, had stepped a few feet away to confer in private, but Reddick took care to keep his voice down, anyway.

'For what they did to you. Perry and his friends.' She paused. 'It was incredibly cruel, so ... I'm sorry.'

Reddick started to say thanks, just nodded his head instead.

'Of course, they didn't know who you were.

What you'd already been through, I mean.
Maybe if they had—'

'What? They would have treated me differently?' Reddick had to snort at the thought. 'I
don't think so. I think you give them too much
credit, Clarke and your fiancé, in particular.'

'Please. Don't call him that.' She glanced at
Cross's body, still waiting under a blood-soaked
sheet on the floor for the coroner's man to finally grant its removal from the room.

'Cross wasn't your fiancé?'

'He was, but that's not the point. I'd just prefer
not to think of him in those terms, anymore.
When I do, I feel unbelievably ... *stupid.*'

She hugged herself for warmth, Reddick
saying nothing.

'Are they going to be OK? Your wife and little
boy?' Iris asked.

The cops had let Reddick speak briefly to
Dana on the phone, and she'd put Jake on the
line for a split second, just so he could hear for
himself that his son was really alive and well,
and emotionally unscathed from the day's events
at the motel.

'I think so. They're both pretty tough. They
might have a sleepless night or two for a while,
but with any luck, that'll be about it.'

'I'm glad. How—'

Reddick shook her off, said, 'I think we'd
better keep what happened at the motel between
me and the detectives. The less you know about
it, the less reason they're gonna have to think
you were an accessory to all this.'

He was right. If the man who'd killed Ruben at

305

the motel down in Irvine had been placed there by Reddick himself, as she suspected but no one would confirm, it would hardly help her to know all the hows and whys of it, no matter how badly her curiosity called out for such disclosure.

'What about you?' she asked. 'Will *you* be OK?'

'I'll be fine.' He didn't look fine or feel fine, but this was the kind of false optimism he had to put stock in now.

'What do you think they'll do to you?'

'If I lawyer-up well? I might get off with ten or fifteen years. Maybe see the outside again just in time to attend Jake's college graduation.'

'And if you don't?'

He smiled. 'I think you can guess the answer to that. Two counts of murder, throw in a couple for kidnapping and B and E ... They'd have to send me the graduation video, something I could watch in my cell until I passed on.'

He chuckled to ease the severity of the joke, but Iris couldn't manage doing the same.

'Whatever I can do to help you, I will,' she said.

Reddick nodded, turned grim again. 'You've already done more than enough. But thanks.'

'You can't really be serious?' Winn asked.

Lerner looked away, toward Reddick and Iris Mitchell on the other side of the room, both of them just sitting there looking like survivors of a coal mine disaster. 'I don't know. Maybe I'm just getting soft in my old age,' he said.

'You mean soft in the head, don't you? We

can't just let this guy skate. Even if we could pull it off—'

'Yeah, yeah, OK. I was nuts to even consider it, you're right.' He tipped his head in Reddick's direction. 'But I mean, look at the poor bastard, No. You know what his story is, what those two just told us happened here. You telling me he's the bad guy in all this? Hell, the bad guys in all this are *dead*.'

'And exactly whose fault is that? By his own admission—'

'It's his fault, sure. Technically, anyway, in two out of six cases. Or seven, if you count this guy Lizama down in Irvine.'

'"Technically"? Norm, do you hear what you're saying?'

'Yes. Yes!' Winn was looking at him like he'd just grown a striped horn in the middle of his forehead. 'Like you said, I asked for a homicide and, Jesus, Mary, and Joseph, No, did I ever get my wish. We've got seven assholes known dead, including Rainey, and Reddick did at least two of 'em. If it were anybody else, I'd be as ready as you to lock his ass up and throw away the key, but *this guy*—'

Lerner was preaching to the choir and didn't know it. Winn was only slightly less conflicted about Reddick than he, because Lerner was right: Assuming the statements they'd just gotten from Reddick and Iris Mitchell were to be believed, the only real victim in this whole mess was Reddick. Perry Cross and his friends had themselves been murderers of a sort, the apparently accidental nature of Gillis Rainey's death

307

notwithstanding, and Reddick had had every right to believe they would kill again, given sufficient excuse.

Going vigilante on four people to protect his family had been a tragic error on his part, and criminal by any definition of the word, but considering the man's history – the unthinkable loss he had suffered once already at the hands of an animal not unlike Ben Clarke or Ruben Lizama – it was hard, if not impossible, to condemn his actions. Winn herself could not say with any degree of certainty that she would have done differently, under identical circumstances. That didn't make Reddick innocent, but it did make it easy to wish that Lady Luck would get off the poor bastard's back and give him a fucking break for a change. Now and forever.

'What are you suggesting we do?' Winn asked. 'Even if we were stupid enough to try, how in the hell do we explain seven dead vics without pinning at least two of them on him?'

Lerner couldn't hide his surprise, nor his elation. The intransigent hardliner their fellow officers all liked to call 'No Winn' was actually acting as if she could be coerced into straying from the letter of the law for once. It was probably just a mirage, he knew, but Lerner went with it anyway, said, 'Ruben Lizama and his big buddy over there. If what Reddick and the lady say about them is true, they were a couple of really bad hombres. Really bad. Lizama in particular.'

Winn didn't need to hear another word to know where this was going, but all the same, she

308

said, 'I'm listening.'

Lerner checked to make sure no one was close enough to overhear, lowered his voice to just above a whisper. 'Well, Lizama and his boy being responsible for the murders of Cross and his three friends wouldn't exactly strike anybody as highly improbable, would it? They owed him money and couldn't pay off. Mitchell said the debt was over two hundred and fifty Gs, for Chrissake. Hell, what happened to those guys is what always happens to people who stiff Mexican drug families out of a quarter million bucks. Am I right?'

'You are. But—'

'I know what you're gonna say. You're gonna say the evidence won't add up. And for the most part, it probably won't. But a dirtbag like Lizama, assuming he's everything they say he is, who the hell's gonna care? The Feds? The authorities down in Mexico? I don't think so. They've probably both been trying to put this guy out of business for years. We hand them his head on a silver platter – four homicides he's tailor-made to fit – I kind of doubt they're gonna spend a whole lot of time worrying it might be a frame-up.'

Lerner was oversimplifying matters, to be sure, but Winn couldn't argue with the crux of his logic. Given a choice between two ways to close the books on Ruben Lizama – one imperfect but quick and dirty, the other a convoluted, open-ended mess that could take months of investigative legwork to resolve – what cop in his right mind, regardless of the agency in-

309

volved, would choose the latter? Especially when a killer like Ruben Lizama, who was dead and beyond giving a damn, was the only one likely to be hurt?

'Even if all you're saying is true –' Winn said, 'and I'm not deranged enough yet to admit that it is – you seem to be forgetting one thing.'

'Yeah? What's that?'

Winn tipped her head in the direction of Reddick and Iris Mitchell. 'Them. They'd have to go along for the ride. Almost none of what they've just told us would jibe with your "Lizama wasted them all" scenario. Would it?'

Lerner shook his head. 'No. You've got a point there.'

'Of course, people's stories change,' Winn said. Imagining what Reddick's wife and kids, butchered in their sleep, must have looked like nine years ago in Florida, and how trying to live with that kind of memory might have tested her own ideas about the senselessness of street justice. 'If we interviewed them again, they might remember things differently. Maybe a lot differently. That's how it usually happens, isn't it?'

Lerner gave his partner a long look, trying to spot some telltale sign that this was not Finola Winn speaking at all, but an identical twin born on another planet who'd taken her place while his head was turned. 'Only one way to find out,' he said.

Reddick didn't know what the hell was going on. He should be getting booked right about now. Instead, he was still here at his home, watching Winn and Lerner break up their little chat and head back his way, looking like they hadn't already been given enough information to ensure his conviction, ten times over, for the murder of two men.

'We're going to need to go over a few more things with the both of you,' Winn said, speaking to Reddick and Iris Mitchell as if they were one and the same person. 'Starting with Andrew Baumhower.'

'What about him?' Iris asked.

Now Reddick knew for certain something was up. One of the cops should be taking Iris aside to question her individually, while the other remained here to do a one-on-one with him, just as they had earlier. Questioning them together, the two detectives working as a pair, was nothing short of inept, an invitation for Reddick and Iris to listen to each other's answers and tell a story to match.

Winn consulted her notes. 'You said Mr Reddick here admitted killing Mr Baumhower in your presence. Is that correct?'

Iris gave Reddick a sheepish glance, apologizing the only way she could. 'Yes. But—'

'Did he describe the killing to you? Can you remember exactly what he said?'

'Look—' Reddick said, not wanting to see Iris harassed on his account any more than she already had been.

But Lerner said, 'You'll get your turn to speak shortly, Mr Reddick. In the meantime, kindly keep your mouth shut, OK?'

Reddick started to argue, decided to hold his tongue.

'Ms Mitchell?' Winn said, turning Iris's attention back to her question.

Iris gave the matter some thought. 'I can't remember exactly, but I think he said...' She took her mind back to the morning before in Reddick's car, after he'd dragged her out of Cross's condo and she'd posed the question to him, point-blank: 'Did you kill Andy?' What had he answered?

And then it came to her.

'Oh, my God,' she said.

Winn studied her. 'What?'

'He never answered the question.'

'Excuse me?'

'He never actually said he killed anybody. I realize now I'd just assumed he killed Andy because he kept avoiding the question.'

'You're saying he *didn't* confess to Baumhower's murder?'

'No. I mean, yes. That's what I'm saying.'

'Then you can't say for certain that Mr Reddick was the person who broke into Mr Baumhower's residence and killed him Friday evening. For all you know, that individual could have been someone else.'

'Someone else?'

'Like this Ruben Lizama character, for instance,' Lerner said, looking straight at Reddick as he did so. *Are you paying attention, sport?*

'You've both told us Baumhower and your fiancé, Mr Cross, along with Mr Clarke and Mr Sinnott, owed Lizama a great deal of money,'

312

Winn said. 'Money they apparently didn't have. Isn't that right?'

'Yes. Perry and Will both told me that was the case.'

'So isn't it possible – or more likely, even – that it was Lizama, and not Mr Reddick, who broke into Mr Baumhower's home and killed him, in an attempt to retrieve what Baumhower and the others owed him?'

Reddick couldn't believe what he was hearing, but hell if he was going to question it. One wrong word and whatever spell Winn and Lerner were under might break, bringing them all back to reality with a vengeance.

'Is it possible?' Iris asked Winn. And then, finally and inevitably, the clouds parted and she was able to see the door that was not only being held open for her, but through which she was being masterfully steered. 'Yes, of course,' she said. She turned to Reddick, braved a small smile. 'In fact, I'm almost sure that's what must have happened.'

Lerner stole a glance at his partner, who betrayed no indication of noticing. Instead, her stoic expression never faltering, Winn flipped to a new page in her notebook and, in a perfect imitation of a boxer too tired to answer the bell, said to Iris and Reddick, 'In that case, I guess we'd better get your statements all over again. Just to be sure there's nothing else you two might have remembered, for lack of a better word, "incorrectly."'

She didn't wink, but she didn't need to. Reddick caught her meaning just fine without.

THIRTY-FIVE

Jake and Reddick were four frames into their second game, Jake having bounced his bowling ball off the bumpers in the gutter fortuitously enough to roll his second strike of the day, when his son pointed at somebody behind Reddick and said, 'Hey, Daddy! There's the man who hugged Mommy at the motel!'

Reddick turned around and saw Orvis Andrews entering the building, scanning the lanes at Jewel City Bowl in Glendale for the man he'd come here to see. Reddick raised an arm to wave him over, then said to Jake, 'You go ahead and keep playing, OK? Mr Andrews and I have to talk for a quick minute.'

'What are you going to talk about?' Jake asked.

'Just things. I'll be back in a second.'

Reddick went up to meet Andrews halfway and the two men shook hands, then found a table. Mid-morning on a Saturday, there were a lot of empty ones to choose from.

'This is your idea of a joke, right?' Andrews asked. Reddick couldn't tell if he was amused or not.

'Let's just say, I thought it would be an appropriate setting.'

Andrews nodded, taking no offense, and looked casually over at Jake. 'How's little man doing? OK?'

'He's fine. Been asking a lot of questions I can't answer, of course, but other than that, he's good.'

'And the wife?'

'She's good, too. Thanks for asking.'

Andrews nodded again, let out a sigh. 'I've been thinkin' about it a lot. What might've happened to 'em if I hadn't been there. 'Cause that cat Lizama, he was really bad news, wasn't he?'

'Yeah. He was,' Reddick said.

Andrews grinned. 'Course, people say the same shit about me. Which is why you gave me the job in the first place, I suppose. You knew I could do what might need doin'.'

'Something like that.'

Six days ago, when Reddick had shown up unannounced at Andrews's front door seeking his help, he had told the big man in no uncertain terms what he wanted done. He needed somebody to go down to the Embassy Court Motel in Irvine and watch over Dana and Jake; take a room of his own and exchange it with theirs. But all that was the easy part, the part any thug with a gun and a mean streak could probably handle. The hard part would be following Reddick's instructions, regarding what to do if anybody – *anybody* – walked into room 108 without invitation, to the letter: *blow their fucking brains out.* No questions asked, no hesitation. If Andrews wasn't down with that, Reddick had come to the wrong address.

Andrews had said he was down with it, no

315

problem.

Reddick was, after all, offering him a deal he could hardly pass up: His assistance in exchange for all the video Reddick had shot of him rolling the rock out at Arrowhead Lanes in Lancaster four days earlier. Using an arm his eleven million dollar lawsuit against the city of Los Angeles claimed he couldn't use anymore. If Andrews went down to Irvine, Reddick had said, he'd make sure the City Attorney never saw the video, and hell if that didn't strike Orvis as a better than fair trade.

'You know what they're going to do with you yet?' Reddick asked him now. 'They gonna violate you or...?'

It was the great risk Andrews had taken in helping Reddick out, violating his parole by getting caught holding – let alone actually using – a loaded handgun.

Andrews laughed. 'Shit, they like to talk like they might,' he said, 'but they ain't foolin' nobody. Lizama killed that poor girl in the office and then broke into my room, big ass knife in his hand, hopin' to do the same to some other de-fenseless lady. How the hell they gonna explain violatin' my parole to all the people think I'm a hero for wastin' the crazy motherfucker?' He paused, laughter petering out until only a wide grin was left. 'Man, you should'a seen the look on that fool's face when he seen me step into that room. It would've made your fuckin' day.'

Reddick couldn't help but smile at the thought. 'Yeah. I bet it would have.' He looked over at Jake, found himself tickled by the sight of him,

316

hunched down low, trying now to roll two balls down the lane at one time.

'So how 'bout you?' Andrews asked. 'Guess they ain't gonna lock you up either, huh?'

'I think they'll get around to it, eventually,' Reddick said. 'They just haven't figured out the best way to do it, yet.'

It was the most honest answer he could give. He really didn't know what was going to happen to him, whether he'd be a free man for the rest of his life or would be sitting in a holding cell tomorrow, awaiting permanent residency in the state pen. Winn and Lerner had given him every break possible but the task of saving his sorry ass was monumental and there was only so much they could do without putting their badges and pensions at risk. If the Feds or the DA's office decided not to play ball, knowing as they surely must that what they were being asked to do was give a murderer a free pass out of the goodness of their hearts, the whole apparatus of lies and half-truths being told for his benefit would collapse and Reddick would go down with it. Nobody involved was a fool. The only question was how much currency Reddick's tragic past – and present – would hold with them all, and for how long.

'Daddy! Come on!' Jake called.

'Hey, that's my cue to jet, I guess,' Andrews said. He slid a small digital video camera across the tabletop at Reddick, the same one Reddick had used to record his bowling performance in Lancaster almost two weeks ago. Reddick had given it to him Sunday afternoon as his part of the bargain they had struck.

'I'm not gonna find any homegrown porn on here, am I?'

'Naw. You ain't gonna find nothin' on there. You can trust me on *that*.' Andrews laughed and eased his way up from the table, demonstrating a renewed reluctance to ever use his 'injured' arm for leverage. 'You sure you ain't got no other copies somewhere? You didn't make at least one?'

Reddick shook his head. 'Not a chance. Looks like I'll just have to tell the City Attorney that all that video I shot of you throwing strikes with that right arm out in Lancaster last week just got erased during transfer to my computer. Clumsy me.'

'And if he don't wanna believe that?'

'Then he can kiss my ass. And for that matter, so can you.' Reddick stood up and shook Andrews's hand again, more warmly this time because he expected it to be the last. 'You're quite the gangster yourself, big man. I've got no illusions about that. But you came through for me, big time, and I'll always be grateful for that. Good luck, huh?'

'Yeah. You, too, brother. Tell the little lady I said hi.'

Andrews waved to Jake with his left hand and hobbled out of the bowling alley, right arm held close to his side like a clipped wing.

Later, as Reddick drove Jake back home to Dana, he thought about the words Andrews had used for her: *the little lady*. Was that what she was to Reddick? His little lady? Or was she just somebody who had been, once? Even that part of Reddick's life remained undecided. His wife hadn't yet retracted her declared intent to divorce him, so as far as he knew, the divorce was still on, but it seemed the last twelve days had somehow calmed the waters between them, given them both a greater appreciation for what they had as a couple and as a family.

Dana had always loved him, just as he loved her; it wasn't a lack of affection that had come between them. It was his smothering over-protectiveness, his crazed belief that it was his duty to shield her and Jake from all harm, no matter the cost. He was overcompensating, try-ing to do for this family what he hadn't been able to do for his first, and the effect on her was stifling. But now Dana had been given a good, long look at the flip side to his madness; she had seen for herself that, under the right set of terrible circumstances, there could indeed be some value to her husband's particular brand of obsession. Perhaps, Dana thought now, the world was too horrible a place for her and their son to go on living in without a man like Red-dick watching over them.

Maybe he and Dana still wouldn't make it, Reddick didn't know. But what he did know was that Dana understood him better today than she ever had before. And what she surely understood most clearly of all was something he had told her from day one, something that was as true at this moment as it had been then.

He had her back. Now and forever.